Praise ...
A Shred of ...

...ng! In *A Shred of Truth,* Eric Wilson delivers a twisting tale of sus-
...w, and repentance that will grab you from the start and keep your
...pied well past the turning of the last page. Aramis Black never
...good. Warning: reading this book may be hazardous to your sleep

—SHARON CARTER ROGERS, critically acclaimed author
of *Sinner* and *Two Graces*

"Eric Wilson can flat out write!"
—CRESTON MAPES, author of *Nobody*

"*A Shred of Truth* serves up another cup of addictive suspense from author
Eric Wilson. The adventures of Aramis Black read like successive shots of
adrenaline, offering readers fresh takes in Christian suspense."
—SIBELLA GIORELLO, author of *The Stones Cry Out*

"Eric Wilson possesses a profound power of prose and dialogue that kept me
riveted to the last, remarkable page. A great work from one of our most extra-
ordinary writers of suspense."
—JAMES BYRON HUGGINS, author of *A Wolf Story,*
The Reckoning, and *Leviathan*

"Wilson has done it again! *A Shred of Truth* is a highly textured, superbly crafted
story that will resonate with readers long after the last page has been turned."
—BRANDT DODSON, author of *Original Sin, Seventy Times
Seven,* and *The Root of All Evil*

"Eric Wilson continues to amaze me with every novel. *A Shred of Truth* grabs you at the first page and never lets go. From a hero who is flawed yet admirable to the demented evil out to destroy him, Wilson has given us his best work yet."

—BRIAN REAVES, author of *Stolen Lives*

"Now that I've had my second cup of coffee with my favorite bad boy turned java-shop host, I'm hooked on Aramis Black. *A Shred of Truth* gives us a heaping spoonful of terrific writing, a double dollop of historical intrigue, and a custom blend of danger, mystery, and family drama. Is there any question that Eric Wilson is one of the best suspense writers around? Not by me—I'm ordering another cup!"

—KATHRYN MACKEL, author of *Vanished*

A
SHRED OF
TRUTH

A NOVEL

A SHRED OF TRUTH

ERIC WILSON

WaterBrook
PRESS

A Shred of Truth
Published by WaterBrook Press
12265 Oracle Boulevard, Suite 200
Colorado Springs, Colorado 80921
A division of Random House Inc.

Most Scripture quotations are taken from the Holy Bible, New International Version®.
NIV®. Copyright © 1973, 1978, 1984 by International Bible Society. Used by permission
of Zondervan Publishing House. All rights reserved. Scripture quotations are also taken from
the following: The King James Version. The Message by Eugene H. Peterson. Copyright ©
1993, 1994, 1995, 1996, 2000, 2001, 2002. Used by permission of NavPress Publishing
Group. All rights reserved. The Holy Bible, New Living Translation, copyright © 1996,
2004. Used by permission of Tyndale House Publishers Inc., Carol Stream, Illinois 60188.
All rights reserved.

The characters and events in this book are fictional, and any resemblance to actual persons
or events is coincidental.

ISBN 978-1-57856-912-0

WaterBrook and its deer design logo are registered trademarks of WaterBrook Press,
a division of Random House Inc.

Library of Congress Cataloging-in-Publication Data
Wilson, Eric (Eric P.)
    A shred of truth : an Aramis Black novel / Eric Wilson. — 1st ed.
        p. cm.
    ISBN 978-1-57856-912-0
    1. Country musicians—Tennessee—Nashville—Fiction. 2. Brothers—Fiction.
3. Coffeehouses—Fiction. 4. Nashville (Tenn.)—Fiction. 5. Psychological fiction.
6. Domestic fiction. I. Title.
    PS3623.I583S48 2007
    813'.6—dc22

                                2007015532

Printed in the United States of America
2007—First Edition

10 9 8 7 6 5 4 3 2 1

Dedicated to

my sister, Heidi,
for late-night talks and memories of Brazil
and for yelling at me when my life depended on it

and my brother, Shaun,
for adventures together around the world
and for being a brother who sticks closer than a friend

He was a killer from the very start.
He couldn't stand the truth because
there wasn't a shred of truth in him.

—JOHN 8:44, THE MESSAGE

PART ONE

BITTER BREW

*Good faith…is a weapon
which scoundrels very frequently make use of
against men of honor.*

—Alexandre Dumas, *The Man in the Iron Mask*

1

Put to the test, Johnny Ray Black failed and got cut—a literal, skin-splitting ordeal at the hands of a killer. One minute he was mingling with producers and industry insiders, drinking Jack Daniel's, and giving an acoustic performance of his first Top Ten single, "Tryin' to Do Things Right." The next he was bound to a statue and bleeding.

Still alive though. Thank God.

It was supposed to be a celebration. A party for the rising star. In a park at the north end of Nashville's Music Row, I jostled elbows with his fans while bursting with pride. After years of honing his skills and playing small shows, my older brother had beaten the odds by signing with an independent label and charting a hit single.

He'd made a mistake, however, by admitting his weakness for redheads in an *Entertainment Weekly* interview.

She came to him that Friday evening in Owen Bradley Park.

A test in red.

Beneath a moon turned soft and buttery by Middle Tennessee's humidity, propped on high heels, she nudged between caterers in ruffled white shirts and bypassed the open bar. I'm told she wore a shimmering dress. She managed to evade my attention—a minor miracle, but recent experiences have made me wary of the opposite sex—and brushed up to Johnny as he finished his acoustic set.

Coy smiles. A whisper.

Johnny finished another shot of Jack, then stumbled off with her beneath tree branches strung with party lights, toward the darkness of the nearby ASCAP Building.

I didn't realize he was missing till a half hour later. Considering it was his own party, his disappearance was a bad publicity move. Where was his manager anyway? I'd seen Samantha Rosewood hurry away minutes earlier with a cell phone pressed to her ear, eyebrows knitted in worry.

My gut clenched. What kind of trouble had my brother gotten into this time? I searched the crowd, then stopped near the publicity tent and tried to recall when I'd last spotted him.

"Mr. Aramis Black." A stubby man appeared in front of me. "You look lost."

"I'm fine."

"Bet it's hard on you."

"What?" My gaze zeroed in on this slick-haired booking agent, with his goatee and ostrich boots. Every year Music City draws thousands of country-music wannabes, easy prey for men such as this. Who'd invited him anyway?

"All the attention your brother's getting. Must make you jealous."

"Not at all. He's worked hard for it."

"That he has."

"You know where he is by any chance?"

The agent chuckled. "In the stratosphere, that's where. And still rising."

I gave a weak smile, scanned the cluster of partygoers at his back.

"You ever think of sharing the spotlight, maybe singing as a duet?"

"Nope."

He tapped my chest. "You've got the look, my friend. Maybe we should talk."

"Not gonna happen. Johnny's the one with the voice and the guitar."

"What about some harmonies? Think Montgomery Gentry or Brooks and Dunn. Those boys won't be around forever, and we're always looking for—"

"I'm not the type." With a tug on my shirt sleeves, I revealed twin tattoos of banners wrapped around double-edged swords. *Live by the Sword* on one forearm, *Die by the Sword* on the other.

"Come on now." The dude winked—actually, full-on winked at me. "These days, country fans aren't afraid of a little ink. Why live in your brother's shadow?"

"Go away. Please."

"Just think of—"

"Before I hurt you."

"Oh. I… Okay." He swung round and bellied his way back into the crowd.

A voice from my right: "Aramis, you got a minute?"

"What now?" I turned to find myself face to face with Chigger.

The man's mouth is curled into a perpetual sneer, and we eyed each other like wary boxers. He wore a ball cap, faded jeans over thick legs, and a Lynyrd Skynyrd hoodie. With his good ol' boy quality and electrifying stage presence, he's been a mainstay in the country scene for the past couple of years. Come Monday morning, he'd be joining my brother as lead guitarist for the first leg of a national tour.

"Got somethin' to show ya."

"Show me then."

"This your brother's?" Chigger lifted a black Stetson into view.

"Could be."

"Found it lyin' out in plain sight near a bench. Not like Johnny Ray to leave his hat behind, so I figured you might wanna hold on to it till he gets back."

"From where?"

Chigger shrugged. "Ain't seen the man since he got up and sang."

"Me neither." I took the hat, noted the initials JRB inside. "Appreciate it."

Chigger nodded and moved on without another word.

I wandered toward the sidewalk that edged the park, my fingers rubbing the Stetson's brim. Jagged flaps in the material signaled to me that something was wrong. On a roundabout across the street, spotlights pointed up at a forty-foot statue, and I examined the hat against their glow.

Five slices in the brim, two letters:

Through the narrow slits, my brother's form came into sudden focus. He was tied to the statue, chin down, golden brown hair glued by sweat to his neck.

"Johnny?"

Dread tightened its grip around my stomach.

2

The statue is called *Musica*. Created by a local artist, it features bronze subjects meant to represent racial diversity and artistic inspiration. Five are caught in a dance on the perimeter, while the three in the center lift a woman toward the sky. In her hand, a golden tambourine serves as a fitting token for Music City USA.

Only one problem. All nine of the figures are naked—or "nekked," as some Southerners might say. Since its unveiling in 2003, *Musica* has symbolized this city's clash between creative expression and conservative values.

And there was my brother, strapped to the monstrosity.

"Johnny Ray!"

No response. Not even a hint of movement.

I dashed toward the statue. Why had I let him out of my sight? At age six, I'd watched a killer pull the trigger and send my mother tumbling into a river below, and that memory still coursed through my veins like a poison. I'd wasted many years dabbling in drugs and anarchy on the streets of Portland, Oregon, wallowing in violence, leaving others with bruises and me with overlapping knuckle scars.

Recently, I've been trying to turn things around. Take flight. Break free. Yet seeing Johnny's immobile form, I had to wonder if this was retribution of some sort, my sins coming back to haunt my family.

God, no. If anyone deserves this, it's me.

My dash was halted by a Hyundai circling the roundabout. Aimed for Demonbreun Street, the car slowed as though bent on blocking my path. Moonlight and shadows flowed over its shiny surface, turning the vehicle into an otherworldy carriage of gloom.

Come on, come on, *come on!*

With macabre stealth, it rolled along. At the Hyundai's wheel, the driver was hooded, faceless, studying me with fiendish concentration.

No. My head was playing tricks on me. Nothing I'd experienced—except a few ill-advised narcotic episodes—suggested that economy sedans could transport demons of hell.

"Outta my way," I yelled.

I scampered behind the vehicle, then darted through a ring of low hedges to the monument's base. My brother's body faced the downtown skyline, the cords pulled tight across his chest, lashed around his wrists, and threaded between the bronzed dancers.

"Johnny!"

He groaned. He was alive, at least.

"Who did this to you?"

"Hey, kid."

"How'd this happen?"

"Should get me some…good publicity for the gossip papers."

"That's not funny."

His weak snicker sent a whiff of liquor my way.

Maybe that was it: he'd tossed back one too many, and his rowdy band had roped him up as a practical joke. Chigger'd probably given me the hat as a clue. Hey, for all I knew this was common hazing for chart-topping artists.

"The guys in the band do this to you?" I dropped the Stetson to try to locate the knots. "Gotcha good, didn't they?"

He tried to focus. "Nuh-uh."

"You sure? You sound pretty drunk."

"I'm…I'm A-okay."

"Don't smell like it." The ropes were a tangled mass. "Who did this?"

"She…she was pretty. We wanted to be alone."

"She?"

In my peripheral vision, I noticed the Hyundai circling again. I craned to get a glimpse of the driver, but the car veered off down a side street. The rear bumper and license plate remained shrouded in darkness.

"You recognize that car?"

"Car?" my brother muttered.

"It's gone now. Tell me what happened. What'd this girl look like?"

"A redhead and…whew, hot as they come. Big blue eyes. Soft lips. We were this close and then"—he tried to snap his fingers—"lights out. Just like that."

My hands were fumbling at his restraints. "Somebody hit you?"

"Clobbered me good…and here I am."

"You didn't see who did it? Could it've been the girl?"

"A pretty young thing like that? No way."

"How can you be sure? Bet you didn't even get her name."

"Wasn't nothing but a kiss, okay?"

I decided it was the wrong time to correct his grammar—all part of his country-music persona, he claims.

"Was she wearing a rock?" I ventured. "Maybe you upset her old man."

"You and your…ideas."

"Did you even check?"

"For a ring?"

"Did you?"

"Hey now, don't you go judgin' me. She…she made all the moves."

"Fine." It wasn't like I'd figure this out crouched in the dark beneath a monument to creative freedom. I wrestled with the final knot. "Look, I've got you loose. Let me help you down."

He winced, gritted his teeth, as I eased him over my shoulder. Although I'm younger and stronger—my broad shoulders came with my mom's Mediterranean heritage—it was tricky shuffling him down to the lawn. Not that I had any right to complain. Over the years, he's had to cart my drunken butt around a time or two.

Settled on the grass, he let out a moan. I pulled my hands away and noticed in the spotlight's glare a tacky red-black substance between my fingers.

"You're bleeding."

"S'all right."

"Where is it? Lemme see the wound."

My words had a strange effect on him, stiffening his neck and his arms, injecting his eyes with nervous energy. He mumbled something.

"What'd you say?"

"Courage," he repeated, "grows strong at a wound."

"Where'd you hear that?" I knelt to assess the damage.

"A phone call, just yesterday… Thought it was some prank."

"Here. Lift your shirt so I can have a look."

"I'll be fine."

"Courage, huh? Cut the tough-guy act."

When he refused to cooperate, I peeled the denim shirt over his head, eliciting from him a raspy grumble of pain. On his left shoulder, the wounds were thin but deep, still dripping. Someone had gone to work on him with a blade. In the amber moonlight, I grabbed the Stetson and stretched the material over the incisions. Whoever had carved up the hat had done the same thing to his back.

Five cuts. Two letters.

Anger flared in my chest as I used my own shirt to dab at the blood. If I found the person responsible, so help me...

"Why, Johnny Ray? Who would do something like this?"

Despite the late-night humidity, he was shivering.

"You have no idea? The letters AX mean anything to you? Talk to me."

"The man on the phone," he said in a husky whisper.

"The prank call?"

Johnny nodded. "I think he knew about the gold."

"The inheritance? How could he?"

My mind raced through memories of last year: the discovery of my kinship to Meriwether Lewis, famed nineteenth-century explorer; the handkerchief given me by my mother that had held the map to Lewis's hidden cache. Like my mom, I'd nearly paid for that secret with my life.

My mom. Dianne Lewis Black...1959–1986.

There was no part of me that wanted to touch that blood money. Instead I'd left a clue for my brother, spelled out in the pages of a book. Coming from a different father, Johnny had none of Lewis's DNA, but I figured if he located the gold, fine. He could do with it as he saw fit. I'd left it at that. No questions asked.

Until now.

"Did you find it?" My words were barely audible.

"Mm-hmm. Few months back...in Memphis."

"You figured it out?"

He recited the clue I'd left. "In a cave where the wolf's mouth opens and Indians bluff."

"You're not as dumb as you look."

"Just like you said—near Chickasaw Bluffs, north edge of the Wolf River."

"So you've been there. You've seen it."

"Twice."

"Have you told anyone?"

"'Course not."

"No one in the band? None of your girlfriends?"

"Not a soul."

"Then who was this guy on the phone? A relative?"

"Said something'd been stolen from him."

"Great."

"Told him he had the wrong number, and he started threatening me—'the wages of sin is death' and that sorta thing. Right before I hung up, he said, 'Courage grows strong at a wound.'"

"You ever heard that before?"

"Never." Johnny Ray wobbled to his feet and arched his back in pain as his shirt fell against the fresh incisions. "Let's get outta here."

A few excited yells carried over the trees from the well-lit park. Chigger held a beer bottle aloft, surrounded by a bevy of women.

"I'm running you to the hospital."

"What do you take me for, some kind of wuss?"

"Now that you mention it."

"Just help me to my pickup, idiot."

"Keys first." I held out my palm.

Half-sloshed, he handed them over. "Get me home to my bed."

His uncharacteristic surrender worried me. "What about the police? Shouldn't we report this?"

"It's midnight. We'll be stuck sitting around, answering questions, and all they'll do is file a report and forget about it. We don't got any witnesses, weapons—nothing."

He had a point. I surveyed the nearby environs for any sign of a razor blade or knife, any evidence that might help us pinpoint his assailant. Nothing but soda cans, concert fliers, and a few cigarette butts.

"We do have two initials," I pointed out. "And these ropes."

"Later, kid."

"Not to mention a good lead on a redhead who might've been an accomplice."

"Or a victim. What if they knocked me out to get to her?"

I paused, then slipped my arm under his to guide him toward his truck. "Okay, I didn't think of that."

" 'Course you didn't."

"What's that supposed to mean?"

His gaze turned my way, full of that watery-eyed wisdom of the inebriated. "Shoot, I can't blame you for being suspicious of women, Aramis, not after your last go-around."

"What?"

"Fact is, you're bitter."

"I am not." I helped him into the pickup and slammed the passenger door.

Bitter. A strong word describing bad coffee and lifelong grudges. I couldn't deny I'd had my share of trouble with women, creating some trust issues, but the fact was someone had sliced up my brother. Whether man or woman, it didn't matter.

When I found the responsible party, I'd hit hard and hit fast.

We followed West End Avenue toward our brownstone, with the moon slipping behind the Parthenon in Centennial Park and silhouetting stone griffins along the ramparts. I thought about my homeless friend, Freddy C, who often sleeps here. During daylight, I love to walk around the structure—the world's only full-scale replica of the famed Grecian complex—but nighttime gives it a menacing feel.

"What if it's a stalker, someone jealous of your success—that guy who called? You're out in the public eye now and going on tour in three days. Which means"—I slapped at the steering wheel—"we need to track down and *nail* this whack job. What kind of person goes around slicing people up?"

"If you knew that, you'd be as twisted as the one who did it."

"What if they've done it before?"

"That's where the policemen come in, little brother. Give 'em a heads-up in the morning, maybe talk to that detective friend of yours."

"Detective Meade."

"That's the one. You fill him in and let him do his job." He ignored my noncommittal grunt. "Appreciate the brotherly concern, I really do, but I know how you can be, always pokin' around. Nearly got yourself killed last year."

"What about your back?"

He blew air from the side of his mouth. "Maybe you're right about some jealous husband or whatnot. Soon enough I'll be on tour, and it'll all be forgotten. Just promise me you won't go stirrin' up trouble. That a deal?"

"Look. We're home."

"Promise me."

We pulled into our parking lot, and the dipped entryway made Johnny grimace as his back bounced against the seat. I eased into a space. My thoughts turned to Meade, my unlikely friend, the unflappable detective who'd lent his capable assistance in the past.

"Deal," I said.

"Which means you'll keep your nose clean while I'm gone?" He waited for me to nod. "And you'll also stay outta the cops' way?"

"Yes, already. I'll be a good boy, I promise."

We headed up the brick steps and locked and deadbolted the door behind us. Johnny moved into the kitchen to put on a pot of herbal tea. I popped open a can of Dr Pepper, ignoring his look of dietary concern, and chugged it.

"Ahhh." I crumpled the can in my fist. "Good stuff."

"Sugar water's all that is."

"Better than killing a million brain cells." I dropped the can into the waste bin under the sink and grabbed the first-aid kit. At the dining table, my brother laid his head on his arms while I dribbled hydrogen peroxide on the cuts. "Sting?"

"Not too bad."

"Be worse if they'd used a dull blade." I finished with the A, then dabbed at the X where his tanning-booth brown gave way to raw layers of tissue. I did my best to draw together the severed skin with bandages. The smell of antiseptics clouded the room. "Just be careful," I said. "Try not to brush against anything."

"I'll keep that in mind, Nurse. Where's your little white outfit anyway?"

"Sicko." I shoved at his chair. "Go get some sleep."

Stretched across my bed, I blew out a minty breath of toothpaste and hoped my rest would be undisturbed. The A/C kicked on, the cool air sweeping the swampy warmth from the room. My eyes began to lock up for the night.

Instantly the cuts on my brother's back snapped into view.

"Please, God." I stared up at the ceiling.

Since childhood I've been plagued by nightmares and dreams. Sometimes I see my mother at the riverbank—crying out, falling. Other times I'm racing through tall grass, pulse pounding. Recently I've had a recurring vision of my last girlfriend, half-hidden behind a handkerchief as she raises the polished barrel of an automatic.

Brianne... Seems like only a few weeks ago.

I closed my eyes again. Pushed away images of Johnny's incisions. An old Radiohead song played through my head, leading me into a dream...

I'm walking across a bridge. Fog surrounds me, muffles my steps as I cross. I see a shape rising ahead, a circle around three stars, emblazoned over a double-edged sword—the emblem of the Tennessee Titans.

This is good. I love my Titans.

A loud crack tears through the air. What now?

The sword is falling, plunging, sharpening into substance. As I turn, I see it swoop along the earth and head my way. I run back toward the bridge, the blade singing through the air behind me. My feet slap at the soft ground. I'm getting nowhere fast. Gasping.

Where's the bridge? It's gotta be close.

"You're no good, Aramis," a voice hisses. "We're giving you the ax."

I stagger and sprawl headlong across the pavement. The sword zips overhead.

"Who are you?" I cry out. "Leave me alone."

Rolling onto my side, I try to spot the speaker. That voice. Do I know it? Nothing but a slim, fading shape. And a strong sense of déjà vu.

3

Detective Meade stepped into my espresso shop the next morning, set a hand on the bar, and turned to scan Black's dining area. His skin was darker than my mahogany counter, his eyes black as coal, revealing little. A member of the old school, Meade's never been the warm, fuzzy type. We met last year during the investigation of a murder that happened in my shop, and he proved to be a man of dignity, of restraint—a person I could learn from.

"The usual, please."

"It's been awhile, Detective."

"Work and more work."

"Know how that goes. One Hair Curler coming right up."

I pulled two shots of espresso, poured them into a cup of dark roast, topped it off with a squeeze of lime. It's my own concoction, loosely based on a *cafe romano* served in Rome but unknown to most in the US of A. Not for the faint of heart. Which, I'm sure, is why Meade likes it.

He said, "You free for a moment?"

"You bet."

I removed my apron and passed off counter duties to my morning crew. I used to run the place with one other person, but all that changed a few months back when a brief stint on a reality TV show, *The Best of Evil*, turned me into a reluctant star. Channel Five News did a follow-up segment; the

Tennessean did a write-up; I was even billed as a local celebrity at a charity auction in nearby Franklin.

Though I still pull shots behind the bar, I've become more of a true owner of Black's, managing my employees and tending to administrative duties. Some days I miss the customer contact. Other days not so much.

I joined the detective in a window booth.

He set down his cup. "I received your message this morning. You say someone attacked Johnny Ray with a knife?"

"Tied him up and cut into his shoulder." I provided details in a voice low enough not to upset customers at neighboring booths and tables.

"You should've called from the park when it happened."

"It was late. I thought it was a prank or some crazy initiation."

"Until you saw his injuries."

"Exactly."

"A code thirty-seven."

"Which means?"

"Aggravated assault."

"Johnny said he had an ominous call a few days back, some stranger speaking in riddles, talking about courage and wounds. Think it rattled him."

"No caller ID?"

"Unidentified. We could probably go back through the calls. He'd recognize it."

"Could be helpful. We can subpoena phone records too. What about this party?"

Detective Meade took notes on a pad while I told him about the Hyundai at the *Musica* roundabout, the names of the attendees, the music execs, and the catering outfit. I handed over the severed ropes in a garbage bag.

"You took these?" He frowned.

"Hey, don't criticize my methods. That stuff could've been long gone by this morning."

"Which is why you should've called it in." Meade leaned back and smoothed long, large-knuckled fingers down his ruby-colored tie. His gaze shifted toward the shop's front door as though willing a suspect to enter and confess.

Along Elliston Place, cars and pedestrians streamed by from nearby clinics, Baptist Hospital, eateries, and Vanderbilt University. A set of slender female legs jogged past, and I looked away. Beauty's made a fool of me one too many times.

"I wonder about you," he said. "You seem to be developing a pattern of stumbling into trouble, and—"

"Dude, tell me about it."

"And then calling my office."

"Uh. You told me to call if I ever needed anything."

He waved off my defensiveness. "Anytime."

"Growing up, I wasn't a big fan of the cops. It's a positive step for me."

He sipped from his mug, watching me.

"Are you superstitious?"

He set down the drink. "Why?"

"In your line of work, I'm sure you've seen people with bad luck. Always stepping into stuff they can't wipe off."

"Think that's you?"

I looked out the window. "I've stepped in my share of it."

"I've seen some. That Michaels kid last year—he didn't have much of a chance. Way I read it, that kind of bad luck is the consequence of people's choices."

"Cause and effect. My brother calls it karma."

"Reap what you sow, sure. Most religions have something like it, and it's the foundation of any good legal system. A price must be paid for wrongs committed."

"Trust me," I said. "If I find out who did that to my brother—"

"You'll report it to me."

I pressed my lips together and wrapped a hand around the back of my neck. I remembered my vow to Johnny Ray.

"You don't need any more bad luck."

I nodded. Smiled.

What I wanted to say, what I suspected in my gut, was that bad luck had latched onto me back in Portland during my years of less-than-admirable behavior. My brother thinks people use the idea of a Supreme Being as an excuse, a crutch. Others say God is all about love and forgiveness, wanting to help, just waiting to be asked.

Deep down I believe the latter. It's like a knowledge that blew in on a soft wind and took root in my chest.

There is also this weed called doubt that tries to choke it out.

"I see those wheels turning, Aramis. Please listen to me, and refrain from any vigilante fantasies. I'll speak with your brother, interview those who attended the party, and follow up on any leads. We'll stay in contact, and—I hope you're listening here—you let me do my job."

"Yes. Of course."

"I'll hold you to that."

"I know you will. Thanks for coming by." I extended my hand and rose from the booth, but he held me in place with an iron grip and a coal black stare.

"One more thing. Does your brother know a woman named Nadine Lott?"

"I… He's never mentioned…"

He released my hand. "You remember the homicide victim in the news last year, the one burned beneath a pile of trash on the north end of town?"

"The homeless lady? Yeah. She came into the shop a time or two."

"It's a nice thing you do, giving coffee to the less fortunate. As for Miss Lott, her cause of death remains undetermined, despite toxicology and tissue testing. She had an extensive arrest history—theft, prostitution, and criminal impersonation. Detectives from North Precinct believe the fire was set to destroy evidence, though they did find some drug paraphernalia in her sweatshirt."

"And—"

"It could be related."

"To the attack on my brother?"

Meade leaned forward, delivering data in his smooth baritone. "Tests show that Ms. Lott had consensual sex in the hour before her death. The coroner found massive cranial hemorrhaging caused by a blunt object—"

"No! Johnny Ray had nothing to do with her. It'd go against his whole concept of karma."

Meade help up a hand. "If I can finish."

I crossed my arms.

"He found something else, which we kept out of the newspapers. Abdominal wounds. Initials carved by a knife and nearly burned away."

"AX?"

The detective's grim expression confirmed my guess.

"So Johnny's not a suspect."

"Should've made that clear up front."

"And you never caught her attacker?"

"We had few leads, but this makes it look like the perp's still in the area."

"And local records—"

"Were searched, yes. For anything related to AX."

"Nothing, huh?"

"Without substantial evidence, you can link two letters to pretty much anything."

"And you're sure the American Xylophonists weren't involved? Those boys can be dangerous."

Meade's expression remained flat.

"Bad joke. Sorry. You still haven't learned to relax, have you?"

"These days, Aramis, relaxing's not an option."

"Must get to you after a while." I recalled sitting in the Charlotte Pike station months ago, spotting photos of his wife and a daughter dressed in pink. "I'm sure it gets to your family at times."

He leaned back in the booth. "They're the reason I do what I do, Mr. Black." I saw his eyes narrow as a vintage Corvette convertible zipped by.

"Sweet car," I said.

"Moving too fast. Just another cage of death."

"Dude. You *seriously* need time off."

"Please tell me you don't drive at excessive speeds."

"In my beater Honda? I wish."

Jaw muscles clenching, he stood and smoothed his shirt. "I'd like to take a statement from your brother. Does he have a reliable contact number?"

"Here." I speed-dialed and handed over my cell. "If he doesn't answer, my guess is he's headed to DAD's studio."

"Your dad's a producer?"

"No. Desperado Artist Development. It's over on Music Row."

"I see."

"It's been Sammie's brainchild from the start."

"Samantha Rosewood?"

"The one and only. Manages my brother's career and of course helped finance this place. Pretty amazing lady."

"Hmm. And, as I recall, quite attractive."

"Wuh—um, right."

"Answering machine." Meade closed the phone and handed it back.

I dropped it into my pants pocket. "He's trying to finish up a new single before hitting the road. Drop by the studio over on Sixteenth. Can't miss the black and silver sign."

"I may do that."

"So tell me. Straight up. You think my brother's still in danger?"

"In light of the way you found him and the wounds you've described, it's a possibility. Miss Lott's abdominal wounds never went public, so it's unlikely we have a copycat. It's possible this murderer has come out of hibernation, and he may have intended your brother as his next victim."

4

The detective headed out, while I stood and watched traffic move along Elliston. Was there really a connection between Nadine Lott and Johnny Ray? Why would someone kill a transient woman, then follow it a year later with an attack on a rising country star? Had my search at the park halted a more lethal plan?

I thought again of the Hyundai sedan circling like a hearse.

If I could just find that car, find that sicko…

No. I couldn't give in to my "live by the sword, die by the sword" retribution. I imagined taking sandpaper to my skin, scrubbing away the words in raw, bloody patches. But they would still be emblazoned on my heart.

I pressed my head back against the padded seat, closed my eyes.

Since childhood, the closest I'd let a woman get to me was my girlfriend back in Portland. Felicia Daly—intelligent, nurturing, two years older than me. After living together a couple of years, she said she'd had enough of my self-destruction. She worried I'd end up another statistic if things didn't change and—as if to underscore her point—admitted she'd started seeing someone else.

"Who?" I demanded.

"No one," she fired back. "Someone who listens, who actually cares."

It got ugly, and I stormed out, afraid of what I might say or do.

The next morning her haunting prediction came true in an abandoned warehouse off East Burnside, with a rival's Glock jammed against my skull. I realized in that moment the shame I'd brought upon my mother's memory. All her love. Her prayers. And I'd done nothing but coddle my own pain.

Three days later I was on my brother's doorstep in Nashville.

I began turning things around—with Sammie's help. Opened up Black's espresso shop, started reading the Bible and trying to follow its instructions. I began to sense there was someone with me, holding me up, giving me strength.

But last year my past started catching up again. Old enemies. Family secrets. A FedEx envelope from an Oregon penitentiary. Some of those memories still rumbled through my head, including an evening at Brianne's condo in which she was attacked with scissors while I was brought to my knees by a street thug's Taser.

Dark thoughts and temptations crept back in, and it felt good the day I visited a gun show at the Davidson County Fairgrounds and bought a Desert Eagle .40 caliber.

Back on top. In charge.

One clear shot was all I'd need to take care of whoever had hurt my brother.

Shaking off these thoughts, I faced the dining area. College students conversed at a window table. A guy in tattered jeans and Birkenstocks sat on the edge of the corner stage, picking out a tune on his guitar. At the counter, customers waited for their caffeine fixes.

Way I see it, coffee's better than the stuff I used to deal. Cheaper. Cleaner. And except for the one time last year, it's kept me out of the line of fire.

I was heading to join my employees behind the bar when my cell vibrated against my leg. Was it Sammie? I'd left a message for her on my way in this morning, worried by her early departure from last night's party. I looked at the line of customers. Debated. Flipped open the phone.

On the screen an icon blinked. A new e-mail.

From the subject line, one word screamed at me: AX.

"Everything all right?"

I looked up from the message on my phone's screen. "Everything's fine, Anna."

"My, your detective looked stern as he left."

"Meade's a good guy. Just got a lot on his mind."

"I'd venture to say he's not the only one." Anna Knight's concern was evident in the creases of her matronly face. Twenty years my senior and a recent divorcée from Florida, she has a valiant smile that matches her work ethic and attitude. She closes weekdays, claiming it helps fill in the empty spaces in her evenings. "Something you want to talk through, hon?"

I rolled my shoulders. Shook my head. Tried not to think about the e-mail inviting me to a rendezvous only hours from now. I picked up a cup and saucer from a table nearby.

"You wouldn't lie to me, would you? I have four sons of my own, so I—"

"Appreciate it." I moved to place the cup in the dish bin. "Just not now, okay?"

"Have it your way then."

"Thanks for holding down the fort. Didn't mean to leave you hangin'."

"You owe me one, I'll have you know."

"Big time. Listen, have you heard from Sammie?"

"Rosewood? Not since yesterday." She handed a customer his change and smiled. "You sound concerned."

"I am."

Anna arched an eyebrow. "Why, Aramis Black, you like her, don't you?"

"Why wouldn't I?"

"I think you know what I mean."

"She's a good friend."

"And that's why you share dinner on a weekly basis?"

"We talk business. She helped me get this place off the ground."

Sammie Rosewood was one of the first Nashvillians I met—in the business aisle of Davis-Kidd Booksellers, of all places. Born and raised here, she graduated with honors from Vanderbilt, with family money, and her soft heart still intact. A Southern belle in designer jeans, she's unassuming and generous.

And single.

Although she exudes an air of indifference to the men around her, it's more the result of her steady stream of projects than any intended snobbery.

"So it's all about her money," Anna said. "Is that what you'd have me believe?"

"You little matchmaker. Don't you have some cleaning to do?"

"I'll have you know that despite my own experiences in the marital department—or maybe because of them—I have to believe in the possibility of true love."

"Yeah?" I huffed. "Good luck with that."

She blinked twice, then started scrubbing the espresso machine's steam wand. Any thought of an apology on my part was cut short by a customer's arrival at the counter. As I took his order, my mind returned to what lay four hours ahead. A showdown. A rendezvous with my brother's attacker. A chance to settle a score. My fingers itched for the cool grip of my Desert Eagle.

I poured the drink and rang it up. "Anna, I'll be in the back. Got some paperwork to do." As I turned, my other employee appeared from the storage area with a container of chai.

"You leaving us again?"

"S'up, Diesel? Yeah, I have a...meeting this afternoon."

He dropped the chai on the counter, causing utensils to rattle in the drawers.

"Careful there." I pointed to a pallet of recently delivered supplies. "Think you can unload that while I'm gone?"

"Why not? I'm used to picking up the slack."

"Slack? You did get your paycheck yesterday, didn't you?"

His cold and translucent eyes glanced up, then looked away. With his habit of chugging ahead regardless of consequences, Diesel Hillcrest's nickname fit far better than Desmond. A lumbering kid from Ohio, he has the stocky look of a farm boy and a deep voice that I suspect hides scars of a rough childhood. He also possesses a restless intellect, which helped him get into the local Psi Chi honor society. We first met in my social psych class at Lipscomb University.

"Here." I grabbed a pair of tin snips. "Gimme a hand."

"Don't worry, boss. I've got it covered."

"C'mon. Things'll go faster with both of us."

After a couple of minutes of stacking boxes of Ghirardelli chocolate under the counter, his demeanor turned playful. He pointed at me and cocked his thumb. "Okay. Pop quiz."

"Right now?"

"No fear," he goaded. "Just sharpening you for Monday's final exam."

"Don't we have a study session tomorrow? Over at Sara's?"

"Figure you could use extra help, being the oldest in the class."

"I'm twenty-eight."

"Like I said. So here goes."

I groaned and handed over another load.

"Choose the true statement: chewing gum takes seven years to pass through the digestive system, the first TV couple shown in bed together was

Fred and Wilma Flintstone, or Osama bin Laden was once slated to be *Time* magazine's Man of the Year."

"That one. About bin Laden."

"You sure?" He waited for my nod. "Wrong-o! But thank you for playing."

"Number two then."

"Wrong again." A high-pitched buzzer sound. "None of them are true. Two days till our group final, and you still can't tell falsehood from fact?"

"Watch it now."

"All right. All right."

He backed off, but I had to admit he had me. I'd been a victim last year of a deception that had stirred all sorts of questions and murky emotions. What made us tick? What drove some people to murder and betrayal? And why did I always seem to attract trouble? In a move my mother would've endorsed, I enrolled for night courses at Lipscomb to see if an education in Christian truth and principles might provide a beacon of hope.

A few weeks back our professor had assigned us a project titled "Legends and Lies: Cultural Susceptibility in a Secular Age." He'd told us to create an urban legend to disseminate via word of mouth and on the Internet. Diesel and I were teamed up with Sara, a girl from East Tennessee, and we brainstormed and voted on an idea to float in online chat rooms, forums, message boards, and mass e-mails. Diesel even submitted it to Wikipedia, carefully couched among actual facts.

Ironic, huh? I was trying to understand truth by perpetuating a lie.

On Monday at last we would unveil our legend to the class and receive our score on its plausibility, scope of propagation, and an oral presentation exploring the public perception that determines a legend's success.

"Diesel, listen. I won't let you down."

"We're counting on you, man." He put away another box. "I know you're taking this class for your own enlightenment or whatever, but I need an A. You hear me?"

"Shouldn't be a problem. You're already acing the class."

"Try telling that to my parents. They just got here from Columbus for the weekend, and my dad's already reminded me twice of the money they saved for years to get me here. Like I'm their prize racehorse waiting in the gate. Go, Desmond, go!"

"Dude, that's not right."

"It's no wonder you're on edge," Anna said, rejoining the conversation.

"And I'm telling you, Professor Bones has it in for me."

Anna frowned. "Bones?"

"Our substitute," Diesel said. "The guy's drier than day-old grits. He's got these narrow shoulders and a hollow face and wears tortoise-shell glasses that make his eyes bug out."

"But please tell me you don't call him that to his face."

" 'Course not. Only when his back's turned."

"Well then. Spoken like a true Southerner."

"I'm learning."

"Professor Boniface Newmann," I explained to Anna. "That's his real name."

"Oh my. Parents can be so cruel."

Diesel guffawed. "Tell me about it."

"Okay, boys, here's one for you." Anna started stacking clean mugs. "True or false: daddy-longlegs are the world's most poisonous spiders?"

"True," Diesel jumped in. "But their fangs are too small to inject the poison."

"You agree, Aramis?"

"Nope. That one's a myth."

She grinned. "A myth it is."

"Ahh." I pointed at Diesel. "Now who's slipping?"

"I swear I read about that somewhere."

"Heard it from the 'friend of a friend,' huh?" I wagged my head. "That's why they call them FOAFs. Don't you listen in class? Mix in a few lies with a shred of truth, and these things slip right into our culture's collective database."

"Surely there are ways of checking these things," Anna probed.

"Of course," I said. "There are a few debunking sites, but most people are lazy. You ever get one of those chain e-mails from exiled Nigerian royalty asking for money? People still think the Mormons own Coca-Cola."

Diesel yawned. "I never believed that, not even as a kid."

"C'mon."

"I didn't. You can ask my mother."

The door chimed as two businesswomen entered, and I smiled to welcome them. In unison, they each raised a finger to silence me while they finished their cell-phone conversations. My smile started to cramp.

"Go on." Anna nudged me. "I'll take it from here."

"You sure?"

"Hon, do I look helpless to you? I know you have paperwork. Go, go."

Before slipping back through Black's kitchen, I turned to Diesel. "You need anything, I'll be in my office."

"Your broom closet, you mean."

"The very one."

We both laughed. I moved on past the freezer and storage shelves.

"Don't forget, boss. Tomorrow at Sara's. We're counting on you."

"You know," I said, "growing up I used to get a beating for anything lower than a B."

"Do any good?"

"Dropped out my junior year of high school. Had to go back and earn my GED."

"Well, there you go." Diesel's eyes turned dark. "It would have been worth trying, just to see the look on my dad's face. School is like life and death to him."

His words caused images to churn in my head: the charred body under the overpass, a sliced Stetson, a pair of letters carved in my brother's skin.

I cracked my knuckles and marched off.

Nothing could keep me from making that appointment today at four. This AX character had no idea of the trouble he'd called down upon himself. I'd be there, locked and loaded, to show him a little urban legend of my own. Soon he would be in my arena.

5

Time to zero in. Confined by brick walls and the stale tennis-shoe odor of my back-room, broom-closet office, I plopped onto a three-legged stool. A dented file cabinet in the corner held hard copies of till reports and credit-card receipts. A safe sat beside the computer tower beneath my metal desk, while on top, stacks of Jack London hardcovers served as the base for my monitor.

Here's the thing: I'll read the classics someday, but for now I've got spreadsheets and bills to worry about.

At this rate, I'll be a toothless wonder by the time I finish *White Fang.*

I waited for the ancient computer to boot up. Clicks and whirs preceded the monitor's gradual awakening. I logged on to my e-mail account and found a smattering of messages, including a response to my complaint about a recent eBay purchase, but that could wait. The ultimatum from AX was all that mattered.

I moved the mouse, let the cursor hover.

Click…

The sender's address was one of those encrypted accounts that requires no ID and makes it difficult to trace. My heart rate kicked up a few notches as I read the words once more.

Chop, chop, Aramis. Your sins are the razor that will slice you deep.

"The ax is already at the root of the trees, and every tree that does

not produce good fruit will be cut down." 4 p.m. Go to Cheekwood
Gardens, the Fabergé exhibit. For the sake of your loved ones, I
suggest cutting off all contact with your colored detective friend.

Had he seen me talking to Meade? What was his objective here? My
brother had mentioned the caller's comments a few days ago, about something stolen. Was it connected? Or a false lead?

I hit Print, and my ancient IBM printer snorted, brayed in protest, then
sent dots galloping across the paper. The message was evidence, a glimpse into
the mind of some sicko. Was that scripture he had quoted? I thought of
Johnny bleeding under the statue. Anyone willing to slash his fellowman and
torch a homeless woman was either severely lacking in moral fiber or…

Or just seriously screwed up in the head.

I dialed Johnny's number, then Sammie's. Left messages for both. Didn't
they ever answer their phones?

My fingers tapped at the keyboard, shooting off a reply to the threatening e-mail. Contact the cops? I asked. No. I could deal with this one on my
own. I'd get some solid answers, or I'd rip out someone's throat.

Call it a character flaw, but I don't have it in me to play into fear trips. I
have no problem defending those I love, and with a quick jaunt back to my
place, I'd arm myself for the approaching rendezvous. Johnny Ray and I may
have our differences, but he's family.

"Aramis? Knock, knock."

"Hey." I stuffed the printout into my pocket. "Need help with the lunch
rush?"

"Pretty dead actually."

"Bet a lot of our business is over at the festival at Centennial Park. What's
going on?"

Diesel glanced over his shoulder and punched at the doorframe. "Anna won't quit with the mothering stuff."

I smiled. "She's got a big heart, Diesel. She cares."

"Like I don't get harped on enough already."

"She's your shift supervisor, so work with her the best you can."

"If you say so." He mumbled something unintelligible, then diverted my attention with a finger pointed at the monitor. "You seen how our urban legend's doing?"

"Let's take a look."

With a quick Google search, we found links to the Wikipedia article, a genealogical site, even an editorial from a respected local newspaper. The legend had also been noted by Snopes.com with a yellow bullet to indicate "undetermined veracity."

"Hey, that's better than a red bullet," Diesel said.

"Not bad so far, huh?"

Within a few weeks, thousands would be spreading the rumor that one of the founders of the Ku Klux Klan, Civil War general Nathan Bedford Forrest, had been the product of a tryst between his dirt-poor white mother and a strapping young slave from a nearby plantation. The KKK's secrecy would only muddy the waters regarding his bloodline.

"Think we've got a winner," I said.

"Bones better give me an A."

"I'll warn him to grade wisely," I kidded.

"He's a blow-hard. This is between him and me."

Diesel's intensity sounded an alarm in my head, but I saw no need to get involved. It was his life to lead, and I had my own blow-hard to warn off, with our introduction fast approaching.

Cheekwood Botanical Gardens would close in less than an hour, which meant most of the Saturday visitors were wrapping up their self-guided tours of the massive estate. I paid the fee at the gate and drove the long approach between the brick pillars, past the Pineapple Room Restaurant and the greenhouse, to the museum's parking lot.

Was the freak watching? Did he know my Honda Civic?

I parked in the shade of an elm tree. Keeping my arms low, I double-checked the safety on my Desert Eagle before shoving it into my jeans, where it'd go unnoticed beneath my black T-shirt and the untucked button-down.

A dangerous combination, me and guns, I'm well aware. My heart pounded as I climbed from the car, and I cautioned myself to keep cool.

"Ready or not."

The tranquil scenery lent a hand at calming my senses. Slopes of grass swept beneath Japanese maples and curled around terraced gardens, providing bright green contrast to tulips, violas, and pink and yellow trillium. From the herb garden, spicy whiffs mixed with the fragrance of roses, while bubbling fountains enhanced the serenity.

I'd done some quick reading at the Cheekwood Web site, gotten some history and an idea of our rendezvous point. Fewer surprises the better, right?

Annually, the estate draws over 130,000 visitors with its trails, gardens, and statuary. Totaling thirty thousand square feet, the original Cheek Mansion displays European and American art, a collection of Worcester porcelain, and rotating temporary exhibits.

While the Cheeks may not be familiar to most Americans, the source of their fortune is: In the 1920s, Joel Cheek developed a blend of coffee that was served in Nashville's premier hotel, the Maxwell House. Postum, now known as General Foods, bought the business from him for forty million dollars, enabling the family's purchase of this vast woodland on the west side of town.

Forty mil. And here I was, trying to pay off loans at my espresso shop.

I surveyed the rolling hills that surrounded the mansion and narrowed in on the massive structure. If this confrontation resulted in any damage, the Cheek family and their art foundation could afford the repairs.

I checked the museum's rows of windows as I made my way along the curved drive. Was AX already up there? The gun—fully loaded with ten rounds in the clip, one in the chamber—poked into my stomach with each step. Overhead, clouds had formed a cast-iron lid over the Cumberland Basin, and the day's heat simmered.

Cautious steps carried me through the entry into a two-story foyer, where an English mantel clock showed I was a few minutes early.

My cell rang. It was the number at Black's.

"Hello?"

"Aramis. Diesel here. Guess who's standing at the counter."

"Listen, can I call you back? I'm in the middle of something."

"It's Professor Bones. In the flesh. Get it?"

"Ha, ha."

"Says he needs to talk to you. You must've missed class one too many times. Here he is."

I sighed and waited.

"Hello, Mr. Black."

"Professor Newmann?"

"You know, as we speak I'm indulging in one of your famed white mochas."

"Glad you like it."

"Of course, this'll play no part in your final grade."

"Sure." I followed the foyer staircase to the second-floor landing. "Professor, not to be rude, but I've got a meeting in five minutes."

His voice was reedy, breathy, like a woodwind instrument barely holding its tune. "I stopped in, hoping to speak with you in person. It could wait until

Monday evening, I suppose, but the classroom setting's never ideal for one-on-one discussion."

"Am I supposed to know what this is about?"

Tension filled the silence. "Excuse me," Newmann said at last. "Listening ears, you understand."

"Not exactly."

"Were Desmond to know what I have to share with you, it might only increase the pressure on him to achieve scholastic excellence." He paused again. "I've received threats from his father."

"You're kidding."

"I'm half inclined to report it to the university's president."

"You should. But why're you telling me?"

"Because Mr. Hillcrest mentioned your name as well. Apparently he blames you and your brother for his son's struggles."

"I've never even met Diesel's dad. And what's my brother got to do with it?"

"You're welcome to ask. He's just now come through the door."

"There? At my shop?"

Scratching on the other end. Some whispering. "Howdy," Johnny Ray said. I sighed in relief. "Sorry I didn't get back to you earlier, kid. Been in the studio. You oughta hear this new track we're layin' down."

"Did you get my message? I've been…you know…"

"Worried about me?"

"Yeah."

"Still in one piece. My Palm Pilot slid under the bench in my truck. That thing's nothing but a distraction."

"Did Detective Meade swing by?" I scanned the museum's foyer, feeling as if I was being watched.

"Yeah, but I was recording. I think they told him to come back later."

"He was looking for details about last night. I'm thinking maybe you should lie low for a while."

"Not gonna happen. With my tour kickin' off next week, this was just some free advertising. My publicist sent out a press release: 'A Cutting-Edge Artist.'"

"That's sick and wrong."

"Hey, we're already getting calls from CMT and *Access Hollywood*."

"Happy for you. But you make me a promise this time."

"Yeah?"

"Stay put, and don't leave the shop till I get back."

"Nice to know you care, but you're talkin' to a hungry man here."

"Grab whatever you like. It's on me." I saw a figure flit through a doorway on the second floor. "Do me a favor. I've got to go, but call Sammie. See if she knows anything about that redhead last night."

"Good thinkin'. She knows just about everyone in this town."

"I'm worried about her. She hasn't called me back."

"That's not like Sammie. Is this about that urgent call she got at the park last night?"

"Yes yes. Call her for me. Gotta go."

"You wouldn't be getting into more trouble now, little brother? You promised."

"Back as soon as possible."

I snapped the phone shut and looked up at the mantel clock: 3:59 p.m. One minute to showdown. An elderly woman stood nearby, a museum volunteer with kind eyes and powdered cheeks. Behind her, a large-bellied security guard was making his rounds. After asking for the Fabergé exhibit and being given the option of an elevator or the sweeping staircase, I felt my .40-caliber gun jostle against my skin with the ascent of each stone step.

Time to do this.

I was armed, feeling justified and vindictive.

Nothing prepared me, though, for the sight of the person turned away and slightly bent at the waist, hands clasped behind the back, eyes gazing at a Fabergé imperial egg. The slender frame made me hesitate, but the face reflected in the glass case caused me some real confusion.

elicia?"

My former girlfriend straightened and swiveled toward me. We hadn't seen each other since Portland, and volatile emotion whipped through my chest. What was she doing here, this woman who'd left me for another man? Had she sent the e-mail?

A part of me wanted to throw out hurtful words and head back the way I'd come. Another wanted to pull her into an embrace and keep her close, bury my nose in that shiny blond hair the way I used to do.

I stood riveted to the hardwood.

"Aramis, you look good."

"What're you doing here? You live in Nashville now?"

"Just visiting for a few days actually." She tilted her head back, looked at me from beneath her straw hat tied with a yellow ribbon. Her knee-length spring dress was circled by a white belt matching her gloves. "I was hoping to see you."

"Here I am."

"You sound upset."

"You cheated on me. Remember how we ended this two years ago?"

She took a step toward me. "You weren't the same person I'd fallen in love with. And I lost everything trying to make it work."

"And then you left. Didn't seem you hoped to see me again."

Another step. "Maybe I was hasty. You gave me no choice."

"Hey, I didn't tell you to go."

She was three feet away now, her cobalt blue eyes studying mine. They were darker than I recalled, more melancholy. "I heard a rumor you'd changed."

"From who?"

"Is it true?" she persisted.

I looked past her. We seemed to be alone in the exhibit hall, yet the threat of evil still lingered. What were the odds of her being here at this time? No, she had to be connected—maybe even responsible.

But that couldn't be.

During our relationship I'd never seen her swat a fly, much less carve initials into human flesh. As for quoting Bible verses in e-mails, she'd come from an overbearing religious background but never been the Bible-thumping type herself. Far from it.

"It's true," I said. "I have changed."

She stood a foot in front of me. "Your response here leaves some doubt."

"Got a lot on my mind right now. Don't know what to think."

"Then stop trying so hard. I see that hasn't changed. You always wanted to analyze everything. Are you still trying to escape all those thoughts beneath that wavy black hair?" In moderate heels, she barely reached my shoulders as she stepped closer and pressed herself against me.

It felt nice. Soft in all the correct places.

"You had every right, Felicia."

"Hmm?"

"To leave." I swallowed and let my arms encircle her waist. "It was easier to be mad at you than accept my own faults."

"I made mistakes too."

"That doesn't make me feel any better."

She leaned back. "You're still bitter, aren't you?"

"Why do people keep saying that?"

Her face turned up, lips parted. Something there worried me, but I brushed it aside.

"You look nice," I said.

"You like it? I dressed up for the steeplechase."

"The Iroquois. That was today?"

"It was magnificent. The horses, the colors… I could feel their hoofs pounding the ground, right up through my legs."

If she meant to draw attention to her toned calves, it worked. I envisioned her up on her toes, cheering with the thousands of spectators, the racehorses thundering past the stands.

The race was held at neighboring Percy Warner Park, named after the first American-bred horse to win the English Derby. In the late 1800s, he'd been the country's leading sire, stabled at Nashville's Belle Meade Plantation. The glory days had faded when strict rules against racetrack wagering went into effect.

"You always were a horse lover," I said.

"You remember that? I'm touched."

There was a lot I'd tried to forget, but I knew that, as a girl, Felicia had ridden an Appaloosa mare and tacked posters of stallions on her walls. She'd begged more than once to go riding on the beaches, but I'd never made it happen. Too busy with spoons and needles.

"I was a real loser, wasn't I? Back in Portland."

"You know I still loved you, doll."

"Is that why you're here?"

Her eyes grew moist, and she looked down.

"What's going on, Felicia?"

Blond tips stroked her collarbones as she shook her head, and I fought the impulse to run my fingers through her hair. I'd come expecting a show-down with a killer, not this reunion in a museum. In a rush, logic pushed back up through my spinning thoughts, shoving my suspicions to the surface.

"Who put you up to this?" I breathed. "How'd you know I'd be here?"

"I… It started a few months back."

"And?"

"I saw you on that reality show, and it set me thinking about all the times we'd shared. I guess…well, I wanted to see you again."

"So you sent me the e-mail this morning."

"E-mail?"

"Did you… Are you carrying a knife?"

"No. *Gosh,* no."

I scanned the exhibit area again, then took hold of her slender arms. The image of my brother's sliced shoulder filled my vision, followed by a descend-ing curtain of red. I slid my fingers down. Stroked her warm skin. Was she the culprit? The question had to be asked, but our years of shared history were all the answer I needed.

She simply didn't have it in her.

Really? You've been a fool before, you know.

My fingers tightened into cuffs around her wrists. "There's something you're not telling me, Felicia." Twisting her around, I pressed her against the wall and put my mouth close to her ear. Her hair smelled like flowers—or was that only the scent of the gardens outside?—and my rough actions sent a pang of guilt through me. "Cough it up. Just tell me why you showed up here today."

"Please, doll, don't treat me like this."

I tried to recall my training in social psych. Had I learned anything about sifting out falsehood from fact? She yelped as I pushed harder. "I want some answers, darlin'. You hear me? The truth. Did you hurt my brother?"

"Why would you ask such a thing?"

"You didn't cut him up last night?"

She stiffened. "Have I ever hurt anyone?"

"He was attacked. The letters AX mean anything to you?"

"Like an ax?"

"You heard me. Someone told you to come, am I right?"

She fell silent.

"Who sent you?"

"This guy."

"What guy?"

"I can't say. It wouldn't have been his real name anyway."

"You can't? Or won't?"

"You're hurting my arm."

"Have you seen him? Seen his face?"

"I… He said his name was Axman. Please, Aramis, you're hurting me."

"What's he look like? Sound like? Describe him for me."

"There's nothing to say. We talked on the phone. He told me he'd kill me if I didn't do as he said or went to the cops. I wanted to see you, and at first he made it sound like you and I might work things out. He said he knew you. He sent me cash for my airfare, told me to buy some new clothes and come meet you."

"There must've been a catch."

"You were the catch. He was going to hurt you."

"No, that was your job."

"I know I left you, but please believe that I never stopped thinking about us."

"Blah-de-blah. So what's this guy want from you?"

"I'm supposed to give you this." Trapped in my grip, she leaned her head forward against the wall. The hat scooted back off her head and onto my chest.

"Is this a joke?"

"He taped something inside." Still captive, she craned around with a pleading look. "You have to obey the instructions if you want to know the truth."

"Whatever."

I released her to search the hat, telling myself it had nothing to do with the tears. Nothing at all. Not her quivering lip or the memories she sent racing through my head.

Footsteps clicked down the hall, and I caught a glimpse of the security guard's polished shoes. A rent-a-cop? Or the real deal? The museum contained a fortune in art, but I'd never heard of a theft occurring here. What would he think of a crying woman pressed against the wall by a swarthy-looking man with tattooed forearms?

I corralled Felicia into an embrace and planted a long kiss on her mouth. Call me quick on my feet. Call me unoriginal. Either way, it worked. Despite our age difference, she'd always been submissive. Even now, her stiffness melted into a willing response, and I discovered the hopes still trapped there, written across her lips like heat-activated ink.

"Folks." The guard cleared his throat. "We'll be closing in fifteen minutes."

I disengaged, waved a hand. "Thanks."

"We do suggest visitors leave before the gates lock at four thirty."

"Okay."

"And please," he said with a frown, "don't brush against the walls."

"Yes sir. I mean, no sir."

He walked away with clicking strides toward the next room.

Felicia put both hands on my chest. "That was nice."

"Tasted salty to me."

"Oh, quit it. I see through the macho facade."

"Macho. That's me."

"You haven't changed." She pushed away. "I wanted to believe otherwise. I really did."

With the yellow-ribboned hat still in my hand, I watched her march off and wondered if she was right. The impulsive lip lock, the protective sarcasm, and emotional walls. Had I just hidden my old ways behind a wall of good intentions?

I turned the hat over and peeled off a small envelope taped to the straw. As I stood among the pristine displays of sparkling Fabergé creations, fear swelled against my rib cage. I removed a note and a blood-crusted razor blade, imagining the silver edge splitting my brother's flesh. Flashing in the moonlight. Dripping red.

"Felicia, wait!" I darted toward the hallway.

"Whoa, slow down." The guard appeared and blocked my path. "We're closing, so you're going to have to mosey on toward the parking area. Maybe save yourself some heartache."

Not likely. The man's advice went against the note's instructions.

7

The note was a typed clue: "Hit the trail, but keep the razor. You'll need it to find piece at the steeple."

Find *piece*? I doubted that was an accident.

In my mind's eye, I pulled up the Cheekwood map that I'd seen on the Web site. The Woodland Sculpture Trail ran along the back edge of the mansion, with sites on the path numbered according to the presiding displays.

The *Steeple Dance*. Third on the list.

With the clock ticking, I'd have to move quickly and avoid a confrontation with the estate guards. Though worried about Felicia's safety, I was driven by a greater need to discover the identity and motive of the person behind this stupid game. He might be out there, waiting for me among the trees.

"Nice exhibit," I said to the security guard.

He eyed me with distrust as I moved as nonchalantly as possible down the spiral staircase in the center of the mansion. I pretended to turn toward the front foyer, then cut back through a passageway that led to an outside arbor. He hadn't followed me. Good. I padded up a stone walkway, then sprinted across the back lawn, past a swan fountain. Following directions. Heading for the trail.

Only minutes until closing. What would I find back here? Another person tied to a sculpture and bleeding onto the forest floor?

Felicia's words: *obey the instructions if you want to know the truth.*

The truth. About what exactly?

I tramped through the underbrush. Darkness deepened beneath the merging clumps of trees, offering at least some concealment.

The trail. There. Should I veer left or right?

Left.

I ran now, envelope and razor in one hand, Desert Eagle in the other. I knew where I was headed. The straw hat fluttered from my grip, but it didn't matter. On either side of the path, the woods were so still I could hear my shirt swishing with each pump of my arms, my feet padding over bark and turf.

BEAR: *breathe, evaluate, act rapidly.* I'd learned that from one of my street pals as a teenager.

In the clearing ahead, rusty-orange spires stabbed at angles into the gray sky. I'd seen the *Steeple Dance* sculpture online and in the brochure. What I hadn't seen was the object swaying on a cord from a branch of a cedar tree. A casual passerby would've missed it.

I took a deep breath, peered around, listened. As far as I could tell, I was alone. I walked closer and reached for the object. Too high. I tried to gauge the distance.

Seemed innocent enough. A small bag cinched with leather straps.

Find piece at the steeple…

A piece of what? I paused. A finger? An earlobe?

Whatever this was, whatever was in there, it was all part of the sicko's game.

I glanced around the clearing and walked to the back of the sculpture into the thickening shadows. With a good jump, I might be able to snag it. But what would I be grabbing? Last fall I'd found the horror of a clump of hair in an envelope that sent shivers through my limbs.

C'mon. Just grab the thing. Get this over with.

I told my feet to back up and get a running start, but they stayed planted like tree roots—heavy and thick.

What was wrong with me? Was I turning soft? For years rage had fueled my confrontations, erasing all other emotions while focusing my energies on rib-cracking victory. I'd taken on bigger men. I'd learned to throw the switch, cutting off any thoughts of injury or pain or consequence. I'd been unstoppable.

Eighteen months ago I'd made the decision to give up all that and start honoring my mother. Time for a change. Time to start thinking of others, not just myself. In choosing the high road, though, I'd been burned both literally and figuratively.

I looked down at my hand that still bore the scars. Apparently my psyche wasn't faring much better.

I scanned the clearing. This was me, Aramis Black, gathering evidence, reconnoitering, considering his next move. This was *not* a moment of weakness.

So why couldn't I budge?

———

PS3414—Social Psychology.

Lipscomb University, College of Natural and Applied Sciences.

In last week's class, Professor Newmann had addressed the mental hurdle of limb-numbing fear, reminding us that public speaking—forget spiders or heights—was Americans' number-one phobia. This set off a lively debate. Most of us could recount paralyzing incidents—two hundred feet up the face of a cliff, a chance at a game-winning free throw. One boy even admitted to freezing up during his first kiss and got a rousing laugh from the class.

"Look at Professor Bones," Diesel prodded me. "He's not even smiling."

"Probably still waiting for his first kiss."

"Naw. He was married once."

"Really? Now there's an urban legend for you."

Newmann's attention swiveled our direction. Behind tortoise-shell glasses large enough to frame a…well, a tortoise…his eyes locked on to mine. Above thin lips and pasty eyebrows, his hair was plastered across his forehead by one of those hair sprays that smells like something you'd use to polish your tires. His outdated tweed jacket didn't do much to hide an almost anorexic frame. Poor guy. Even his role as a sub was nothing more than a scrap thrown his way after our original teacher was pegged and hospitalized by a hit-and-run on South Twenty-First.

"Mr. Black, is there a comment you wish to add to our discussion?"

I started to zero in on a snappy comeback to send the class into howls. I imagined this slightly graying man at home alone with a microwave dinner, listening to Michael Bolton. Could he be any more pitiful? And then something moved in me: empathy maybe. Or godly compassion. How pathetic to ridicule a man I knew so little about.

"No sir," I said. "Sorry for interrupting."

Newmann studied me, testing my sincerity. Nervous giggles flitted about Ward Lecture Hall 150, but I remained stone faced.

Bones turned back to his notes on the lectern. Head down, he said, "We have ten minutes remaining before dismissal. Would you please stand, Mr. Black, and give a summation of our discussion?"

"Uh. Okay."

"No reason for a show of shyness. Speak for all to hear."

I rose and cleared my throat. I was working without a script, and the class probably had some perverse desire to see me fall.

Time to face the nation's number-one fear.

"Professor, can I address the class from the podium?"

"You *can*. More accurately, though, you'd need permission to do so."

"*May* I?"

He peered over his glasses. "Yes, you may."

I strode to the front and faced my peers. Nabbing bits of info from our past hour of interaction, I layered them with facts uncovered in my weekend homework, including recent theories that human DNA is encoded with ancestral memories.

"You're losing our attention," Newmann said. "Perhaps you can clarify."

"Okay. Who in this room is scared to death of cats?" I paused for a show of hands. "No one? But if a rat came skittering in under our desks, I bet this place would go crazy." The mere mention caused a group of girls in the front to lift their feet and shudder. "What if there's something in our collective heritage that triggers such reactions? Rats helped spread the Black Plague in the Middle Ages. Maybe the nightmares of previous generations passed down through our DNA."

The lecture hall was with me now.

"And think of déjà vu. We've all experienced it, right? Well, what if a particular bend in the river or a curve of the road seems suddenly familiar because Grandma saw that place years ago and passed that memory through her genes?"

Eyes were round with contemplation.

"Fear is a tool," I said. "A warning mechanism to aid our survival. DNA, genetics, maybe even your grandparents' memories play a part. Of course it gets tricky when it filters from our logical side into our intuitive side. A mom sees her kid run into the street, and she finds superhuman ability to protect her young. But emotions can also get in the way. Who was it who mentioned shooting free throws? You, Derek? I bet you wouldn't have frozen at the foul line if your dad hadn't been watching."

"Probably not."

"Bottom line," I concluded, "in this age of science and rationalism, we can't forget that the heart and brain are connected. They work in tandem. When we *feel* afraid, it only serves to underline that fact."

The professor's jacket swept against me as he retook the stage. The applause and whoops from the class faded, and he threw me a scowl. "Speaking of feelings, how do you *feel* you just did with your little discourse?"

"Pretty good."

"And how do you *think* you did?"

"All right, I guess."

"Which simply proves, Mr. Black, that thoughts and feelings don't always coincide with reality."

All this raced through my head in seconds.

Fear is a tool. Feelings don't match reality.

I shook my arms and took a step back. The ground was spongy, an unstable springboard. To my left, the *Steeple Dance*'s orange spires stretched upward. Straight ahead, the felt bag still dangled from the tree.

BEAR...act rapidly.

I made two running jumps, but my fingertips only raked along the soft material and set the object swinging back and forth above my face, taunting me.

The cords were wrapped around the branch, defying my efforts.

The razor. That was it. The freak had provided the necessary tool.

I shifted my gun back in my waistband, held the blade between my teeth, and grabbed hold of a lower branch. I tried not to close my mouth on the bloody metal.

To find piece...

I braced a foot between the tree trunk and a branch, stretched my leg to reach the next. A grunt. Another stretch, and I reached the limb that held the bag. Gripping the wood between my thighs, I scooted out to the cord. I saw it was knotted, damp and thick, almost impossible to loosen by hand.

After a few seconds of my sawing, the bag plummeted to the forest floor where it hit with a metallic clink. Didn't sound like a body part.

Other sounds now, not too far off.

Heavy breathing. Pounding feet. *The security guard!*

I dropped the blade and eased my legs over the cedar limb. My fingers released, and I landed in a crouch on the twigs and leaves below, the Desert Eagle squeezing over the rim of my jeans and thudding on the ground. I snatched it up, found the blade and the bag, and sprinted away as the guard came into view.

"Hold it right there!" he called.

He was no match for my speed, and he was in need of serious meds if he thought otherwise. Daily sit-ups, push-ups, and walking the mile to Black's most days—and now riding my mountain bike to class at Lipscomb—kept me lean and mean.

See ya.

Without slowing, I crashed through the bushes and swatted away the branches that slapped at my face. Give the guard some credit for recognizing pursuit was futile. Behind me, I could hear him yakking into his handheld radio.

high-stepped through dense underbrush, my mind racing.

Would they try to stop me at the gate? Was there an alternate exit? Aside from some suspicious behavior, I'd done nothing wrong. Maybe I could get to my car and simply slip away.

Nope. Couldn't take that chance just yet. If the bag clutched in my hand contained more clues on this little treasure hunt, it might lead to another spot here on the grounds. I couldn't mess this up. The bag's contents warranted at least a few seconds of investigation.

Still running, my feet hit a slope of grass and slipped from beneath me. I landed hard, juggling and cradling the stuff in my hands, careening on my backside toward the base of a fountain. With a bone-rattling jerk, I came to a stop.

As good a spot as any. You take life's lemons and make lemonade.

I loosened the bag's leather straps and peeked inside. Something glittered. Something smooth and polished. My cupped fingers brushed against paper before scooping the item into the daylight.

A Fabergé egg?

I'd seen many just like it in the exhibit hall, but this couldn't be an authentic one. The shape, size, and array of gemstones around the deep blue oval all looked genuine and expensive, but it seemed too light. And I knew from the brochure how rare they were. Fifty-odd imperial eggs existed in the entire world, and only a few remained unaccounted for after the assassination of the Romanovs during Lenin's revolution.

Sure enough. On the bottom, a sticker read "Fauxbergé." A clever fake. It was probably available at the gift shop in the restaurant.

What was the point of this then? Was there another message inside?

In the museum's exhibit, plaques explained how Fabergé's master craftsmen had designed these things originally to hold trinkets and treasures, revealed by the use of concealed mechanisms. I ran my fingers along the row of fake diamonds, felt for a seam in the translucent enamel surface.

Nothing obvious. Maybe this jutting jewel on top?

The squawk of a radio just up the hill interrupted my search.

I pressed back against the cool stone of the fountain, felt the spray dotting my face. No doubt the rent-a-cop was gathering his buddies, tightening the trap. My Honda was close now, but even if I reached it, I'd still have to pass the guards at the front gate. And, of course, ditching the car to escape on foot would leave my license tag to be traced, like a giant finger pointing to the place my brother and I share off West End Avenue.

Not much time. My options were limited.

I wrapped the razor in the envelope and stuffed it in my pocket. I removed the clip from my gun, ejected the chambered round, then slid the deadly components far back beneath a bush that bordered the fountain, and scooped dirt and bark over the pile. I marked the location in my mind for later retrieval.

Breathe, evaluate, act rapidly.

As the guard's large gut came into view, I realized my way out. Standing, I smoothed my shirt and headed toward his voice.

"Sir," I called out. "Excuse me."

"Take it easy now! Hold it right there."

"Did you see where she went?"

"Where she… Listen, bud, you keep your hands where I can see them." The security man puffed out his chest, sucked in his belly, then brought his hand to his mouth and spoke into his transmitter. "Yes sir, cornered him over here near the Perennial Garden."

Cornered me? I'd practically hopped into his lap.

In a show of remorse, I let my shoulders slump a little and said, "Should've kept my mouth shut. That's what I should've done. But no, I went and told her everything. You know the girl I'm talking about, the one I was kissing in the museum."

The guard studied me with obvious misgivings.

"She just left in a huff. Can't blame her," I continued. "I should've never said a word, especially after last time."

"Last time what?"

"It's a free country, right? So what am I supposed to do, never look at another woman? Impossible, right? Tell me that's possible."

"You admitted to looking at other women?"

"Honesty's the best policy. Isn't that what they say?"

"Now hold on. I saw the girl leave out the front, but you went hurrying out the back. And why'd you run from me when I told you to stop?"

"Ah, that's what this is about." I chuckled. "Sorry for the confusion. I wasn't running from you, not intentionally."

"I saw you with my own two eyes, so don't even—"

"I was trying to find her."

"Out the back door?"

"First I had to go find the gift I'd hidden for her."

"On the trail?"

"It was supposed to be romantic. A surprise."

"You trampled the flowers and ignored me to grab a gift? Didn't I tell you to save yourself some heartache?"

"Well, look. Now she's gone."

The guard showed no sympathy.

"This is her last day in town," I explained. "I wanted to make it special."

He shook his head, and his cheek bulged where his tongue worked its way around. As another guard arrived at his side, his nostrils continued flaring like bellows, wheezing with each intake of air.

"Trouble?" the reinforcement asked.

There was that word again.

"This man"—the guard lifted his meaty arm in my direction—"ran off from the museum and refused to obey my orders to stop."

"He's not running now."

"Well, I wasn't going to let him get away, Jerry. Look at his pants. The grass stains. He was up to something."

"Didn't mean to cause such a…a hullabaloo," I said.

Hullabaloo? Where had that word come from? I'd hoped to sound less threatening, but that was bordering on backwoods.

Jerry lifted his eyebrows. "What's that in your hand?"

"This?" I removed the Fauxbergé from the bag. "A gift for my girlfriend."

"So he says." The first guard huffed, then gave a recap of my story.

Jerry's face took on a bemused expression, and I got the feeling that a power play of sorts was at work here, that the first man had a habit of exaggerating situations to boost his own stock with his boss—cool-headed Jerry— who to his credit, listened all the way through before taking a step toward me, his palm outstretched.

"If I'm not mistaken, that's from our shop. Let's see a receipt."

Home free.

"Here you go." I fished the paper from the bottom of the bag, handed it over.

"Well, there you go. Purchased this afternoon in cash. See, Chuck? Nothing to get worked up over."

"But he was running away! He—"

"Look at him." Gazing my direction, Jerry draped a hand over his subordinate's broad back and spoke in a winsome tone. "He's a lovesick soul, Chuck. Maybe, just maybe, he can still catch up to this girl and win her back."

I nodded. "I appreciate that, sir."

"Just a bit of advice: think before you speak next time, and wear blinders if you have to." Jerry gave a melodramatic nod to the gardens on his left, to the daffodils on the right. "Beautiful flowers are easy enough to find. But true love? That's something special. Don't go tossing away a rose for a peek at the latest blossoms."

"Easier said than done."

"But worth it, son, I assure you." He tapped his wedding ring. "Nineteen years."

"Wow. Way to go."

"Like anyone wants to hear this," Chuck interjected.

"Thanks," I told the other man. "You're a true romantic."

"Actually, just another wannabe songwriter. Hey"—Jerry lifted a shoulder—"doesn't hurt to dream."

We all laughed, even taciturn Chuck. Guitar-packing troubadours come to Nashville by the thousands, many to be quickly chewed up, spit out, and crushed underfoot. Stardom's a fleeting thing, as my brother can testify. He spent years paying his dues, earning his keep, sharpening his chops.

Johnny Ray. I'd left him waiting at Black's. At least he'd be safe.

And what about Felicia's part in this?

I thanked the guards for their understanding, then darted toward the parking lot—the picture of a man chasing lost love. The contents of the bag in my hand demanded more exploration. Still muddled by a kiss and the events of the last twenty minutes, my mind was a blur.

coasted through the front gates and past the guard post. I turned onto Page Road, took a left onto Belle Meade, where frolickers still spilled from the Iroquois Steeplechase, then headed into town on Harding Pike.

Outside the windshield, a dragonfly buzzed along, iridescent, staying a foot or so ahead of my Civic. I watched it for a while until for some reason it struck me funny, and I laughed, bleeding off the past hour's overload of adrenaline.

On the seat beside me, the felt bag waited.

I pulled into Elmington Park before the I-440 overpass and killed the engine. Three boys in baggy shorts kicked a soccer ball and laughed as a mom watched from a picnic table, her hand rocking a baby carrier beside her. I recalled the park where my mom had taught me how to swing. Those twinkling eyes when she tousled my hair.

Six years compacted into one corner of my memory. So little to hold on to.

I traced the felt bag with my fingers, realizing its contents could shake things up all over again. Despite promises to my brother, there might be more trouble ahead.

A chance I'd have to take.

I removed the Fauxbergé from the bag. The jewel on the sphere's top caught my eye once more, and I twisted it, hearing the soft click of a lock opening. The egg's upper third fell open on a golden hinge to reveal a hollow space inside.

A bullet casing rested on the velvet lining.

What in the...

When I tipped the jeweled egg like a tiny teapot, the tarnished shell rolled into my palm, and I noticed a slip of paper tucked inside it. What if I ignored the note? I could just refuse to play this cat-and-mouse game.

But I knew better. I had to do this for Johnny: *for the sake of your loved ones...*

And Felicia.

Whether innocent or involved, Felicia Daly was my best link to the culprit. I'd manhandled her, allowing the resentments of our breakup to take over, and now she was gone. I should've run after her. For her sake and mine. Of course, the guard in the hallway had put a stop to my meager attempt.

Against my skin, the casing was warm. I tried to extract the paper, but it was furled and wedged in at an angle. I plucked at it. Attempted to grip it with my short fingernails. I pinned the sheet against the metal and began edging it out, millimeter by millimeter, until it popped free into my hand, and I spread it open on my leg.

Chop, chop, Aramis. Here's a piece of your mother's past. "Where, O death, is your victory? Where, O death, is your sting?" Yes, by falling forward before the trigger was pulled, she cheated the grave. If you help me, you'll get to see her again and earn your way back into our family circle. Perhaps you should give me a ring.

"Sure," I grumbled. "It'd help if you left me a number."

Our family circle? Who did he think he was? And this continued twist-

ing of scriptures seemed an intentional affront against the respect my mother
had shown for the Good Book.

Obvious lies. I wasn't falling for any false hopes.

Could my dad be responsible? He seemed as unlikely as Felicia.

I studied the cartridge's tarnished brass, found myself reliving the moment when the gun had exploded and sent my mom reeling forward. An earlier shot in the thigh had brought her to her knees, and she'd cried out, black
hair clinging to her cheeks. Then…she was toppling, falling, vanishing
beneath the river's dark currents.

I have no memory of any blood. Or an impact wound. Her body was
never recovered from the water. From previous discussions with Meade, I
knew most police departments destroyed evidence long before two decades
had passed. What were the chances of this casing being the one from that
Oregon riverbank?

Surely it wasn't possible she had survived, was it? What if she…

No! Stop!

I stiffened in the driver's seat. "She was shot," I whispered. "She refused
to give in to greed, and she paid with her life. I watched it with my own eyes."

If you help me…

Why should I do anything for this deviant? He was an extremist, nothing more than an urban terrorist using Scripture and sick-in-the-head means
to justify his actions.

You'll get to see her again and earn your way back into our family circle…

The words were barbed arrows dipped into the disease of deceit. They
had no effect on me. I was inoculated against the stuff.

I read the note a second time and a third.

See? No problem.

I folded the paper and tucked it into my pocket along with the empty cartridge. The Fauxbergé went under the seat. I turned the key in the ignition, adjusted my mirrors, backed out of the parking space, and threaded my way through Saturday's late-afternoon traffic toward Black's.

———

"Pop quiz."

"Not right now."

"This one's easy, a simple true or false."

I surveyed the shop. "You want true or false, Diesel? Here ya go. I told my brother not to leave before I got back."

"True."

"So where is he?"

"Last I looked, he was there at that table."

I followed his pointing finger to a lone salad plate beside a glass of melting ice.

"He's real down to earth," Diesel continued. "One cool cat. He was telling me all about this latest song he's been working on, but then Samantha came in."

"Sammie was here?"

"Ohhh, yeah. Hard to miss. If you don't mind me saying so, she's got a nice—"

"Stop, Diesel. Think. Was this five minutes ago? Ten?"

"Been busy cleaning, boss. I don't know. Maybe they headed back to the studio. Isn't she Johnny Ray's manager or something like that?"

"Something like that."

"Beautiful *and* talented." He gave a low whistle. "How old is she?"

"Too old for you. Shouldn't you be working?"

He poured water into the coffee machine. "Shoot, if I showed up on my parents' doorstep with Samantha on my arm, my dad would fall all over himself trying to welcome her in. He's got it bad for women, young or old. Maybe it's wrong to say, but that's a fact. My mom was barely nineteen when they got married."

I dialed my brother, got his voice mail: "If you would like to leave a message…"

Diesel said, "Would you want a serious relationship with a nineteen-year-old?"

"No, I would not." I slapped the phone shut. "Thank you very much."

"Me neither."

"Wait. I wasn't—"

He carried on while scooping coffee into the brew basket. "Guess Dad had to find out the hard way. He and Mom, I've never heard them raise their voices at each other, but it's this constant tug of war, all these unspoken politics. What about your parents?"

"Don't have many memories of them together."

He shot me a glance. Turned away. The whole country had seen the reenactment of my mother's death played out on my segment of *The Best of Evil*, but most people still seemed uneasy mentioning it around me. What? Like I had to pretend it never happened?

He fidgeted. "What was your mom like anyway?"

"She was great." I rolled my neck. "Very loving."

"And?"

"Strong in a quiet way." My hand brushed the old cartridge in my pocket. "And she loved her morning coffee. She cleaned houses to put food on the table for us."

"Johnny Ray's told me stories."

"About my mom?" I wheeled on him. "Since when?"

"I…I don't know."

"Listen. My family's none of your business. And while we're at it, tell me why your dad's been making threats against me and Johnny. What's that all about?"

"That's crazy. Dad's never even met you guys."

"But he's in Nashville, isn't he? Gimme one good reason why."

"I am their only child, if that counts. He and Mom drove down to visit." Diesel kicked at the rubber floor mat. "Forget I said anything. I was just trying to be a friend."

"This is work. You're on the clock."

"But at school, we—"

"That's different. That's college. Here I'm your boss."

"Ohhh." Above solid shoulders, Diesel let his expression turn bland. "I get it."

"What?"

"You're afraid."

I coughed out a laugh. "What?"

"It's just like the stuff we've been talking about in class. Fear and lies."

My arms felt charged at my sides. In times past, less provocation would have led me to do severe damage to someone's face. It cured the red and black squeezing in on my vision every time.

"Shouldn't have said anything," Diesel mouthed. "I'm getting back to work."

"You do that."

Heading back into the kitchen, I found Anna Knight at the stainless-steel triple sink. Even with elbows deep in suds, she had a glow that seemed to fill the room and draw me toward her.

"Just finishing up," she said. "You need help out there?"

"Diesel's got it covered. Any idea where my brother ran off to?"

"Sorry. I've been busy washing up. How's your day going?"

"Fine."

"Hardly a convincing answer." Anna peeked past me. "Is it Diesel? He's been in a mood all afternoon, and nothing I say seems to placate him. He's really not interested in taking orders from me."

"When I'm gone, you're in charge," I assured her.

"Yes, but…I think he resents it a bit."

"And you thought you were done raising kids. I'm afraid you've got your hands full with me and Diesel."

"You? Hon, you're a piece of cake."

I put a finger to my lips. "Careful. I've got a reputation to protect."

"Heaven forbid." Anna slipped her hand from the soapy water and set it on my forearm. "You do know, don't you, sometimes women like to see a soft side, some vulnerability?"

"I don't do 'vulnerable.' Made that mistake not too long ago."

"You'll have to do it again."

"Who says?"

"If you ever hope to find true love."

"Been there. Right now I'm just hoping to find Johnny Ray."

From Anna's fingers, a caravan of soap bubbles trekked down my skin and washed over the edges of my tattoo. I ripped a paper towel from the dispenser above the sink and mopped at the suds.

There it was, my call to action, in glistening green and blue.

Live by the Sword…

In the span of eighteen hours, someone had carved into my brother, blackmailed my ex-girlfriend, spun lies about my mother, and tried to snare me with empty promises. I could not sit by. I would not. Axman wanted me to relive my pain? Good. I would run to embrace it.

Die by the Sword…

Yes, I'd pull my memories close and squeeze every drop of grief from them until they were dead and gone, unable to harm me. No more waiting. Time to act.

I marched out the door, got in my car, and peeled away from the curb. At the first intersection, a traffic light came slowly into focus through my quagmire of emotion. Red light…red light…red…

Brakes!

I mashed the pedal to the floor and corrected the Honda's rubber-burning slide. A horn blared, and a man in a yellow hard hat gave me a one-fingered salute as his SUV slid by.

"Same to you, pal!"

I checked my mirrors, panned the traffic for any glimpse of a Hyundai sedan. Why had AX cut my brother? Why had he turned his attention to me? If he was after Lewis's centuries-old gold, how had he known to come knocking on our door?

The dash clock said it was a quarter past six.

Okay. Forget playing nice. The moral high road sounded so smug, so righteous—until the threats became personal. First I'd find Johnny Ray and Felicia, take them down to the station, and place them under police protection. Then, after nightfall, I'd sneak onto the Cheekwood estate to retrieve my gun. Prey would become predator.

New ways, schnew ways… I'd do what had to be done.

Chop, chop.

On the steering wheel, my fingers itched for the weight of my Desert Eagle, for the familiar resistance of the trigger.

10

*D*esperado Artist Development. Johnny had to be here.

I parked along the curb on Sixteenth. Clouds hovered over the treetops, and I rolled up my windows. A warm gust stirred freshly cut grass around my feet as I got out and headed past DAD's black and silver lawn sign. Though the studio occupies a two-level brick home, it's all business inside. The living room's been converted into a front lobby, the upstairs into offices, the downstairs bedrooms into a soundproof studio and mixing room.

At the steps of the wraparound porch, I turned toward Sammie's late-model Mustang in the driveway. No sign of my brother's pickup. She must've given him a ride.

"Got a kickin' set of wheels, doesn't she?"

"Huh?" I looked up. "Oh. Hi, Chigger."

Johnny's goateed guitarist was leaning against a porch post, taking drags on a cigarette between sessions. He was in faded jeans, a paint-splattered hoodie, and a baseball cap sporting the initials C.S.A. over a Confederate flag.

"Ever had yourself a ride in that car?"

"Couple times," I said. "Went out to Percy Priest Lake in it last year."

"You and Sammie? Not gonna lie to ya. I'm jealous."

"Johnny was with us."

"Johnny Ray Black." Smoke writhed from the man's nostrils, through his sideburns. His mouth curled into its standard sneer. "Can't begin to tell ya how many times that boy's come between us."

Meaning the car? Or Samantha?

"He's keeping you employed," I pointed out. "Is he inside?"

"Whoa now, let's get one thing straight. Chigger keeps *himself* employed, and if Chigger's not feeling it, he's got other places he can go."

"I'm sure you do."

"Man's gotta take pride in his work." He swatted his cap against a thick leg. "Can't let no one push him around."

"What do the initials stand for?"

"C.S.A.?" He looked the hat over as though contemplating things best addressed in reverence. "Confederate States of America."

"You into all that?"

"All what? I'm proud of my heritage. My great-great-granddaddy, he gave his life for this land. Fought for his loved ones."

"Sure. You gotta protect your family."

"A God-given right, yes sir. Says it there in the Con-*stee*-tution."

"And then there's the whole thing against slavery, right there in the Bill of Rights."

Squinting, he took a long drag, then dropped and crushed the cigarette with his boot. His next phrase rang like a battle cry. "Mark my words: the South will rise again."

Though numerous responses rushed to my lips, I couldn't pretend to have a grasp of the Southern psyche. I do know slavery was wrong, but I also know Union troops were as guilty of wrongdoing as those they fought against.

"So have you seen my brother?" I stepped onto the porch. "Is he in there?"

"He's here, all right, and he's gonna regret it if he doesn't start showin' a li'l appreciation. Chigger's about artistic freedom. Maybe you could go in and bend his ear. He might just listen to his kid brother."

"Name's Aramis." The steps lifted me onto the porch.

Situating the cap back on his head, Chigger droned on. " 'Tryin' to Do Things Right,' my foot. Johnny Ray's more about doin' what suits Johnny Ray."

"That so?"

"A blind man wouldn't tell ya no different."

My fists swung like hammers as I moved toward Chigger's leaning post. "That's my brother you're talking about."

"Doesn't change the fact. He thinks he's above listenin' to Chigger—one of *the* best guitar players on Music Row. Man's gonna learn the hard way that ain't how things work. Hear this: I can knock 'em down as quick as I build 'em up."

"You wanna talk about knockdowns?"

With chests almost touching, we locked gazes. His left eye twitched.

"Not that I meant nothin' by it, Aramis."

" 'Course not."

He backed into the railing. "You smoke?" He tapped his pack on his wrist, extended it my direction.

"Been a year and a half. Things'll kill you."

He put the pack back, tugged on his goatee. "You know, you're bigger than your brother."

"Just looks that way."

"Johnny Ray's in there and Sammie too. Get on in."

"I'll do that."

"Door's unlocked."

"Hey." I ordered my fists to loosen. "No hard feelings?"

He lit another cigarette and studied the glowing tip. "You talk to your brother for me." Then he turned and propped both elbows on the railing, hiding his face from me.

In the darkened hallway, the walls glistened with autographed photos and
certified gold albums. I stood at the thick glass, watching my brother belt out
the chorus to his new song. He stopped once to discuss vocal arrangements
with the producer in the booth, then closed his eyes and faced the suspended
mike again.

Even through the hall speaker, his intensity reached my ears:

It's true you left me years ago, travelin' long dark roads.
But in my heart we're not apart, I've been livin' with your ghost.
Your love, it's always been here, faithful to the end.
In these eyes there's no surprise, because an angel's what you've been.

I'd never known him to use religious symbols in his lyrics before, and I
wondered what this new direction indicated. As he repeated the chorus, the
words seemed prescient, strangely fitting.

But in my heart we're not apart, I've been livin' with your ghost...

For most of my life, I'd pushed my mother's absence to the back corners
of my mind. There was no replacing the loss of a parent. Sure, the past year
had reconnected me to her in ways I never imagined, yet the unveiling of her
secrets also had led to hard truths about my biological father, the abuse I suffered as an adolescent, even the bond I shared with my brother.

Johnny seemed to be processing similar things through his music.

A hand on my shoulder snapped me back to the present. I turned to find
Samantha Rosewood, slender and frail looking in the corridor's shadows.

"Sammie. Didn't hear you come in."

Accentuated by honey-colored hair, her hazel eyes trailed up to mine.

"You okay?" I asked. "What's going on?"

Her gaze slid off to my brother in the studio. "Doesn't he sound good? Try as they might, they just can't manufacture that kind of conviction."

"Where've you been? You haven't answered my calls."

She faced the glass.

"Hey," I urged. "Did you get my messages? Is something wrong?"

"It's Miss Eloise," she said.

Miss Eloise: Sammie's lone remaining grandparent, a gentle woman whose medical issues had been an increasing cause for concern.

"Is she…" My breath caught in my throat.

"She passed during the night."

"Sammie, I'm sorry. Have you told Johnny Ray?"

Sammie moved her head up and down. "The funeral-home director left this afternoon, and I went over to the shop. Johnny was so sweet, even offering to sing at the memorial."

"He's a good man."

"He told me you were off on another of your escapades."

"Escapades? Actually I was…"

"You were what?"

"Never mind."

She scanned my face. "What is it?"

I shook my head. I knew it was her nature to try to take on my burdens, and that was something she didn't need at the moment.

"Did she go in her sleep?" I inquired.

"Peacefully, yes, thank the Lord."

"I'm sorry."

"It wasn't totally unexpected."

"Still."

Never one to wallow in emotion, Sammie laid a hand to her heart, and her eyes bored into me with a brief unguarded look. "Thank you."

She was alone, I realized. On her own. After she'd lost her parents to health problems a few years back, she used her trust fund to further her education—as stipulated by her father—and to volunteer regularly in the community. On a more personal level, she shared her parents' sprawling Tyne Boulevard estate with Miss Eloise—bathing, feeding, and nursing her grandmother without complaint.

That security was now stripped away. Aside from distant cousins and an uncle in Cades Cove of East Tennessee's Smoky Mountains, her immediate family was gone.

I opened my arms to draw her in, and she didn't pull away. For a few moments, we stood there together, her pulse feathering against my chest. In increments, her stiffness melted.

"What can I do to help?" I whispered.

She shook her head.

"Anything. You just say it."

"I appreciate that. I do. But no, there's nothing at this point."

"Are you okay to drive? You need me to take you somewhere?"

Though her lips turned up in a brave smile, her eyes were round and moist. She pretended to brush something from my shirt, then moved back a step. "I'm not the one who was ailing," she reminded me. "I think I can operate a vehicle just fine."

From the hallway speaker, bits of Johnny's vocals washed over our conversation:

"an angel...oh yes, an angel...an angel's what you've been."

Sammie's chin shifted, then recentered itself. Seeking balance.

I said, "If you need to…you know, talk—whatever—call me."

"I will."

"You're not alone."

She rubbed a finger against her temple, looked off past my shoulder. Her face softened as high cheekbones caught the glow of studio lights.

"I mean that," I reiterated.

"You've gone through your own loss, Aramis, so I know your sentiments are heartfelt. In all honesty, I'm just not sure I'm ready to hear it."

"Understandable. You want to skip our dinner tomorrow?"

"Our Sunday supper? We still have business to discuss, don't we?"

"It's your call."

"Let's go ahead. There's always comfort in routine."

"Is J. Alexander's still okay?"

She lifted her chin as though catching a breath. "If you'd reserve a corner booth, that'd be wonderful."

Her show of strength riveted me. How she does it, I have no idea. Occasionally I spot a carefree spark in those eyes, and I imagine under there, somewhere, a little girl who once dove into piles of leaves and ran through sprinklers with abandon. She may be hidden for now, but she's still there. I have to believe it. "Six o'clock," I said. "I'll try to be on time."

"You're usually pretty good about that."

In my pocket, the brass bullet casing pressed against my thigh, a reminder that I shouldn't be making promises on a day like today. "Listen, if I'm held up for some reason, you go ahead and order without me."

"Now you have me worried."

"I'm sorry. It's nothing."

"And I'm to believe that? You seem anxious. Does this have something to do with your escapade?"

I mumbled an affirmative.

"Something important?"

"Could be."

"Well then, Aramis, I will be patiently waiting. You do what you have to do."

11

On the streets, if you cave to intimidation, you're as good as gone. That's the law I grew up with. On my desk in Black's office, my New Testament reminds me of a different law: the law of forgiveness. I often think about how, even when he was under arrest, Jesus refused to retaliate, and the apostle Peter took matters into his own hands, drawing his sword and slashing off a soldier's ear.

Now there was a man I could relate to. Three cheers for San Pedro.

Except Jesus wasn't pleased.

With one touch, he healed the wounded man and instructed Peter to put away his weapon. He told him, "Those who use the sword will die by the sword."

Yeah. I knew all about that. Even got the tattoos to prove it. Sometimes I wonder if I'll ever escape the old patterns that seem etched into my being.

Although I'd promised my brother and the detective that I would stay out of trouble, it was Sammie's concern in DAD's studio that caused me to reconsider. By putting aside her own grief, she released me to do what had to be done and unknowingly infused me with a sense of responsibility. I thought of Mom. I thought of Sammie. It was time to resolve this issue with AX, yes—but not the way I'd planned.

Forget the Desert Eagle. No .40-caliber revenge this time.

Once Johnny Ray and Felicia were tucked away under the cops' watchful eyes, I'd turn over the evidence—the stained razor blade, the empty casing, and the note—and let Metro's finest take over.

I'd do it to honor my mother. And Sammie too.

End of story.

After Johnny's recording session, I told him the bare bones of my Cheekwood encounter, and he agreed to go directly to the West Precinct, where Detective Meade would take a statement.

One down. One to go.

Armed with the yellow pages in DAD's front lobby, I began my search for Felicia. She'd worn a dress provided by my foe, flown here on his tab, and it seemed feasible he could've put her up in a local hotel.

A long shot, sure. But what else did I have?

I flipped through pages of listings, punched in numbers on my cell. One hotel. And another. On my umpteenth attempt, a front-desk woman greeted me with rehearsed politeness as I made my request to speak to Felicia.

"D-a-l-y," I spelled the last name. "She may be a guest there."

Expecting yet another strikeout, I was skimming down to the next listing when she said, "Thank you, sir. I'll connect you now."

There was no answer from Felicia's room. The phone went to a message service, and I asked her to call my cell when she came in.

Not that I had time to wait.

With the hotel address jotted down on my palm, I grabbed my keys and headed for my car. I sped through a few turns until I was traveling east on Lafayette. Considering its location on the lower boundary of Nashville's sprawling airport, the hotel was most likely a ramshackle joint. In recent months that area had played host to police raids targeting gang activity, drug transactions, and worse.

Hardly the safest arrangements. If AX *had* paid for her room, he was not only a cheapskate, he was heartless too.

Least he would be. Once I tore it from his chest.

I braced my arms against the steering wheel and shoved my head back against the headrest. No. Couldn't let my thoughts go running down that warpath. I had to resist, for Sammie's sake.

Lord, help me keep it in check here. Please.

A slight easing of tension. Meet the new-and-improved Aramis Black.

As Lafayette merged into Murfreesboro Pike, the evening sun broke in final judgment through the clouds behind me and speared the city with bronze shafts of light. Between buildings, through windows, colors merged and bled onto the streets. There was a terrible beauty to it, which pressed upon me again the unfathomable aspects of God's nature. If he knows all, if he sees the calamity caused by his headstrong humans, why doesn't he step in more often? What makes him hold back his wrath?

Shoot first. Ask questions later. That would be the policy if he left it up to me.

Which is why he didn't, I suppose.

Twelve minutes later I spotted the hotel's flickering sign too late and had to make a U-turn. In a space far from the manager's office, I idled the engine and weighed my options as the sunset washed my face.

The desk clerk might not give me a room number, but I could try bluffing. Or knocking on doors until I got lucky. Or...

What if Felicia had been forced to share a unit with the scumbag? What if he was in there now? My unexpected appearance might put her in even more danger.

I killed the ignition. Something had to be done.

I was grabbing at my door handle when the arrival of another vehicle stopped me. I lowered my head and waited for it to park. Then, just above the dash, I got a good look at the car.

Same make, model, and color as the death hearse. Hyundai. Sedan. Dark green.

AX had come to keep tabs on Felicia? Was she already bound and gagged in the room? Maybe that's why she hadn't answered the phone.

Of course, the car could be just a coincidence.

No. My gut and my brain told me this was a bit of crucial information. Professor Newmann's words played through my head: *thoughts and feelings don't always coincide with reality.*

Guess I'd have to find out for myself.

The Hyundai rolled closer. If I'd had my gun, I would've challenged the driver to a duel, much the same way Tennessee's own Andrew Jackson, seventh president of the United States, did with opponents in his era. Nicknamed Old Hickory, he'd even killed a man in such a gunfight, with the location of the victim's Nashville burial site remaining a mystery to this day.

A duel? No. Remember, the path of peace.

My gaze was fixed on the nearing vehicle, waiting for a telltale glimpse of the driver. In seconds my vigilance was rewarded as the last of the sunlight skipped sparks along the car's hood and broke over the windshield, illuminating the face at the steering wheel.

"No way," I said. Not that it was a huge shocker.

Brake lights flashed, and the car came to a stop.

Felicia Daly climbed out.

Holding a grocery bag and a Dean Koontz novel—she'd always had a fascination with dark and suspenseful tales—my ex-girlfriend made her way up metal stairs to a second-story unit. Number 212. She tucked the book under her chin, fiddled with the key, then, with a half spin in her knee-length dress, disappeared from view.

12

S he's in the room, you say?"

"That's right. Didn't seem worried or nervous. Nothing."

Through the cell, Detective Meade had listened to an overview of my day, and now he met my alarm with a steady voice. "And she shows no indication of leaving?"

My position in the parking lot provided easy observation of her room. The door had remained closed since her arrival, and the encroaching night would be unable to conceal her departure now that globe lights had flicked on above the second-level walkway. On the far end of the landing, an ice machine labored in the sticky air. On this end, a large woman filled a lawn chair, swigging beer from an oversize çan while a diaper-clad toddler played at her feet.

I tensed at the sight.

"Aramis? Tell me what you're seeing."

"I'd say she's turned in for the night. A good book. Bottle of wine. That used to be her thing."

"When you were...cohabiting."

"Seems like a lifetime ago."

"So let me clarify. You believe she's driving the same vehicle you spotted last evening on Demonbreun right after the assault on your brother."

"I never saw the plates. But, yeah, that's what I think."

"And you want me to do what exactly?"

"I don't know. What can you do? Either she's responsible for the attack on my brother or she's an accomplice."

"We have no proof of that, no evidence. Do you know of any motive? As a protector of the law, I'm not given wholesale permission to do as I choose. Calling a judge for a warrant on a Saturday night requires probable cause."

He had me there. In fact, at Cheekwood, Felicia had denied any culpability. I raced through the day's events, grasping for a clue, any lead I might have missed.

"Mr. Black?"

I noted the switch from friendly to formal. "Yes sir?"

"May I ask why you're even at this woman's hotel? I thought we had an agreement you wouldn't take matters into your own hands."

"Still do."

"You think me a fool? Clearly, you've decided to—"

"No, Detective. It's not that way."

"Enlighten me then."

Shifting in the Honda's cockpit, I sighed and stretched my legs. Bugs moved in hazy orbits around the landing's globe lights. "Thing is, Felicia told me she'd been threatened. I wanted to bring her in and make sure she was okay. Only now I'm not sure what to think. Maybe she's working with him, the attacker."

"At this point we really don't know, do we?"

"Hey. Why don't you meet me over here? Then you could question her."

"On what grounds? To be honest with you, I'm off duty in a matter of minutes. My wife's made plans for us tonight."

"A hot date. Ah, that's a good thing."

"A play actually. At the Darkhorse Theatre."

"Never been there."

"It'd be a cultural experience for you, I'd think. Listen, your brother stopped by a short while ago. I took a statement from him and recorded his injuries. I appreciate your encouraging him in that. The number of this anonymous caller, it's assigned to a phone booth in Atlanta. So not much help there. I did discover something you'll no doubt find fascinating though. Are you familiar with the phrase *Virescit Vulnere Virtus*?"

"Uh, not offhand."

"It means 'Courage grows strong at a wound.' Back in the sixteenth century, Mary Stuart—known to us as Mary, Queen of Scots—embroidered the phrase into a cloth, and it later became the motto of the Royal Stuart clan."

"And?"

"Our perp could be a Stuart."

"Or just a Latin-spouting sadist."

Meade refused to be derailed. "In my cursory research, I found that the Stuarts were protectors of the Knights Templar. Considering your recent entanglements in history, you might see a connection."

"Not…really."

"Pretty nebulous, I admit."

"My brother's more the history buff anyway. Unless we've got a Stuart Axman wandering the streets of Nashville, I doubt there's anything there."

"I checked some variations of the name. Nothing seemed to match up."

"Well, thanks for looking into it." My gaze ran along the hotel's second-floor landing. "You'd better get going. Your hot date."

"What about you?"

"Me?"

"Your brother's gone home for the evening, and you'd be well advised to follow suit."

"What about police protection? Did Johnny show you the e-mail I printed out?"

"He did."

"And that qualifies as a threat, right? Especially after the attack at the statue."

"It raises concerns, certainly, and I understand why you'd be upset, but please, try to relax. For a number of reasons, though, Metro can't respond to every incriminating letter. There are financial factors, legal ones too. Domestic-violence victims can be referred to safe houses, but that's generally the extent of it. Hate to contradict the movies, but that's the facts."

"So there's nowhere Johnny can go for the night? He needs to be hidden until you find his attacker."

"He could check himself into a hotel. Or stay with a friend or family member."

"You're telling me you won't do anything for him." At the hotel's street entrance, a pair of headlights dipped, bounced, then flashed across my car window. I turned from the glare.

"On any given day there are a dozen threats of this sort."

"In other words, your hands are tied until a crime's been committed. Meanwhile, this AX person gets to roam around. What about the aggravated assault? Or Nadine Lott's murder? Don't those factor into this?"

"If it's any comfort, I did request increased patrol on your block tonight."

"Thanks." The car was pulling in three spaces away, and I hunched down with the phone pressed to my ear.

He sighed. "You have to understand my position."

"Yeah, I get it. You need a corpse before you can act."

"Mr. Black, have you ever contemplated killing someone?"

"What?" Memories of my youth caromed through my head, years in which vengeance and survival had kept me tightly wound. My tattoos had been a strident warning to friend and foe: don't mess with Aramis Black.

"It's a straightforward question," he prompted. "A simple yes or no."

"You're a cop. What do you expect me to say?"

"I'm off duty, remember? I'm not asking for a signed confession."

"Okay. Sure. Who hasn't?"

"Which explains why we can't assign round-the-clock protection every time a citizen of Davidson County considers such things. It'd be a logistical nightmare."

His words became garbled as I lifted my head and identified the newly arrived vehicle—the curve of the windows, the size of the chassis, the shape of the brake lights. Felicia's car had raised all sorts of questions, but this recent arrival elevated them to neon paranoia. Was my own imagination getting the best of me?

"Did I lose you?"

"Still here," I said, staring in surprise at the new car.

"Please assure me that you won't disregard everything I've said."

"Dude, not at all." I tried to sound calm. "Sorry for bugging you."

"Considering the day you've had, I suggest getting a good night's sleep."

Deep breath. "Yeah, and you have a nice date with your wife."

"Mm-hmm." He seemed wary of my sudden attitude change. "Take care of yourself."

"Peace." I closed the phone.

Three spaces away the latest arrival was another economy-sized Hyundai sedan, dark green. A duplicate of Felicia's. Apparently, now that I had this specific car on my mental radar, I was spotting them everywhere. We'd discussed this phenomenon in social psych. Such heightened awareness was a well-documented trick of the human brain.

But two of them? In the same lot on the same night?

Don't let down your guard. Not yet.

From the cockpit, a middle-aged couple emerged. They lumbered toward their first-level room and disappeared inside with nary a hint of affection.

While I respect their generation's desire to "keep things proper"—and I admit my age group has cheapened the whole business—I couldn't help wondering if anything went on behind those closed doors.

Again I studied the matching cars. Gave a caustic chuckle.

Stickers in the left corner of the rear windows indicated that both Hyundais came from a rental agency at nearby Nashville International Airport.

Odd coincidence, yes. Earthshaking evidence, no.

Suddenly my accusatory thoughts seemed silly and circumstantial. I had to get a grip here. I was becoming a full-on head case.

Still parked in the hotel lot, I decided to give it a few minutes. Lamps cast an inviting glow against the drawn curtains of room 212. What was Felicia doing up there all alone? Curled up with a suspense novel and a bottle of white zin?

At the museum, she said she still thought about me. How would she react if I went to her door? What would she be wearing?

Boys who grow up without a mother often crave female attention. Perpetuating the generalization, my brother and I became relational pyromaniacs, using behavior justification like matchsticks to start fires for the raw excitement of it, for the breathtaking heat of the flames. And yet we remained oblivious to women's inner workings. By the time we realized the dangers of our activities, we'd burned and been burned numerous times.

Johnny considers it all part of life. Animal instincts will have their say. I, on the other hand, have been trying to die to my old desires so that they might be rekindled in a purer form—with drier wood, so to speak, and fuel that'll feed a fire that never goes out. A lady deserves nothing less, right? A lady like Sammie Rosewood.

For the sake of example.

Shadowed movement behind the curtains shot another burst of suspicion through my mind. Was Felicia being held captive? She said her life had
been threatened. Least I could do was go up and knock. Put my fears to rest.

I lifted myself from the Honda and jogged across the pavement to the
foot of the stairway. Insects hummed nearby. Everything in me insisted this
was a bad idea, one I'd come to regret. Black paint thrummed with the day's
heat as my fingers slid up the metal rail.

13

xcuse me." A husky man was coming down the exterior hotel stairs.

"Sorry." I moved aside. "My bad."

It was the middle-aged driver of the second Hyundai. His sagging cheeks and double chin looked freshly shaved. He bore a plastic bucket, and from the bed of ice a foil-capped champagne bottle told me to stop assuming I understood the romantic overtures that played out among my elders.

"Thanks," he said.

"You have a good night."

A mischievous grin tugged at his droopy mouth. The sly dog.

At the top of the stairs, I was next confronted by the diapered boy. Mosquitoes circled his ebony arms and dimpled legs. Through walnut-brown eyes he took me in, then with a wobble he plopped down on his padded backside.

"You okay?"

"He's aw-ight," snapped the woman in the lawn chair. Her girth stretched pink bicycle shorts and a yellow tube top to their limits, while poor teeth and a hair net made it difficult to determine her age. The kid's mother—or grandmother?—challenged me with a bleary, black-eyed stare.

"S'up?" I greeted her. "Nice night out, huh?"

"Hmmm."

"Pretty humid though."

"This?" She emitted a throaty giggle. "Ever been to Louisiana?"

"Love to go someday."

"Y'all think you know, don't you?"

Unsure of her meaning, I said, "Cute kid there."

"My sister's."

"Lotsa bugs out tonight. He's getting eaten alive."

"Nothin' he ain't used to."

When she shifted, I was assailed by a mental image of her collapsing in a heap of bright colors, bent aluminum, and beer-scented curses.

"I know it's none of my business," I said, "but he really shouldn't be out here." I smacked a tiger mosquito that had landed on my arm, held out my bloodied palm as proof before wiping it on my jeans. "We've had local cases of the West Nile virus."

The woman's facial muscles pulled at her wizened cheeks and eyelids. "West Nile? In that Superdome, right after Katrina, we had worse than that. My sister, gone just like that. Left me this kid to watch after and no money to speak of. Don't see how it's your place to tell me where I'm doing it wrong." She ended with a rattling cough.

"I… You're right. I have no idea what you've been through."

She wagged her head, looked away. "Them TV crews move from disaster to disaster, while we in New Orleans still figurin' how to live day by day." She swore through rotted teeth, but it was more fatigue than malice.

"I was outta line," I said.

"Mmm, tha's mighty big of you."

Her defensiveness seemed extreme, but once again I'd judged this person and her situation prematurely. Christ was known for reaching out to the downtrodden, the orphans, and the poor—while I'd planned to step right on by.

"Listen, I'd like to help," I offered. "Mind if I get you something?"

She pursed her lips. Raised an eyebrow. Scrutinized me without a word.

"What if I go and buy you a can of bug spray? My gift to your nephew."

"Jug o' milk. Fetch us some of that, too."

"Done deal."

"You be wantin' somethin' for it?"

"No. It's on me."

"I got my ways, you know." Her eyes clouded over with the same weary knowledge I'd seen on the streets of Portland.

"Your little man there, he needs to get inside."

In a single motion, she heaved from her seat, opened her room door, snagged the back of the kid's diaper, and swung him through. "Satisfied? Now getcha gone."

My gaze slid along the walkway to Felicia's door, then back toward the vision of yellow and pink beside the lawn chair. Would my decision in that moment have changed what was to come?

I still wonder.

Five minutes later I was paying for Purity milk, breakfast cereal, and Off! insect repellent. I drove back to the hotel and handed over the supplies.

"I could spray the little guy, if you want."

"I can take care of my own," his aunt told me.

"Hope it helps."

"Set the milk down there by the door."

"Got you some Cheerios too."

"Cheerios? Hmmm." She called her nephew onto the walkway, shook the repellent, and sprayed his chubby arms and back. "Stuff stinks, don't it?"

"Guess that's why it works."

She gave no response. She finished off her beer, crumpled the can between her palms the way I'd expect a Titans tailgater to do, then dropped it with a clink onto the others by her chair. With one hand tugging at sweat-adhered bicycle shorts, the other at the toddler, she headed indoors.

"Have a good night," I mumbled.

As I reached the bottom of the stairs, my cell rang.

"Felicia."

"How'd you know it was me?"

"Caller ID."

"Silly me. You recognized the hotel's number."

"I'm smart like that." From my vantage point at the foot of the exterior stairway, I could see the glow of her window. On the other side of the parking lot, evening traffic raced along Murfreesboro Pike.

"How'd you find me here? I listened to your message after settling in for the night, and to be honest, I was a bit startled by it."

"As in scared?"

"Uneasy is more like it. Did you follow me here?"

"Not my style." Technically it was true, and this seemed the wrong time to mention my proximity to her room. "But it wasn't hard tracking you down. The unit was in your name."

"Persistent as always, I see."

"It's how I got your attention when we first started dating."

"True enough, doll."

"So. Did you pay for the room? Or did he?"

"He?"

"Don't play dumb." I waved away a swarm of bugs. "Axman. The guy who flew you here, who bought you the dress." There were things to be learned here, and Felicia remained my only direct link to the culprit.

"No call for being rude," she said.

"I'm just on edge, okay?"

"Forgive me if I'm not as alert as usual. I'm starting to fade. In fact, I'm…
I was just heading to bed."

"That's…nice. I'll just ignore that mental image."

"Oh. I didn't realize you still cared."

"This guy," I said, returning to the subject at hand. "He's attacked my
family and seems to know me. Knows stuff about my past. I'm in no mood
for his little game."

"It's not a game to him."

"You sure about that?"

"I think he's more than capable of carrying out his threats. If you want
my suggestion, give him whatever it is he's after so he'll leave you alone."

A nearby cicada added its high shrill to the buzzing of mosquitoes. I surveyed the environs for any larger potential threats. Nothing out of place. Across
the lot my Honda sat undisturbed, surrounded by the evening's other arrivals,
while the twin Hyundais still sat in defiance of my earlier presumptions.

My gaze wandered back to room 212. "What *is* he after? I have no idea.
A person who carves initials in someone's shoulder—that's a narcissist, a guy
who lacks empathy. It's all about him. Believe me, he's only trying to yank our
chains."

"After I left you at the museum, did you check the envelope in the hat?
He must've given you some idea there. What'd you find?"

"More games. And lies."

"Did you perchance keep the hat? I bought it just this morning for the
steeplechase."

"The steeplechase," I repeated. A red flag fluttered in my head.

"The Iroquois. Don't you remember? I told you—"

"I remember. Sorry. The hat just wasn't my color."

This glib response was meant to hide my sudden questions. Was it yet
another coincidence that "steeple" was in the title of the sculpture I'd been sent

to as well as in the name of the race Felicia had attended? Another religious clue? Most likely it had no bearing. Just my overactive mind again.

At what point, though, did coincidences add up to something sinister?

"Too bad," she mused. "I really liked that hat."

"Could be in the museum's lost and found. You can call tomorrow."

"I fly out at five a.m. So long, farewell."

The melancholy in her voice tried to pull me through the phone. She'd been drinking, so her mood was a result of the wine. But what if AX was in there with her? Was she trying to get me to come up for her protection?

"Felicia, listen." I crouched in the shadows, trying to think of questions she could respond to without raising an abductor's suspicion. "Are you alone?"

"You'd like to know?"

"I'm serious. Yes or no?"

"Yes."

"You're not in any trouble?"

"Not yet," she slurred.

"You sound tired. Don't tell me you finished off that bottle."

"Bottle? Did I even mention the wine to you?"

"Uh. C'mon, I can tell."

"You're here, aren't you? Should've expected as much."

"What do you mean? I'm not there." A pathetic attempt.

"Doll, you never were good at fooling me. And truthfully, it's always been a better part of your character, this desire to come to the rescue, to save the fair maiden. I knew you'd want to keep an eye on me."

"I admit, I am worried about you. But you say you're okay?"

"Why don't you come up and see for yourself?"

"What? I'm… How would I know which room to go to?"

A giggle bubbled through my phone. "Don't be silly. You need more than a rusty old railing to conceal that big frame of yours."

An upward snap of my neck gave me a clear view of her window. There, outlined by lamplight, a hand angled through the curtains and waved.

"Hmm. Busted."

"Like a kid with his hand in the cookie jar. It's sweet though. I flew into town hoping we could reconnect. What do you say, doll?"

"I can't stay very long," I replied. "He could be watching."

"Sure."

Flipping the phone closed, I headed up the stairs. Growing dread dogged my steps. I was vulnerable here, visible to the traffic on Murfreesboro Pike. One step. Another. Mosquitoes goaded me along the landing, little vampires craving blood. Their buzzing matched the tension of my nerves, hurrying me forward till I was standing at the threshold of room 212.

I stared at the door, thought I saw movement behind the peephole. I started to turn away. Heard the release of a latch.

"Not leaving now, are you?"

"Hi."

She was wearing a silk robe. "Well, don't just stand there. Come in." She stepped back, the bedside lamp lighting her silhouette.

14

B ack in the day, Portland's dealers and low-level alley dwellers knew me by name. For anonymity, I tried early on to go with a street handle, but it never stuck. Aramis, they called me. Or just Black. Knowing that this bit of personal data floated at the top of the scum pond worried me, so much so that I'd kept a loaded .357 within reach of my king-size waterbed and a sawed-off shotgun above the mirrored headboard.

Not that I ever waited for the cover of darkness to deal with my problems. If heat was coming down, I believed in head-on damage control—in broad daylight or in the pouring Oregon rain. Long-term security was a demanding job.

Which meant hitting hard, hitting fast. But playing fair. Down in the gutters, even your enemies expect the game to be played by certain rules.

Then everything changed. Or at least I did.

I haven't talked much about this new faith of mine. I'm not one for spouting spiritual slogans. One thing Mom taught me was that actions speak louder.

There was something wrong, though, about Felicia's words.

In the softly lit hotel room, she stretched out atop the comforter and propped herself on an elbow. Blond hair followed the gentle swell of the pillow while her free arm draped along her hip. "Don't be shy, doll."

"I…just wanted to make sure you were safe."

She moved her hand on her thigh. "Does everything look okay to you?"

On the nightstand, the paperback was opened facedown beside a wine bottle. There was the phone, the TV remote, hotel stationery. A coffee maker and plastic-wrapped glasses on the vanity. A damp towel was balled at the foot of the bed.

"I guess so."

"You guess?" She pouted. "Is there any chance of us working things out?"

"Uh. What're we talking about?"

"Please don't be dense. You know I care about you."

"That's why you left me."

"*Yes.* Yes, exactly. Can't you see? I needed all of you or none at all. When you started drifting away, it broke my heart wide open. You were coked out of your head, unavailable, and I had to talk to someone. But I never meant for anything to happen—you have to believe that."

"Doesn't matter. It's done."

"Have I lost you?"

My hand remained frozen on the knob, leaving a slight gap in the doorway. The fresh air made the room's stale smells more pronounced, as well as the contrasting floral perfume. And yet there was no mistaking the inebriation in Felicia's eyes and the weariness that went well beyond the wine.

"I shouldn't have come up here," I told her.

"But you did. Maybe you should let your heart guide you more often."

"Our hearts are what got us into trouble before."

"It's my last night here."

"I told you. I've changed."

"Hmm. I'm not so sure."

"Nothing like a vote of confidence."

"Surely you won't deny that our kiss at the museum brought back memories. We're being given a chance to start over."

"By some freak's manipulations," I noted. "You wanna talk about start-ing over? This very night there's a woman here in Nashville, another old flame of mine, who's sitting behind bars because of what happened last year. Did you know about that?"

"We all have our sins. Don't punish me for hers."

"That's what I'm trying to tell you. I've punished myself, Felicia, by fol-lowing my heart and making some really bad choices. Someday I hope to find the one for me, sure. But she'll have to respect the way love works. She'll..." My voice trailed off.

"Is there someone else?"

"What? No." My hand flexed around the doorknob. "I'm just...still learning, I guess. Or unlearning."

"Wow. Okay, maybe you *have* changed. What's happened?"

"Honestly? I'm trying to follow God."

"Aramis Black's found religion. There's one for the front pages."

"No, it's not religion. It's more like... Well, I want to be who he created me to be. Back in Portland, I was destroying myself."

"There's an understatement."

My hands fell to my sides, and I leaned back against the door till it latched. "If you can, please forgive me for the junk I put you through. You didn't deserve any of it. I think you need to hear me say this. I want you to be able to move on."

"If only you knew." She clasped the folds of her robe. "It's too late for that."

"Why?"

She looked to the ceiling. Closed her eyes with a heavy sigh.

Footsteps approached on the landing, and a flurry of activity started in my head. I spun to latch the chain. My hands pressed against the metal door.

I was an idiot for coming up here. No doubt AX had warned her not to let me in.

"What is it?" Felicia sat up, alert.

"Someone's coming. I need to hide."

"Probably just a guest who checked in or someone getting ice."

Was she covering?

"I don't think so," I said, slinking past the bed. A loud rap on the door stopped me in my tracks.

"Oh!" Felicia sat up and looked at me.

Putting a finger to my lips, I eased into the bathroom. The odor of cigarettes clung to every air particle. I turned to peek through the door, but the angle allowed only a glimpse of an armchair, peeling wallpaper, and a kitschy painting next to the TV.

Another knock. What had I gotten myself into? The whole purpose in coming here had been Felicia's safekeeping, but the matching Hyundais had thrown me, and the conversation with Meade had pushed me into breaking my promise to Johnny Ray.

Knock, knock, knock…

Felicia's robe swirled by. "Be there in a moment."

No! She had always been too trusting. But before the command could travel from my brain to my mouth, a familiar voice bellowed from the doorway. I recalled pink bicycle shorts and a strained yellow tube top.

"He's in there, ain't he?"

"Who?"

"You can't fool me, missy. I know what I seen."

"No one else is here," I heard Felicia respond.

"Then why's you wearin' that little robe, hmmm? You think I'm blind?" A pause. "I can see through them curtains, you know."

I heard the curtain being readjusted.

"If he's wantin' attention—"

"I'm sorry, but I think there's been some misunderstanding."

"You just watch yourself. You don't be cuttin' in on my corner, flashin' them skinny legs. No man wanna cuddle with no bag o' bones. You wastin' your time here."

Despite myself, I stifled a chuckle.

"We're old friends," Felicia said, "and I'm leaving in the morning."

"Durn straight, you are."

"You have a good night, ma'am."

I heard the New Orleans woman *humphhh* and pound away down the landing. As I leaned back and took a breath, my eyes slid to a pile of clothes at my feet. My silent mirth vanished. There, along with the spring dress I'd seen at Cheekwood, a wig of long locks glistened red.

Johnny Ray's test last night at Owen Bradley Park. His weakness.

All along it had been Felicia.

15

Here was the proof. Plain as day. She'd cozied up to Johnny and kissed him just to lure him into a trap. His shoulder bore the wounds of that encounter.

Virescit Vulnere Virtus…

Was she a helpless accomplice? Or an instigator? Either way, she'd lied to me.

She was relocking the hotel-room door. "Did that lady know you?"

"I bought her nephew some bug spray."

"Nice of you," she said. "You can come out now."

"Gimme a minute."

I closed the door, turned on the light, banged the toilet seat against the porcelain tank. The worry in her voice only fueled my anger. My pulse beat against my eardrums, and the bathroom's small area felt suddenly claustrophobic—as though someone else were here with me.

With my right fist cocked, I raked aside the shower curtain. A tiny shampoo bottle rattled into the tub.

Nothing. No ax-wielding foe.

"Doll?"

"Be right out."

I could try sneaking the wig out, but lifting fingerprints from it seemed unlikely.

Wait. My cell phone.

I snapped a photo of the wig, then sent it to Meade and myself. On my way out, I'd get a shot of the Hyundai's license plate. It could link Felicia to last night's events and possibly lead to the true culprit, especially if he'd paid with a credit card.

I stepped from the bathroom. Pretended to wash my hands at the sink. In the mirror I could see Felicia's eyes on me.

"Everything okay?"

"You tell me." I turned toward her. "What's going on?"

"Aramis? What're you talking about?"

"Oh, I think you know."

Her shoulders slumped. "You found the wig, didn't you?"

I strode toward her and snatched her arm, eliciting a short gasp, then headed for the exit. The flimsy chain snapped from the wall as I yanked open the door. She followed along, feet scrambling to keep up but giving no resistance.

My plan was simple. Take her back to our brownstone, let Johnny confirm her identity, then keep her secured until morning, when I would turn her in.

Her fate would be in Meade's hands.

At the top of the stairs, I slowed. Felicia wasn't dressed for this, and I had no interest in injuring her. I guided her back to the room, gave her a moment to slip into her shoes and a light jacket. From the base of the steps, we crossed the lot to the passenger door of my Honda Civic.

"Get in."

"Let me explain."

"You almost got my brother killed. Why?"

"To tell the truth, I'm relieved that you know."

"The truth." My fingers tightened around her wrist. "Okay, let's start there."

"Yes, I drew Johnny away from the party, but I had no idea he was planning to attack him. And honestly, my main hope at the party was to bump into you. I saw you once through the crowd, and I—"

"Enough. Just tell me why."

"Why do you think? He said he'd hurt me if I didn't. It didn't sound like an idle threat."

"Right. And where is this mysterious Axman? Can you tell me that?"

"Next door. Across town. I don't know, but probably not far. If he finds out I told you anything—"

"He'd probably kill you anyway."

"Aramis!"

"You don't think so?"

Her eyes blinked back tears. "I hate him, I really do."

The parking lot was a maze of shadows capable of concealing a watcher. My scan over the tops of vehicles revealed nothing. No movement. Nobody in sight.

"Get in," I repeated. "We'll talk in the car."

I shut her door, then crossed to her Hyundai. After snapping photos of its plates and the other rental's too, I slipped the phone into my pocket and heard it clack against the empty brass casing.

She cheated the grave...

It was a lie. A tiny seed. Growing, twining through my head.

If you help me, you'll get to see her again...

Time to shut off these thoughts. I'd had more than I could handle already. A myopic determination took over, driving my actions. In the last year I'd been tested by ugly, painful events, and I wondered if I'd ever escape from the consequences. Whatever this new test was, I wanted to pass it quickly and leave behind my past once and for all.

I marched back to the car and dropped into the driver's seat beside Felicia.

"I'm sorry we had to end this way," I said, turning the ignition.

Before I could move my hand to the e-brake, a wiry arm snaked around my neck. I grabbed at it, craning my head to catch a glimpse of the hooded figure in a black ski mask. Suddenly my chin was shoved forward, and a razor blade skimmed along my stubbled face. My eyes darted to the rearview for a better view of my assailant, but the mirror had been snapped from its mounting and tossed to the floor.

"Tell me what you want." I forced the words from my throat.

"He wants you to drive," Felicia said.

"Where?"

"I'm supposed to give you the details as we go."

I tried to turn again, but the press of sharp metal against my cheekbone made my decision clear. So this was my buddy, the axman. How nice of him to make an appearance. But who was he? Had he been watching me this whole time?

"Show yourself, you twisted freak!"

My mind raced through options, evaluating and discarding. There was a slim possibility of deflecting the razor long enough to rip free of the stranglehold, but my escape would leave Felicia alone with this terrorist. Of course, she could be his wicked little partner.

"He can't talk for himself?" I growled.

"You're not supposed to know who he is. Please don't cause any trouble."

"Me?" I laughed. Choked. "I *make* trouble."

"Aramis, I beg of you."

My laughter kept coming, rough stones rumbling from my chest, each new burst knocking my Adam's apple against the man's arm. Yeah, bad tim-ing. No joking matter. Blah-de-blah. I couldn't stop any more than I could hold back a rockslide.

"Tell him," I said.

"What?"

"The way I deal with thugs like him."

"Please, let's just do as he says so we can end this."

"End it. That's right." I shifted my words to the back. "But I don't even know what you're after. You wanna play it this way, throwing out lies about my mother and attacking my brother. Big mistake. I'll come after you and take you down hard."

The arm flexed against my throat.

"You're in deep now," I coughed out. "The cops followed me here, and they're watching us right now. Best bet's to take off now before they get too suspicious. Otherwise, you're toast." A desperate ploy. Most likely this guy had been out here long enough to inspect the area.

Felicia fidgeted, looking back for instructions. An unwilling accomplice?

"But hey," I laughed. "Why believe a thing I say?"

She turned back to me, her eyes animated by the flicker of the hotel's neon sign. "He wants you to drive."

"Oh well. Your call, buddy."

"Just follow my instructions."

I turned on my headlights, revved the motor. "To where exactly?"

The arm cranked back against my windpipe, and shards of color speared the corners of my vision. Okay, so he wasn't in the mood for questions.

"Soon as we start moving," I gasped, "the cops'll be onto you."

The razor's edge moved across my cheek. Pressure. A slice of heat.

"Nooo," Felicia protested.

The cut was clean, nearly painless, releasing drops of blood that spilled along my jaw line and landed in the lap of my jeans. Sticky warmth seeped through the material and oozed onto my leg.

"All right. We'll go." At least I'd have some control at the steering wheel. "But don't forget, we're being watched the whole way."

"Don't do anything else to provoke him," Felicia begged.

"Hey. I always like a nice, close shave."

Slice number two. Slower, more deliberate. X marks the spot.

"Courage grows strong at a wound," I said through clenched jaws.

"*Please,* Aramis. Drop the macho act and just drive."

I drove.

Drip, drip…

Blood forged trails down my neck, beneath my shirt. One branched off over my right pectoral muscle while another pooled in the cleft of my collarbone.

Drip…

None of this concerned me. I'd been cut before, hit, kicked, bludgeoned. In most cases, pain was a temporary thing. The real problem was the powerful organ of the mind that turned traitorous, elevating the fear of pain into something worse than the pain itself.

Superficial wounds—that's all these were. I'd be lucky to get scars out it.

The dash said it was just past ten. Most of the evening's full-bellied diners had already headed home, and Vanderbilt kids were still gassing up their SUVs to go clubbing on Second Avenue. A lull had settled over the streets, and my Honda zipped along unimpeded. Despite my bluster, nobody was following us. Nobody knew where we were headed.

I tried to throw out a silent prayer, but it felt more like an act of surrender, as though I was conceding victory too soon. That just went against my nature.

A primal urge began welling in my belly and surging through my limbs in a chemical cocktail of nerves and epinephrine—a call to arms, a slide back into the familiar survival mechanisms of rage and revenge.

BEAR...

Pinned in the driver's seat by my captor's locked arm, I breathed and evaluated. I considered ramming down on the brakes to loosen his hold, but that could send Felicia's face into the window. What about a backward head butt? No, my headrest was in the way.

The razor blade. It was still in my pocket, wrapped in the envelope.

Yes, that was it. Two could play this game, I decided.

PART TWO

DOUBLE SHOT

*You are about to hear…a secret
which they think buried with the dead
or entombed in the abyss.*

—Alexandre Dumas, *The Man in the Iron Mask*

16

*G*ame on.

At the corner of Elm Hill Pike and Murfreesboro, we passed the dark-ened Purity Dairy plant—source of award-winning ice cream and all things milky—and I slipped into a playful tone. "Cold snacks anyone?"

Silence.

I hoped the goofy comment would divert attention from my left hand easing into my jeans pocket. With a little patience and a couple more min-utes, I just might get to go blade to blade with Mr. Axman.

Chop, chop, you sicko!

My throat worked for oxygen against his arm. His razor angled toward the corner of my eye, scraping past a small mole. Though there was no break in the skin, I made a conscious effort not to flinch.

We continued past the walled entry of Trevecca Nazarene University toward blocks of industrial buildings. On the north end of Lafayette Street, square brick structures housed hundreds of low-income families. Over the project lawns, darkness accentuated erratic sparks of light, which I'd mistaken for flicked cigarette embers when I first moved here from Oregon.

I gestured with my elbow for Felicia's benefit. "See that?"

"Are those fireflies?"

"They're called lightning bugs here."

Another moment. Another diversion. My fingers were now creeping into my pocket, touching the edge of the folded envelope.

Felicia said, "He wants you take a left up here."

How was he communicating this stuff to her? He had on a stinkin' ski mask. If he was whispering, it was too quiet for me to hear. Had he given her instructions back in the parking lot?

"It's a one-way."

"No, not yet. Go under the freeway, and turn at the light."

"Called the interstate here."

"Just do as I say, please."

The envelope was caught in my jeans, blocked by the crease at my hip.

"Left on Fourth," I said. "Got it."

As we approached, a lone figure on the other side of the street took a step off the sidewalk and waited for me to roll by. I tapped the brake to cover the straightening of my left leg. The envelope was out. In my hand. The razor was still wrapped inside.

"Look at that guy." I shook my head. "He's gonna get himself killed."

But I knew this man. It was my homeless friend, Freddy C.

Beneath the streetlights, his ragged clothes and shuffling gait caught my attention, but it was his tapered beard that confirmed his identity. A resident of Centennial Park, most mornings he comes to my shop for the free java, and he always finds a few coins for the orange tip mug. He's a jittery character who's overcome a tainted past. Ever since Nadine Lott's death, he'd been committed to fighting the crime and despair on the streets. His help in the police investigation last year had been instrumental.

"What're you waiting for, doll?"

"Just letting the man cross," I told Felicia. "Is that a sin?"

My Honda inched onto Fourth Avenue South, pointing toward Freddy. What was he doing out at this hour? His watery gaze met mine. Then: recognition. I angled my face to make visible my fresh wounds, and his sandy eyebrows wobbled with alarm.

You're no dummy, Freddy. See this blood? Call the cops.

Attention trained ahead once more, I accelerated by him. My sideview mirror showed him standing in the middle of the street with his hand held high, cupped into the letter C.

C for Crime-fighter.

"You know that guy?"

"I do believe he just gave us an obscene gesture," I covered. "You believe that?"

"Nearly there. I suggest we slow down."

"Rough neighborhood." I tilted my head toward a graffiti-tagged building where two women in miniskirts—one tall and black, the other rail thin and bone white—leaned against a Buick Regal on blocks. Behind them, glass shards glittered across the entrance to an empty lot. "Not the best place for a pit stop."

"Just do it, Aramis. Is this Oak Street? Okay, turn right and park."

"At the City Cemetery?" A chest-high stone wall encompassed crumbling monuments and tilted tombstones while a wrought-iron gate guarded the front entrance. "You sure this is the place? The gate's locked."

"Park."

"If you say so."

"Turn off the engine."

"But of course. Now what, dear?" My saccharine tone caused the abductor's arm to tighten, yanking me into the headrest, forcing my chin up. As Felicia looked back for clarification, my fingers wedged the envelope against the seat and tried to unfold it.

The blade popped loose. Slid down the side into the carpeted space beneath me.

"Hello?" Felicia's hand was extended. "You're supposed to give me the keys."

"My keys?" I nodded at the cemetery gate. "They won't work on that."

"Honestly, you're only making this more difficult."

"Call it a personality defect."

"The keys."

"This car Blue Books at nine hundred bucks. I'll take seven fifty."

Her lips pressed together in exasperation, she waited. At my throat, AX's grip prompted obedience. I surrendered the keys, then watched my ex-girlfriend step from the car, draw back her arm, and toss them toward the graveyard.

From the stone wall came a metallic jingle.

"Oops," I said.

"You're not helping, Aramis."

Still wearing the jacket over the silk robe, she trotted across the lane, located the keys, and lofted them over the wall. She brushed her hands together, but her eyes showed no pleasure in the accomplishment.

Did she know something I didn't? Why were we here?

With the car now immobilized, I'd have to run for it and hope he didn't have a gun. The razor was under the seat, still in the envelope, and my .40 caliber was tucked beneath a bush at Cheekwood.

Trying to prep my muscles for action without telegraphing my intentions, I let my fingers crawl toward the door handle. I could endure the razor as long as it wasn't rammed into my throat or an eyeball. One good yank, and I might just clear the car with minimal damage.

Felicia was stepping closer. She should've taken off while she had the opportunity, but she probably hoped her compliance would ensure my release.

This was it. The handle was in my grasp.

"Run!" I started to yell at her.

The arm cranked back into my larynx and stifled my command. Before I could react, the back door flung open, and AX exited in a flurry of motion that inflicted a nick along my ear's ridges of cartilage. Okay, that hurt. My involuntary pause of pain gave him the half second he needed to grab hold of Felicia and start shuffling her down the street. His mask and hooded sweatshirt disguised his size. As he held the blade against her neck, I saw it was a fully extended razor knife. No surprise there: a terrorist's weapon.

I sprang from the vehicle. "Let her go!"

Felicia offered him no help. Limp prey being dragged off to the lair. I took a step forward, but he arced his arm, and the knife angled toward her throat. If I could just get close enough to tear away his cover, smash my palm into his nose...

"What do you want?" I demanded. "Why'd you bring us here?"

"Stay back." Felicia's throat worked against the razor. "Please."

The distance was growing between us, eliminating any chance for a quick strike. I'd lost my keys, but they could be recovered with a little luck. Lost a bit of blood too, but that was nothing.

What was the purpose behind this? Why had I been forced along?

Felicia and the hooded figure hesitated at the rear of a parked panel truck. There was movement, a scuffle. She let out a gasp. Another. Then, still entangled in his clutches, she was pulled out of view.

The following scream tore at the darkness.

I catapulted forward, stumbled on uneven pavement, touched a hand down to right myself. Back on my feet, I tried to bridge the gap as quickly as possible. Reached the end of the truck. Stopped. Angled wide and low, anticipating an attack.

Whimpers drifted in the stillness.

"Felicia?"

I crouched and ran to her crumpled form on the sidewalk. She was face-down, blond strands splayed over cracks in the cement. She lifted a hand from her shoulder. Something moist glistened in the moonlight.

"What'd he do to you?"

"Don't let him...get away," she sputtered.

I scanned my perimeter. No sign of him. By all appearances, we were alone along this stretch of warehouses where parked commercial vehicles waited for Monday.

I peeled back the shoulder of her jacket and saw the same initials. These were shallower, sliced in a hurry.

Nearby an engine turned over.

"Go," she said. "Before he...takes her."

"Who?"

"Your mother."

What? The note in the bullet casing said my mother was still alive, but that was ridiculous. This surreal drama was trying to override all logic.

"Please." Felicia's back arched as she tried to lift herself. I saw defense wounds on her arms where she'd resisted him. She pulled herself forward and heaved onto the uneven sidewalk.

"Tell me what's going on. Felicia—"

"Hurry." A breath. "You have to stop...him."

"I can't leave you."

"Go."

I started to rise. "You hang on. I'll be right back." I saw an old white Dodge van lurch forward from the curb.

A cocoon of blackness surrounded the driver, shielding his eyes behind the ski mask. His head turned my way, taunting me. Still playing games. With one stomp on the gas pedal, he could be gone.

I tried to breathe, evaluate. What could I do? Maybe if I ran after him, I could reach a door handle before he sped away. Seemed unlikely though, with him watching me.

A visual sweep of the area produced another possibility.

A red tricycle left out on the grass.

I stepped sideways until his view from across the street was obstructed by the panel truck at my side. I grabbed the plastic-fringed handlebars at my feet, hefted the tricycle up on my shoulder, and crossed to the center of the street as he pulled out.

Sorry, kids. Should've put your toys away.

The van, spewing exhaust, squatted on the gnarled pavement thirty feet in front of me. There wasn't enough room for him to turn around, and if he accelerated, I'd have just moments to jump aside, ratchet back both arms, and crash this metal three-wheeler through the glass into the coward's face.

"Bring it!" I beckoned.

Head to head—that's how we'd do this. I bobbed on the balls of my feet, zeroing in on my mark behind the windshield.

One shot at this. Ready now. *Ready.*

The engine roared, and the front end leaped forward. For a moment I was blinded by the sudden glare of headlights. Then sharpened by adrenaline, I registered two things that would be forever seared into my memory.

A woman straining forward in the passenger seat.

And a weak yet distinct cry: "Aramis?"

17

f I'd paid more attention in social psych, if I'd noted the signals of sub-
terfuge Professor Newmann was so adamant about, I might have been prepared there along Oak Street's crenelated cemetery wall.

I wasn't.

Back at the *Steeple Dance* sculpture, I'd grappled with irrational fear and
used it as a tool. A catalyst for action. The emotional numbness that now
took over, however, swept through my extremities like an injection of liquid
ice, undermining any physical response. I was powerless. I stood in the path
of the charging van, unable to breathe.

The Dodge gained speed, an old metal bull charging to gore its victim.
It moved from beneath outstretched tree limbs into the moon's gray yellow
glow. The same guy who'd attacked Felicia and Johnny Ray leered over the
steering wheel.

And in the passenger seat: my mother.

Go. Before he...takes her.

No. This was an illusion, a heartless prank. I didn't believe in ghosts. Yet
there was no denying the black silky hair framing that feminine face, wisps of
gray—but that would be expected after all these years—and those round,
dark eyes seeking mine with the direct attention of a bloodhound tracking a
scent that'd nearly gone cold.

Nearly. But not quite.

No! It wasn't possible!

It could not be real, could not be her. This was a fake, another attempt at fooling me into submission. Some clever makeup and a professional wig.

The van continued, seemingly in slow motion. The woman's gaze locked on to mine. She was struggling, her elbows moving. Were those ropes tied about her chest and arms?

Like a person being buried alive, she lifted her mouth toward a gap in the window and screamed again. One word forming and bursting forth in an unmistakable tone.

"Aramis!"

The weight of more than two decades shifted.

The Dodge hurtled my direction on a collision course. Twenty feet. Fifteen. Twelve. Bridging the gap of twenty-plus years. Smells of gasoline and radiator fluid coiled from the onrushing beast.

My knees buckled.

The woman heaved herself at the driver, bound hands clutching the wheel and wrenching it toward her. The man jabbed his elbow and connected with her head. But she held on. The van jerked from its course, squealing, throwing the rear end to the left so that it sideswiped the parked panel truck. A shrieking wall of metal, it plowed toward me once again.

I remained kneeling on the asphalt, motionless.

Mom?

With another elbow jab, the driver snapped the woman's head beneath a veil of disheveled hair. Her eyes widened in terror, but also concern. She wrenched the wheel again with her iron grip, willing the van to veer away.

The driver roared, this time cocking his arm back and smashing it into her face. Her body flew into the passenger door.

The ice in my limbs turned to fire.

My legs exploded from my rooted position, tendons twanging down my neck and shoulders. The Dodge skidded toward me until its tires started to catch on the pavement and guide it away.

She had fought for me.

She was *alive*. She was *in there!*

"Ahh-*rrrhh!*"

In one sweeping motion, I gripped the tricycle and ran full speed toward the driver's door. My feet pounded over the rough road, and I tripped, nearly face planted, and regained my balance. With every ounce of sinew and muscle in me, I crushed the red trike into his window. Fringed handlebars stabbed at the glass, shattering it into fragments, but the van continued. Behind it, the tricycle clanged to the street in a twisted heap.

On the van's dented license tag were the words Georgia...on My Mind.

I raced toward the cemetery wall. My hands clutched the stone, and I lifted, got a knee on the summit, and vaulted into the territory of the dead.

I paused, trying to calculate the trajectory and distance of Felicia's toss. With my search narrowed, I trampled between grave markers and mausoleums. Scrambled over grass and gravel. Combed fingers through weeds and bunched flowers.

The deceased here along the hem of St. Cloud Hill were governors, mayors, generals, and Confederate soldiers by the thousands. Nearly two centuries of fathers, brothers, mothers.

Please, God. Help me here!

My hand brushed over a cool, dark clump, and a jingle verified my find.

I grabbed the keys, dropped them, grabbed them, hurdled a tombstone, raced toward the wall on Oak Street. Up and over. Hands scraped, bloodied. I landed on the sidewalk, felt my ankle twist. I hobbled across the road, threw myself into the Honda, and fired it up. A squealing U-turn brought me back to Fourth Avenue South, where I turned right and slammed the accelerator down so hard I thought it might punch through the rusty spots in the firewall.

The engine was screaming, nearly hysterical.

"C'mon! Where are you? Where *are you?*"

My throat turned scratchy. Tears pricked the corners of my eyes. I prowled the streets, up and down, back and forth, desperate to locate the woman who'd been taken from me, who'd fallen from a riverbank, who'd managed somehow to find her way back.

She cheated the grave…

At a private graveside service, Johnny Ray and I had watched a casket lower her into the earth—a symbolic ceremony since boats and divers had never found her body.

But somebody *had* found her. How? How could that be?

Someone had to be playing a cruel joke on me, and I was taking the bait, swallowing it whole. The hook was set. Reeling me in. For what purpose? So that some gold-grabbing fool could squeeze me for info about the family cache?

That one word, ringing in my ears: *"Aramis!"*

It was her. I couldn't *not* believe it. Years of an alternate history argued against it, yet we'd locked eyes. Connected. Somehow—miraculously, unbelievably—that was Mom. How could I turn away from that possibility if there was even one iota of hope that it was true? She was in that van, trapped with that sad, sorry excuse for a human being who had struck her full force in the face.

Finding her would be worth any danger, any risk.

Dianne Lewis Black.

Mom's alive! That was her. That was her…

I pounded the words into my mind, nailing them down so that nothing could shake them loose.

Her voice. Calling my name…

I weighed a late-night call to Metro Police, even started to dial Meade's number. But the detective would expect answers, explanations, proof of some sort.

Defying all reason, the driver of the van had paraded my aged, beautiful mother before my eyes. In the course of twenty-four hours, this freak had managed to flip my entire paradigm, handing me a new game with a new set of rules. Unless I played it his way, he'd make certain I never saw her again.

Rule number one: no cops. *For the sake of your loved ones...*

I closed my cell.

Already doubts were prying at my hopes, popping them loose quicker than I could hammer them down.

Where had she been for over twenty years? How had she gone undetected? Obviously, I was falling for an elaborate deception, just as Johnny Ray had been tested by a few shots of Jack, a red wig, and some soft kisses.

He'd failed. He'd been cut.

And my bleeding cheek proved I was no different.

So I'd seen a dark-haired woman in the shadows of a van, heard my name called, watched her fight to protect me. What did that prove, except the lengths to which this guy would go to fool me?

I'd almost bought into it. Almost believed. I'd been fooled before, but this time the stakes were even higher.

I headed back to Oak Street, wondering when I would ever learn.

"Some people never learn," Professor Newmann had lectured the class in his reedy voice. "When a secular mind-set pervades a culture, fact and falsehood become interchangeable. For most people, seeing is believing. News channels parade wholesale misinformation as unbiased fact, and the average viewer suspects nothing. The Internet is equally pernicious." In a habitual tic, he hitched the lapels of his tweed jacket. "Anytime such deceit pollutes one's mind, it weakens his intellectual and spiritual fortitude. And such weakness is inevitably punished."

I remember raising my hand.

"Do you have a question for the entire class, Mr. Black?"

"Not to be rude, but our previous instructor already touched on this subject." Heads bobbed in agreement. "In fact, we turned in reports a few weeks back."

"Two-page reports, if I'm not mistaken. I found them hardly comprehensive." Twiddling his glasses, Newmann mulled an idea. "Why don't you give us a brief recap of yours? Perhaps your summary will persuade me to move on to other topics."

"Okay. I wrote about an investigation of subliminal messages conducted in the fifties. Maybe you remember hearing about it?"

"Not likely. I was born in the early sixties."

"My bad. Thing is, this study showed what happened when the word *popcorn* was flashed between images on a movie screen. Even though it happened faster than audiences could recognize consciously, concessions sales went through the roof."

"Snap," said Diesel. "That must be what happened to me last Friday."

The professor ignored a smattering of giggles. "Fascinating. And the sources you cited? Newspapers? Scientific journals?"

"Basically."

"Did you include the comprehensive findings of the USPA?"

"Uh. You mean, the United States Psychology Association," I improvised. He raised his eyebrows.

"I'm sure I did."

"No, you did not." Newmann rushed forward and hovered over my seat, thin, vulturelike. "There were no such findings, nothing substantiated by reputable publications. This study and its results were fabrications of a mind no more active than your own."

"But I read—"

"Commendable. A skill for all students to master. And in your reading, you may want to check into the history of the USPA."

"Extra credit?"

"Not unless they offer social psych at the U.S. Parachutist Association."

Snickers flitted about the hall, the fallout of my own lackadaisical research. As one who prides himself on critical thinking, I'd been duped by an erroneous article and beaten by a stinkin' sub. Once again, my failures last year to distinguish deception from reality came rushing back.

That evening in the lecture hall, I vowed I would not be made a fool of again.

Felicia was real, of that much I was certain. Minutes ago I'd left her sliced and trembling while I chased after a phantom. It seemed like ages.

Navigating the one-way streets, I returned to City Cemetery. I parked at the corner of Oak Street and Fourth and spotted my homeless friend pacing in mismatched shoes and a tattered jacket. I climbed from the car.

"Freddy C."

"Artemis."

From the start, Freddy's mistaken my name, and I've given up correcting it. "Thanks for coming down here. Guess you recognized me at the corner."

"Saw you bleeding."

"Did you call Metro?"

"No phone. Too late now anyway."

"Don't worry. There's nothing you could've done. C'mon, I need to check on my friend."

I started across the street, but his glazed eyes slowed my steps. He shook his head.

"Freddy, you look scared."

"I letcha down." A pungent odor wafted from him, a mix of salt and onions.

"Not at all. Look. I'm fine."

I continued across, and Freddy trudged after me.

"Who did that to her?"

"Did what?" I asked over my shoulder. "The cuts?"

He pressed a fist to his temple, then pointed at my cheek. "They cut you too."

"Yeah."

"Least you got away."

"If only I could've gotten my hands on that guy—"

"I wanted to help," Freddy blurted. "You believe me, don'tcha?"

"Of course I do. You're a good man, a crime-fighter."

"She was scared of me."

"Not surprising. Alone, on a dark street. I'll let her know you're harmless." I slipped around the parked panel truck, to the place I'd left her. "Felicia?"

"No." He stopped in his tracks. "I told you."

"Told me what?"

"Too late. It's my fault."

"What're you talking about?" I hurried toward Felicia, her legs curled on the sidewalk. "Come over and give me a hand."

"No use. No use."

"We can get her to a hospital."

"She's dead," he barked. "Dead! Don'tcha get it?"

tudies over the years have indicated that psychology students are those with the highest levels of childhood trauma and abuse, damaged souls looking for comfort, for explanations, for a cure.

I don't doubt it.

While I believe this lends credibility to the motives of professional counselors, it may also challenge their level of objectivity.

My objectivity, as I knelt beside Felicia, was already in question.

"I tried to help," Freddy C vowed. "Found her right there."

The pool of blood had grown and oozed over the concrete to settle in the cracks. There were plenty of reasons to leave everything untouched and call the cops. Of course, Meade would eventually connect this with my surveillance at the hotel, so any hopes of my escaping future interrogation were negligible.

I looked down. I had to know. Had to see for myself. My fingers eased around the nape of her neck to her carotid artery.

"She didn't budge," Freddy was saying.

Clammy skin. No pulse.

"Tried talking to her, but not a word. Not one."

"She's gone."

"Didn't touch her," Freddy repeated. "I tried to help."

"I know. I believe you." I lifted my head. "Are we all clear?"

He looked toward Fourth Avenue, where a car sped by. Sounds of drunken bravado rang out, most likely from the strip club two blocks away, the one place open late here on a Saturday night. Along Oak Street, a breeze stirred residual heat and lingering odors.

"I'm gonna turn her over," I said.

My homeless friend filled his lungs, gripped his beard with one hand.

"Felicia?" I rested my palm on her back. She was gone, yet some misguided sense of formality had me talking to her. "Sorry, but I need to see what he did to you."

Freddy tensed. "I didn't—"

"Not you. Keep watching for me, okay?"

My hands moved over her wounded shoulder, took hold, and eased her onto her side. Blond hair dangled over a slack mouth where pinkish blood had foamed.

I blinked. Took a breath.

This afternoon these lips had pressed against mine. Earlier this evening they'd downed white zinfandel. For three years Felicia and I had shared a rocky relationship, and we'd spent the last two apart. I wasn't the man for her—that much I knew—but she'd flown to Nashville to see *me*. All she'd wanted was another chance.

My inexpert examination continued, but the work of the razor knife was clearly responsible for her death. Even with the moon working as a spotlight, the depth of the stab wounds was impossible to judge. Muscle and skin had contracted at these points, her body's attempt to hold itself together. A coppery-blood scent stirred in the breeze, almost triggering my gag reflex as I took in the damage to her midsection.

I winced. *Gimme strength here.*

I knew I shouldn't be handling anything—"contamination of a crime scene" and all that desensitizing mumbo jumbo. Nevertheless, I closed the folds of her robe and draped her jacket gently over her.

I looked up at Freddy nervously shifting side to side. "Let's get you outta here."

"The police. They need to come."

"Yes, I'll call them. First, let me take you somewhere safe. You don't wanna be mixed up in this. You're sure you didn't touch anything?"

"Nothing."

"No blood on your shoes? Double-check."

He nodded and checked. Pointed to me. "Your hands."

"I have nothing to hide."

"But…who did this? We can't leave her. No, we can't do that."

"Doesn't seem right, does it?"

"She's all alone."

"You wanna wait for the cops?"

"Me? I… Maybe you."

"Here's the plan," I said, scrubbing my hands against my jeans. "We rush downtown and make a call before anyone else stumbles upon her. Metro will be here within minutes. They'll take care of her."

Freddy nodded.

We tramped to the car and headed downtown. Soon I'd be a prime suspect. Detective Meade knew of my contact with Felicia. I needed extra time. A police investigation would only complicate things with AX.

Turning onto Sixth, I nearly collided with an old Pontiac GTO descending from the direction of Fort Negley, a Civil War site atop St. Cloud Hill. The gleaming muscle car blasted its horn. Beside me, my friend grabbed his armrest.

"Didn't mean to scare you," I apologized. "My mind's not all here."

I couldn't shake the questions. Had Felicia bled to death? Would I have been able to save her with a makeshift tourniquet? She'd been more concerned that I go after my mother—at least who she thought was my mother. Had she known AX's plan all along?

Go. Before he…takes her.

One selfless act before breathing her last.

Next to me Freddy C was muttering, "Too late. I was too late."

The same self-accusation kept grinding through my head.

Ten thirty-two p.m. I called the cops from a pay phone at Third and Broadway. I spoke anonymously, gave a minimum of details, and prayed they'd respond rapidly.

Driving back toward Centennial Park, we watched a pair of Music City's finest speed by in a noisy bluster of spinning red and blue lights. My heart raced. Freddy flinched in the seat beside me. Minutes later we eased along the park's perimeter.

"Sure you don't want a soft bed for the night?" I asked.

"No, thank you."

"We have a spare room. My brother won't mind."

"I'll be fine, just fine." He waved at a flowering magnolia. "Drop me here."

I braked and watched him clamber out. "Freddy."

He turned toward me with a haunted expression.

"I was with her before you got to her," I told him. "There's nothing you could've done."

"I'll be fine."

"Seriously," I said. "Thanks for waiting there with me."

"That's the way friends oughta be."

"Absolutely."

A police cruiser sat at the corner, with a clear view of our brownstone building. Meade had been true to his word, providing extra patrol on our block. Even with the security cameras watching the property, my brother seemed better guarded by a person toting a gun and a badge.

I could hear it now though: "A call was placed at 10:32, Mr. Black. A woman's body was discovered on Oak Street, with multiple stab wounds. Officer So-and-So reports that you pulled into your residence thirteen minutes later. Circumstantial? Really? And what about the bloodstains on your pants? Or those hair follicles and ski-mask threads in the back of your car?"

I rolled forward. Evidence on wheels.

My course of action was obvious: Proceed directly to Metro. Do not pass Go. Play on the right side of the law. But a different game was already in motion, and until I could track down Felicia's killer, his new set of rules was in effect.

Nosed the other direction, I stopped beside the cruiser. My hands dropped into my lap. The sliced side of my face stayed turned away. No fear. No guilt.

"Hi there."

The cop's window came down, and he gave me a wary eye. "Good evening."

"Everything okay, Officer? I'm Johnny Ray's brother."

"Johnny Ray Black? Good song that boy's got on the radio."

"He's worked for it."

"Catchy, no doubt about that. 'Where'd I go so wrong...'"

I joined him. "In tryin' to do things right?"

"Nothin' like a good country tune. Back in the early days of the Grand

Ole Opry, my mother's cousin played the Ryman a couple of times. Great fiddle player."

Clipped to the man's uniform, a radio squawked. With an uplifted finger, he angled his head to listen. The dash lights and on-board computer painted him in hues of green. Though I don't know much about cop lingo, the subject of the transmission was clear: "unidentified Caucasian female…"

I exhaled through narrowly parted lips.

"Been some commotion over on Fourth." The officer tweaked the volume knob and leaned toward me. "A couple of these dispatchers, they just about yell into the dang radio. I'm getting up in age, true enough, but my hearing's just fine."

"You need to go?"

"Not yet. They've already sent the nearest units by GPS."

"Hi-tech."

"Causes some real mix-ups. A car might be close as the crow flies but on the wrong side of the interstate or miles away."

"Never thought about that."

"Neither did they." He waved me on. "I'll let you get where you were going."

"Thanks for keeping an eye out."

The radio squawked again, and he expelled a tired sigh. By the time I'd parked in the lot beside my brother's Ford Ranger, the cruiser had completed a U-turn and sped away.

Well, his night was about to go down the flusher.

———

Johnny met me in the entryway. "Where've you been? Had me worried sick."

"Don't ask," I snarled at him.

"What's wrong, kid?"

I shook my head as he clapped a hand on my arm. If I'd rehearsed this, I would've looked him in the eye and conveyed the evening's events in a dispassionate voice. Instead, by dealing with Freddy's state of mind and Felicia's fate, I'd sidestepped my own emotions. A knot began to form in my throat. "Forget it."

"You look like you've seen a ghost."

I sniffed. "Maybe I have."

"Now you're talkin' nonsense."

"Probably." I bowed and shook my head.

"What happened to Felicia?" When my eyes snapped up, he added, "You ever manage to track her down?"

At that point I collapsed in his arms and let it all go.

19

A sword dangles over my head. Its razor tip skims through my hair, tingles along my skin. Its shadow sways against the wall that faces me, stabbing down the concrete toward my chair, then pulling away. Shackles hold me in place.

Movement at my back. She's here, strapped to a chair behind me.

"Mom?" Our shoulders are touching. "Where were you?"

"I had to hide."

"Why didn't you come find us?"

"Why didn't you find *me*?"

"You were gone. And I was six."

"I never meant to leave you, Aramis. But I was alone too."

From her lips, the sound of my name is a sweet ointment drawing bitterness from my chest. This is it, our chance to be mother and son again. Her shiny hair brushes against mine with assurance. My eyes cloud. Steeling myself, I sit up straighter, but the overhead sword swings by and splits hot furrows in my cheek. As I slouch to the side, I spot a mangled red tricycle in the corner. Cigarette butts litter the floor.

"Where, Mom?" I insist. "Where've you been?"

Her tone turns frosty. "With him."

"Him?"

In response to my question, a metal door scrapes over the floor. My eyes grow wide.

Who has brought us here? Can we escape?

He is approaching. No, he's here. Already in the room—spying, watching.

"Show yourself!"

"I'm right here."

"Okay, I'll play your game. Just let her go. Please."

"And what gives you the leverage to negotiate?"

"I'll do what you want. You want gold? Fine. Leave her alone—that's all I ask."

His voice is syrupy. "I already told you: I want you to give me a ring."

"I don't even know you."

"Yes you do." From an unseen hand, splatters of red create dripping initials on the wall, with nothing but the sword's thin shadow to divide them.

"AX. I know. But what does that mean?"

"It should be obvious."

"I have no idea."

"Your sins have blinded you."

The door slams, and the taunting presence seems to fade. At my back, my mother quivers with quiet sobs. I lean against her, to comfort her with my nearness, but her sorrow spreads into my own neck and shoulders, shaking me, shaking…

"Aramis, wake up."

My eyelids peeled apart at the sound of my brother's voice.

"Hey there." He shook me again. "You were having one of your dreams."

I lifted myself onto an elbow, found I was wrapped in a blanket on the sofa, still wearing yesterday's clothes. From a guitar stand, my brother's Martin six-string bounced early sunrays onto the living-room ceiling.

"You remember anything about last night?" Johnny probed.

Hotel rooms, wigs, razors, and tombstones…*Mom.*

I rubbed at my eyes. "Can't believe I fell asleep."

"You had a lot on your plate for one day."

"He could be two states away by now."

"Good. The farther away, the better."

"But what if that was her?"

"Look at me." Wearing only Tabasco boxers and the bandages on his shoulder, my brother edged closer. "You swear that what you told me last night is true?"

"Why would I lie about such a thing?"

"You really think she could be alive?"

"I don't know."

"Coulda been a trick of the light. They say everyone's got a twin."

"No. It looked like her. Sounded like her. Felicia believed it."

"You were six, Aramis. No one would expect you to remember those details."

I swung into a sitting position. "You think I don't remember?"

His gaze took in my bloodied jeans. "Put yourself in my shoes. After all this time, years of thinking she was gone… You sure you weren't drinkin'? Maybe you and your ex shared some of that wine and—"

"Felicia's dead!" I shoved him away. "What's wrong with you?"

"With me?"

"Yeah, you!" I grabbed my cell from the coffee table, scrolled through photos, then held it toward my brother. "Recognize that red hair?"

"A wig? That's creepy."

"It was in Felicia's hotel room."

"Hold on. You're telling me that was your ex?"

"She was used to lure you away."

"What with all that booze, I didn't even recognize her."

"It's been years since you've seen her. Not like it matters now."

"Sorry, kid. I really am." He combed golden brown hair from his face and headed to the kitchen. I heard cupboards bang, heard the fridge door open. He returned with glasses of unfiltered grapefruit juice. "One for you. Should help clear your mind."

"If you say so." I took a swig, grimaced.

"How 'bout you change clothes and we ride down to the Pancake Pantry?"

"You don't believe me, do you? About the woman in the van?"

"Listen." Johnny's bloodshot eyes turned away. Had he been up all night, tormented by my story? "I've buried the past, learned to live with it. Scares me to even think of letting those thoughts back in." He folded his legs, pulled his Martin onto his lap. He was in his thinking mode. Most of his songs originate here on the hardwood floor in the morning hours. "Strange, though, isn't it?" He strummed a few chords.

"What?"

"This new single I've been recordin'. I wrote the lyrics a few weeks back—like a premonition or something." His fingers slid along the guitar frets, filling the room with rich tones as he sang:

I know you left me years ago, travelin' long dark roads.
But in my heart we're not apart. I've been livin' with your ghost.
Your love, it's always been here, faithful to the end.
In these eyes there's no surprise, because an angel's what you've been.

"You didn't write that for a girl?"

"What girl in her right mind would leave a guy like me?"

"Dude. I could give you an alphabetical list."

"Wanna know the truth?" He tapped his knuckles on the guitar. "I've just had this sense the past few days that Mom's angel was close by. Maybe you felt the same thing. Maybe you just *wanted* to see her and—"

My whisper cut him off. "It was *not* my imagination."

"I'm just sayin', is all."

These"—I indicated the slits on my face—"are real. My ex-girlfriend's gone. There was a lady in that van who looked exactly like Mom, with gray streaks in her hair. *Gray.* Like my mind would've come up with that in the heat of the moment. She yelled my name, tried to protect me. You think a stranger would do that?"

"Easy there, kid."

"And what about those lyrics? Maybe you've been tapping into something you don't understand. Angels. Ghosts. Since when've you written stuff like that?"

"Hey now, don't nobody know why I write what I do."

"Yeah yeah. Don't wanna jinx the magic."

"Anyway, there's nothing wrong with trying to broaden my appeal. It's country music, buckle of the Bible Belt. Gotta give 'em what they want."

"That's lame."

"Just takin' Chigger's advice."

"Chigger."

"Few days back we were hangin' at his place with some friends and the band. Whew, you should see it—big ol' log cabin off Highway 100, worth half a mil easy. He's done good for his family, made his share of cash."

"He's got an attitude."

"Goes without sayin'. But that boy's a bona fide axman."

My eyes darted to Johnny's.

"Ax, as in guitar," he explained.

"I know what it means. He's going on tour with you, right?"

"Leavin' tomorrow at the crack of dawn. Might not be Music Row's way, but the same boys who recorded in the studio are coming on the road with me. DAD's backing us one hundred and ten percent."

"What if I told you I don't trust that guy?"

"Chigger? He's all bark and no bite."

"He has a thing for Sammie."

"And that's gotcha worried?"

"He thinks you're cramping his style. Professionally. Even romantically."

"So he cut into me outta jealousy, is that it? How's that link him to Felicia or Mom? Far as I know, he doesn't even own a van. Ain't nothing in that garage of his but American-made classics and muscle cars."

"I don't know." My shins jarred the table as I stood. "Just seems to have an attitude is all."

"Okay, let's say you're right about Mom. What kind of motive would there be for kidnapping her?"

"How should I know? To get to that treasure in the cave maybe."

"The prank caller," Johnny Ray mused aloud.

"Does Chigger have any Scottish blood?"

"Whoa now. That's outta left field."

"You're the history buff. You know much about the Royal Stuart clan?"

"Um…I know some of 'em ended up here in the South. They go back hundreds of years, though, to the British monarchy. Had ties to the Freemasons and Knights Templar."

"And their motto is…'Virescit Vulnere Virtus.'"

Johnny turned a blank face toward me, and then understanding bloomed in his eyes. "Courage grows strong at a wound." His hand moved to his bandages.

"And who in our bloodline was a Mason?"

"Meriwether Lewis."

"The one who hid that treasure back in 1809."

"This has got my head spinnin'."

"Join the club." I stood and straightened my shoulders. "Maybe some-one found out about the gold, and they're using Mom to blackmail us for it. All I know is, if there's any chance she's alive, I've gotta do something. Until I know, I've gotta act on the belief that it *was* her in that van."

"It's never been your style to sit still."

"Better freakin' believe it."

"Then let's call your detective friend. The cops got the best chance—"

"No cops. That's his rules."

"They always say that. And how's he gonna know?"

"This isn't a stinkin' movie, Johnny. You should've seen what he did to Felicia—he cut her open!" I flashed on the image and felt the constriction in my throat. My foot catapulted the table across the floor. "What if this really is Mom we're talking about? That means he's got her right now." I paced the room. "You know, it scares me. I thought I had this thing beat."

"What?"

"These!" I slapped at my tattoos. "My old ways."

"So all that Bible reading doesn't count for anything? I've seen you change since movin' here. For the better, I might add."

"If that freak so much as touches her, I'll tear out his liver through his nose."

"Gotta find him first. So we better get movin' since I'm supposed to be on a tour bus to Atlanta in less than twenty-four hours."

"The Georgia license plate. Let's start with that."

He set his guitar back in its cradle. "You know the numbers?"

"Got them burned into my brain, but"—I tossed a notepad from the end table—"I wrote them down just in case. There. Look that up. I'll call Dad."

"Now don't go getting him all riled."

"Maybe he knows something."

"If so, he would've told us years ago, don'tcha think?"

"Considering his track record? No."

"I still think you oughta hold off."

"Fine." I downed the rest of my grapefruit juice, then faced my brother. "Do me a favor."

"Sure."

"Could you pray with me?"

He raised an eyebrow, adjusted his Tabasco boxers. "If it'll make you feel better, I s'pose I could."

20

A hard rapping on the door punctuated our morning. Through the peep-hole, I spied a familiar face on the steps and groaned—torn between wanting to enlist the detective's help and wanting to sneak out the back window.

Sorry. I had my own investigation to pursue.

As the knocking continued, I crept from the entryway and held up a hand to my inquisitive brother. "We have no obligation to speak with him," I whispered. "He's on a fishing expedition, that's all."

"Is it Meade? He could be the answer to your prayers."

"You're a funny man."

"Doesn't he ever take a day off? Why's he here so early?"

"I e-mailed him a picture of that wig. Before everything else happened."

"Could he help us on the sly?"

"No. He's a straight shooter."

"Maybe he's found some helpful info."

"Or maybe he's connected the dots between me and the wig and a mur-der. Which'll only cause more delay."

Johnny Ray wagged his head. "Fine mess you've gotten us into."

"That's right. I'm to blame."

"He's gotta know we're here, considering both our vehicles are in the lot."

"It's only seven twenty on a Sunday. We're sleeping."

"Just go talk to him, and get him off our backs."

"In these?" My pants showed streaks of blood. "I need to clean up first."
Eventually the knocking abated.

"You think he's still out there?"

"I don't know. Don't care." I poured a bowl of Froot Loops, waved off
my brother's predictable dietary criticisms. "Tell me as soon as you pull up
anything on those Georgia plates."

"You betcha, sugar lips."

After sterilizing the cuts on my cheek and washing dried blood from my
chin and neck, I ran a dab of gel through my hair and slapped antiperspirant
under my arms. In my bedroom, I changed into fresh socks and boxers, black
jeans, an "As Cities Burn" concert T-shirt, and a black knit cap. From the
stained pants—which I later shoved into a bag at the bottom of our kitchen
garbage can—I removed the empty bullet casing and the razor blade, retrieved
from under the car seat.

I set the items next to a wooden box on the windowsill and caressed the
smooth ebony. Inside, the pieces of a handkerchief show my mother's initials:
DLB. This box was a gift from my mother on the day she died.

One split second: the pull of a trigger, her body falling, tumbling...
Or?

One split second: her body tumbling, evading, as a bullet spiraled from
the barrel and passed harmlessly through trailing black hair...

Warmed by the morning sun, I stared out over the expanse of Centennial Park, where the Parthenon's griffins hovered atop the tree line. Crouched
and beastly, they seemed ready to devour my fluttering hopes.

If that was her, why hadn't she made contact years ago? Perhaps twenty-
two years ago the physical and psychological trauma had jolted something
loose inside her. Perhaps she'd suffered temporary amnesia.

Okay. But last night that woman had called out my name: "Aramis!"

I pushed back from the windowsill. Time to check my e-mail for any more messages.

———

On my bedroom computer screen, confirmation of Felicia Daly's fate faced me. A news article described an anonymous call and the discovery of the body but no word as to the cause of death. Although the Tennessee Bureau of Investigation hadn't yet listed any "persons of interest," a TBI contact number was given for those with pertinent information.

With my own investigation to conduct, I wondered how long I'd have before the so-called "Toot, Burp, and Itch" fellows offered me to the media as the sacrificial suspect.

Great. I slapped my hands against the desk, and the Nashville Predators bobblehead on my monitor trembled in fright.

"Any e-mails from him?" Johnny Ray asked from my doorway.

"You ever knock?"

"That's what you're worried about right now?"

I massaged my neck. "None yet. He probably wants to make us sweat. I sent him a message telling him I have his license plate and won't cooperate till I know what he wants."

"Risky. Could make him mad."

"I hope so. That's when people start making mistakes."

"Well, you oughta hear what I dug up." He stepped inside as I spun my seat toward him. "First off, the state of Georgia stopped issuing the 'Georgia…on My Mind' license tags at the end of '03. Most of 'em are obsolete."

"Narrows it down some at least. So the van's tags must've been renewed."

"Reckon so. And you'll be glad to know we've got agencies here in Nashville that'll run reverse license-plate searches for thirty-five, forty bucks."

"Let's do it then."

"But why pay when I've already tracked her down for free?"

I rocked forward. "You're kidding."

"Say hello to your older, wiser brother."

"Emphasis on *older*. C'mon, spill it."

"Well, that particular tag was sold on eBay a couple months back. A cheap, ten-dollar collectible. It's out of circulation and no good to anyone."

"Unless, of course, you slap on some fake stickers."

"And drive it outta state, where the cops are less likely to hassle you about it."

"So it's nothing but a dead end."

"Don't you wanna know the name of the buyer?"

"I thought that was private information."

"Private? On the Internet?"

"Who was it?"

"A Miss Felicia Daly. Sorry to get your hopes up, kid. Just like you said, a dead end."

I gritted my teeth and pinned him with a look. "That's not even funny."

"Aramis, I didn't mean it that way."

"Yeah."

"Really. I'm sorry."

My eyes clamped shut, and my head nodded until I heard his footsteps receding down the hall. A gale was brewing inside me. I couldn't trust myself. Couldn't trust my brother. Couldn't trust my own memories. Who could I trust?

"Someone left you a sealed envelope," Diesel told me over the phone. "He came into the shop just a few minutes ago. Said it was important. For your eyes only."

"Who was it?"

"That street bum who's always leaving us tips."

"Freddy C's not a bum. He's homeless."

"Here's one for you then. True or false: on the average, one out of four bums—I mean, homeless men—are convicted felons?"

"Diesel, are you even working? Or are you cramming for our final?"

"Both. Things've been slow this morning."

"I'm heading that way."

"True," he called into the phone as I hung up.

Normally I walk through the park to Black's, threading along the shores of Lake Watauga, beneath the Parthenon's pillars, or alongside monuments honoring Nashville's civic leaders. But not today. Instead, after repairing my rearview mirror with a tube of epoxy, I drove the back streets to the shop. I saw no sign of surveillance, but Meade knew where I worked. I'd hear from him soon enough.

"Well, if it's not Aramis himself," a woman greeted as I entered the shop.

"Ms. Thompson. Good morning."

Dressed in a fitted tan business skirt and jacket, she crossed her legs at her table and cupped her usual mocha. She's a regular customer, the first to spot the camera crews last year when I was selected for the reality TV show. "To what do we owe the pleasure? I thought you did church on Sundays."

"Sometimes I go with Sammie, but I don't exactly 'do' church."

"Please, I didn't mean it as an insult."

I waved it off. "It's all good."

"I'm probing here—you'll tell me if it's none of my business, won't you?—but I know I've seen you reading your Bible here in these booths."

"I love God, definitely. It's just the ritual of it that makes me feel awkward."

"Having been born Roman Catholic, I rather liked the ritual."

"Liked?"

"I haven't attended Mass in years."

"Maybe the ritual's not enough. I guess that's what I'm trying to say."

"Hmm." Sipping her drink, she watched me round the front counter.

I would have loved to continue the conversation, but my thoughts had already jumped ahead to Freddy's hand-delivered envelope.

21

"iesel. What's going on?"

"Oh, hey." He waved. "Just showing my parents around."

I run Black's on a tight budget and can't afford to ignore county health codes or the high standard for roasting, grinding, and brewing in my little space. While employee guidelines are more lax, it didn't keep me from balking at Diesel's parents standing in the work area.

"Uh. No one but staff allowed behind the counter. House rules."

"Sorry, boss. They're just heading out, flying back home."

"Okay, for now."

"Mother, Father, meet Aramis Black."

As the middle-aged couple turned from their tour of the kitchen, I took a quick visual inventory, concerned with good impressions. Anna had closed last night, and the floor still sparkled, the sinks still shone. Everything tidy and in place.

Mental note: *speak to Ms. Knight about a raise.*

"Mr. Black." A small, firm hand was shaking mine. "Heard a lot about you."

"Good to meet you, Missus…uh?" A hint of recognition triggered a sudden memory glitch. I'd seen this woman before…hadn't I?

"Hillcrest," she said.

Diesel stepped in. "Don't take any offense, Mother. Around here, no one calls me by my full name."

"Desmond's a fine name," she huffed.

"As is our family name," his father agreed, heavy cheeks jostling.

I paused, trying to place the man's face. I'd seen him before as well. "Uh, I hope you'll forgive me, Mrs. Hillcrest."

"But of course," she told me. "As for my son's denial of his given name, that's another matter."

"He's a good kid."

Diesel's eyes narrowed at me. His father's did the same.

"A young man," I amended.

"We've raised him to be nothing less."

"You should be proud." I stretched out my hand, found a strong grip attached to Mr. Hillcrest's arm. His husky form must've been rock solid at one time, but the years had taken a toll. "Lipscomb's a good university. And Diesel…uh, Desmond studies hard. Even with the long hours he puts in here at the shop, he still seems to get his schoolwork done. We have a night course together."

"Social psychology. Yes, I've spoken to Professor Newmann."

"In fact, we're working on a class project together."

"Thank you, I'm well aware."

"I'm sure you are. Like any good father."

"Unfortunately, Mr. Black, the statistics regarding fatherhood in our nation don't support your rosy outlook. Marriages are crumbling, and liberalism is corroding our moral fiber. My son's fortunate."

Rosy outlook? What was with this guy? I recalled Newmann's claims that Mr. Hillcrest had not only made threats but had blamed my brother and me for his son's grades. I was forming a question along those lines when the front door chimed.

"Customer," Diesel said. "I'll be at the front counter."

As he disappeared, Mr. Hillcrest trudged on, his double-chin quivering: "Yes, our forefathers are turning in their graves, Mr. Black. My hope for a better future rests on the shoulders of my son and ones like him."

"A better future. We all want that."

"And yet…" He glanced at Mrs. Hillcrest. "The antics of your celebrity brother only serve to undermine our years of personal investment."

"Excuse me? What has he done exactly?"

"Cavorting. Inebriated carousing. I'm concerned that he's influencing Desmond with his decadence and partying."

"Hold on. You're making a mistake."

Mrs. Hillcrest touched my arm. "We only wish that were so."

"This weekend," her husband continued, "has been an eyeopener. No doubt you've been told of Desmond's legacy of academic excellence. I have doctorates from SMU and the University of Houston." His droopy eyes bored into mine. "As parents, we cannot stand idly by. We'd appreciate your help as his employer in redirecting his energies toward more productive pursuits. For the sake of your family, you may also need to intervene in your brother's destructive relationship with our son."

"That sounds like a threat."

"When one suffers, Mr. Black, all suffer."

During class sessions, Diesel had hinted at childhood abuse. I'd heard him describe what I considered to be extreme methods of correction. Now, face to face with this couple, I felt a rush of heat in my neck. I, too, knew the sting of a father's blow and of his glare of disdain. Violence wasn't something I'd learned from TV or the Xbox.

"Okay." One last effort at remaining cordial. "Johnny does tend to enjoy a little too much Jack Daniel's now and then—"

"A little?" Mr. Hillcrest's reaction shot spittle through the air.

"But he is my brother. I care about him."

"Of course you do," his wife purred. "A little tough love might be just—"

"And," I barreled forward, pinning Mr. Hillcrest with my gaze, "if he's had any negative influence on Diesel—which is what we call him around here, and he seems to like it—then I am sorry. I'll look into it. But I won't have you come into *my* shop, behind *my* counter, and bad-mouth *my* brother to my face."

"We're leaving now," Mr. Hillcrest assured.

"Good plan."

"And if I'm not mistaken, your brother will be departing soon too, embarking on his first major tour."

"That's right."

"For his sake and yours, I suggest a tighter leash on—"

"He's not a dog."

"On his activities. The book of Proverbs says that a 'dog returneth to his vomit.' Seems an apt description of a man ensnared. A lifestyle of excess will exact its pound of flesh."

"Pleasure to meet you," I said, crossing my arms.

"Likewise. We'll continue this discussion later."

Long ago I'd learned to keep my hands available during confrontations, ready to strike, to snap up the closest object for attack or self-defense. Now, with a deep breath, I shoved my hands into my pockets. I tried not to think about Felicia's plane, heading back to Oregon this morning with an empty seat.

"Mr. Hillcrest, Mrs. Hillcrest, you have a safe flight home."

They said curt good-byes to Diesel, then, from the large front windows of Black's dining area, I watched them cross Elliston Place to their car.

A rented, dark green Hyundai.

That was where I'd seen them. The hotel, last night.

"They gone?"

I nodded.

Standing at the glimmering espresso machine, Diesel seemed to relax. "They're not always that bad. They were wound tighter than normal this trip, with my finals coming up and everything."

"They're your parents. I'll keep my mouth shut."

"They can be a real pain, but I love them."

"What else can you do? You can't change them."

"Got that right." He wore a rueful smirk. "Nothing's ever good enough."

"Speaking of which, why would someone with your dad's expectations and education settle for a rundown hotel in the seedy part of town?"

"What? How do you know where—"

"Long story. Just answer the question."

"He's a tightwad. They had to fly down because of Mom's circulation problems, and he got the cheapest place possible to get back at her."

"And she stands for that?"

"She has to." Diesel started to say more, but another customer had arrived at the bar. With studious care, he worked on a dry cappuccino. "By the way," he said, "that detective friend of yours stopped by and said he needed to talk to you about some e-mails you sent him."

"When was this?"

"I don't know. Before you got here."

Diesel shut off the steam wand and handed the man his drink. The customer took a sip, then tucked two dollar bills into the tip mug before heading out.

"Nicely done," I said. "And I'll take one just like that."

"A cappuccino?"

"Haven't had my morning coffee yet. Gotta get it from the best."

Diesel looked at me. My expression remained flat. His chest seemed to swell just a bit as he dispensed and tamped the espresso grind, then he flipped a black mug from the grill above the machine and set about his work.

———

Coffee in one hand, sealed envelope in the other, I went back to my office to look through what Freddy C had left for me. Last night's images tumbled through my skull. My pulse pounded like twin mallets against my temples.

For the hundredth time this morning, I shut down.

Or tried to.

The picture of my mom in the seat of that Dodge van was a debilitating thing. What if I lost her again? What if I found her gutted on the sidewalk, bleeding her life away while I crouched helplessly at her side?

Stop. Get a grip.

Or what if it was all just another deception?

Stop!

Beneath stark fluorescent light, I sank into the office chair, pushed aside the keyboard and my pocket New Testament. I peeled open the oversize envelope and shook its contents onto my metal desk.

A pamphlet. A handwritten note. And a piece of torn paper.

The first item was trifolded, inexpertly designed and full of typos. It was a call to arms for "The Kraftsmen," those who wish to "rebuild our Country, taking it backe from the Mongrels and Sons of Ham who pullute our soil." Aside from archaic King James Version quotes, the verbiage was crude and aimed at base fears, but I know from the study of human psychology that—sadly—these tactics often work.

The second item was harder to decipher, penned in shaky cursive from Freddy C's hands. I'd seen his writing during last year's intrigues. His scent wafted upward. In the note he reminded me I had asked why he was out late yesterday evening. He claimed he was investigating "criminals called the Kraftsmen." He wanted me to pass his findings along to the police.

How Freddy knew about these people was a mystery.

My eyes turned to the final item, a torn corner of cardstock. I recognized that it was a tattoo pattern. Most parlors offer huge books of such designs, opened for reverent contemplation like the verses of an ancient monastery's illuminated text. *Write them deeply in your heart...*

Or on your chest, your ankles, your lower back.

I grinned, imagining my homeless friend wandering into a parlor downtown, leafing through pages, ripping out this artwork. "Freddy, you didn't."

My grin froze at the sight of this particular tattoo.

An executioner's ax.

According to his note, this mark could be found on the upper arm of one of the Kraftsmen's leaders. As for what it all meant, I was only beginning to form an idea.

22

harpened by caffeine, I decided now was the time to salvage my Desert Eagle from the gardens at Cheekwood. Nothing like the reassurance of cold steel. Although the Israeli-made components were disassembled beneath a shrub, I was worried about pets sniffing around and kids playing hide-and-seek. What if someone found the gun? I could do without any more complications.

A bitter realization coursed over me, though, as I merged onto West End Avenue, headed in the direction of Belle Meade. I would've had my gun last night if it weren't for AX's shenanigans yesterday at Cheekwood. I could've drilled a round through that driver's side windshield. Unwittingly, he had saved his own skin.

My palms slammed against my steering wheel.

Did the law of peace, of forgiveness, ever fit into real life? What actual power did it have to change any of this?

Live by the Sword…Die by the Sword.

My old credo seemed so much more practical, so potent.

"Come on," I growled at my cell. "Gimme something to work with."

Set to vibrate upon receiving e-mails, the phone had yielded nothing yet from my enemy. No explanations. No instructions. My nerves were steel cables twisting into knots.

The dash clock told me I had a few hours before hooking up with Diesel and Sara Sevier for our study session. After that, I'd join Samantha Rosewood at J. Alexander's for our business dinner.

Supper, I corrected myself. *Sorry, Sammie.*

Before I knew it, I was dialing her number.

"You'll still be able to make it this evening?" she asked me.

"I want to. Definitely."

"Please don't feel any pressure. There's always next week."

"No, I'll be there. It's just that things are…getting complicated."

"You and your escapades."

"Yeah."

"Aramis?"

"What?"

"I didn't mean for that to sound dismissive."

"You're fine."

"Or so you've told me on previous occasions," she teased, and I cheered up at the uncharacteristic playfulness. "Though your lips may have been slightly loosened."

By a couple of glasses of wine, she could have added. But she maintained her Southern decorum.

"Gotta go," I said. "Just wanted you to know you're on my mind. And Miss Eloise, she was probably the sweetest old woman I ever knew."

"Old? You're never one to sugarcoat things."

"I… No, I didn't mean it that way."

"Aramis, you're fine."

"Thanks. That's the first time you've told *me* so."

"But not the first time I've thought it."

She let out a mirthless laugh, and it struck me that she was grieving. Loneliness resonated beneath her tones. Though I was tempted to respond to her rare flirtation, I knew I couldn't take advantage of it.

Even if it was Sammie. Especially because it was Sammie.

"You're right," she said. "There was no one sweeter. Miss Eloise was up every morning at dawn, ready to share a good Southern breakfast and tell me stories of her childhood. Were you aware that she was born the day the First World War ended?"

"I didn't know that."

"What will I do with this huge place now that she's gone? She tended the flowers and fed the horses. She felt it important to do her part."

"I can stop by and help with the horses," I offered.

"I wasn't meaning to burden you with my concerns."

"Don't be silly, Sammie. It's no burden."

"You're such a man."

"Tell me that's a good thing."

"Trying to come up with solutions. But I appreciate it, I do."

"I hope so. Because when it comes to flowers, I'm useless."

"Such a man," she said again.

———

I was cruising past Montgomery Bell Academy, wondering if the same security men I'd faced yesterday would be patrolling Cheekwood this afternoon, when a nondescript sedan slid into the lane beside me. A tap on the horn brought my head around, and I spotted the honorable Detective Reginald Meade.

"Wonder Bread wonderful."

He honked again. I kept driving, watching my mirrors for suspicious tagalongs, checking my phone for messages.

No cops. That was the rules.

Meade kept pace, making his wishes known with chiding stares and shakes of his head. He wasn't going away. After a few blocks, I caved and turned into a gas station. He pulled alongside with his window down.

"Why didn't you pull over earlier?" he demanded.

"Didn't recognize the car."

"And my face? You going to tell me that all black men look the same?"

"Only the ones I don't know."

"You're a regular comedian, Mr. Black."

"Hey. You're the one trying to play the race card."

The detective lifted a palm. "Listen, I'd like to believe we've built some trust here. I need to speak with you."

"You followed me from my shop, didn't you?"

"Would you rather I'd gone in and made a scene? It may be in both our best interests to discuss what happened on Oak Street."

"Oak Street?"

"Runs parallel to City Cemetery. Based on preliminary evidence, it's the site of a criminal homicide. Frankly, with investigative responsibilities already passing over to TBI, I thought it'd be good to speak with you myself, get your version of things."

"My version?"

"Of what happened between the time I hung up with you and the time a Caucasian female was found mutilated and still warm."

"Am I under arrest or something?"

"No, I just—"

"Then I don't have to say a word."

"You're under no obligation, that's true." Meade polished his watch with a thumb. "I just hoped to gather some facts."

"There's nothing to say. I've done nothing wrong."

"You're the last person known to be with the victim."

"You think I'd be stupid enough to dial you up before some violent act?"

"You could've called for that very reason, to create reasonable doubt."

"C'mon."

"Or perhaps it was unpremeditated."

I measured my words. "I did not hurt her, Detective."

"Do you remember the question I asked last night, about whether you'd ever considered killing someone? Do you remember your reply?"

"Hold on! That was just conversation. A rhetorical question."

"Inadmissible in court. Yes, I know."

I put my car into gear. "Big mistake, pulling over for you."

"Is there anything you'd like to tell me about the incisions on your face? And the scuff marks on your hand?" Meade pointed at my grip on the wheel, where the swirled scar tissue of an old burn wound reaches from my fingers to my right wrist. "You look like you've seen some recent action."

"First rule of fight club," I quoted. "You don't talk about fight club."

"Always a snappy reply to avoid dealing with the truth."

"What do you want? Why're you doing this?"

"Because I know you and some of the trouble you've been facing. There's no reason for you to hide anything—isn't that what you've been telling me?—and, in fact, your knowledge could lead to the apprehension of the person or persons responsible." He peered through his open window, waiting for my response. "If you're hungry at all, we could discuss this at Martha's at the Plantation."

"Never been there."

"It's down on the Belle Meade property. Do crawfish cakes and black-eyed-pea salsa sound like something that might interest you? I'm buying."

"Is that allowed?"

Meade's eyes showed little amusement. "I have to eat, same as the next guy."

I glanced back over my shoulder, checked my mirrors, vacillating on my course of action. From the station's minimart, a lady and young child, perhaps six, exited with goodies in hand. She bent to peel the paper from the boy's ice-cream bar, then smiled and tweaked his nose.

"Are we on?" Meade checked.

For Mom's sake, I needed to keep my mouth shut. "No," I said. "I've gotta go. Anyway, you're barking up the wrong tree."

"So you say. There is one thing, Aramis."

"One thing?"

"That irritates me."

"Fine." I rolled my eyes. "I'll bite."

"It seems strange that you still haven't even asked the victim's name."

Ahead of me, the boy stumbled and stared down in wide-eyed dismay as his cold treat hit the pavement.

23

fter you," Meade told me.

A hostess seated us at a cloth-covered table, and I placed my cap in my lap.

Pulled in two directions, I was the flag in a tug of war. If Detective Meade flexed his legal muscles, he could detain me regarding a homicide. On the other hand, if AX realized I was talking to the cops, he might harm my mother. But how would my enemy know? Was he watching even now?

Ridiculous. He couldn't be everywhere at once. Plus, the detective was working in plain clothes, limiting his chances of being ID'd.

On the early end of the Sunday lunch crowd, we were sharing the airy dining room with two giggly women in sun hats and an elderly gentleman toting a trusty Nikon 35mm. The place had that casual yet refined charm that embodies the South.

After sucking down a tea-flavored punch, I passed on the crawfish and ordered a fried-green-tomato salad with horseradish sauce—sure to clear the nasal passages while also meeting my brother's approval. Meade stuck with his standard fare.

"The chef here has never let me down," he said.

I straightened my napkin. Adjusted my silverware. Looked out the window.

"Big guy like you, Aramis—you seem awfully nervous."

"No, not me. Nice place."

"Read all about it." He pushed a brochure across the table.

I scanned the words while thoughts raced. My mom was out there some-where. And there was nothing I could do but wait for her abductor to con-tact me. Couldn't even go looking for clues at the crime scene since cops were all over that and—

Just read, you fool. Disassociate.

Flipping through the brochure, I saw the words "Belle Meade, the Queen of Tennessee Plantations." Once a mecca of thoroughbred racing, she'd en-compassed more than five thousand acres. Her greatest sire, Bonnie Scotland, contributed directly to the lines of such horses as Seabiscuit, Seattle Slew, and Secretariat. Today a carriage house and stables stand on the remaining thirty acres, as well as John Harding's 1853 Greek Revival plantation house, which endured Union occupation during the Civil War.

The ghosts of that War Between the States still haunt the hills and hol-lows of Tennessee, and according to the pamphlet I'd read this morning in my shop, another specter had appeared: the Kraftsmen. Their brand of bigotry was rooted in the Ku Klux Klan's postwar years of propaganda, when certain Southerners feared the loss of everything sacred to them and distilled those concerns into hate.

The South will rise again.

Was Chigger one of the Kraftsmen? Did he have a tat of an execu-tioner's ax?

"Aramis, you look miles away."

"Got a lot on my mind."

I gazed over my glass at the detective's dark brown face. Years ago I'd been shot at by an African American male—now there was a person I didn't trust. But that had to do with lead thudding into the wall behind me, not his skin color.

I could trust Meade. I knew I should just spill it, tell him everything.

"I can only imagine," he was saying. "Seems quite a bit unfolded yesterday in that hour and a half between your call from the hotel parking lot and your arrival back at your place."

"Ninety minutes. Is that all it was?"

"Ninety-one, to be exact. From 9:21 to 10:52 p.m."

"Stickler for details."

"And in that short time you found and photographed the wig."

"Yeah. Seems Felicia was coerced into helping this guy, the same one who attacked my brother and tied him to the statue."

"She was the redhead mentioned in Johnny's statement?"

"You got it."

Meade's forehead furrowed. "I also saw the license tags you photographed. In fact, I ran them this morning and found that they both belong to a rental-car agency out at the airport. The first was signed and paid for by one Felicia Daly. The second by a Mr. Drexel Hillcrest."

"Interesting." But there was no feeling, no surprise in my response.

"Back to the wig. Where did you find it?"

"The hotel bathroom."

"In her room? Is there something you should tell me about your relationship?"

"Completely platonic. I promise."

"Mm-hmm."

"When I confronted her about the wig, she confessed."

"Which made you upset, I'm sure."

This was potential quicksand, one of many leading statements that could drag me under. I glanced around Martha's dining room. The Giggly Girls were still giggling, Nikon Man was fiddling with his camera, and more diners were filtering in. The waitress approached with our lunches. She set the plates before us, refilled our drinks, made sure everything was in order, then floated away.

"Now that's what I'm talking about." Detective Meade breathed in the aroma.

The food was fantastic. For a few minutes, a truce was called.

At last Meade set down his fork and wiped his hands. "There is a witness," he told me, "who claims you forcibly dragged Miss Daly from room 212 to your car."

"Now wait a sec. I was trying to protect her."

"By dragging her away?"

"Johnny showed you a copy of that e-mail I received, right? The one threatening my family if I contacted you? Well, I thought if I could get Felicia and Johnny safely tucked away, then I could get you involved without endangering them."

"A flawed but noble plan."

"What else could I do? I mean, I shouldn't even be talking to you now."

His eyes lifted from his entrée. Two tables away a college kid took his seat.

"Food's good," I said. "Thanks."

"Do you believe you're still in danger?"

"I just…I don't want anyone else to get hurt."

"Anyone in particular?"

The tug of war continued. How much should I explain? Months ago, along with millions of viewers of *The Best of Evil*, the detective had watched details of my mother's death. For me to say that she was now alive and being held hostage would sound lame—and more than a little too convenient.

He leaned forward and lowered his voice. "Miss Daly is dead, Aramis. The media will be all over this, scrutinizing Metro's handling of the investigation, playing to the public's fear and the local ratings. Within the department, certain people will be squabbling for political gain. All that to say, I have one goal and one only—to apprehend the guilty party. Would our shared past lead you to believe otherwise?"

"No," I said. "You've always been straight up."

"I appreciate that. It's my job to suspend blame until all the facts have been gathered, and I have no intention of tricking you or pointing fingers."

I nodded. In my pocket my cell phone remained lifeless.

Why hasn't AX responded? I swear, if he's hurt Mom…

"So by taking Miss Daly to your car you were trying to protect her, correct? The witness saw the two of you get into the vehicle, then head west on Murfreesboro Pike, in the direction of downtown. What made you turn onto Oak Street?"

"She told me to."

"Do you know why she chose that particular spot?"

"No idea. I tried to warn her, told her it was a rough neighborhood. She got out anyway, and there was nothing I could do. I went home, crawled into bed, woke up this morning to the breaking news."

"Did you place a call to 911 last night?"

"You said you weren't trying to trip me up."

"No trickery. Just covering all the bases. You do realize, though, that minutes before my fellow officer noted your return home, an anonymous call led patrol cars to Miss Daly? They found her with multiple stabs to the abdomen, defense wounds on her forearms and palms, and slashes on her shoulder blade—matching your brother's, I might add."

"There. Doesn't that prove my innocence?"

"Raises more questions actually."

"It's the same guy. Don't you get it? He killed Felicia."

"And you witnessed this firsthand."

"No. Remember, I went home."

"Of course."

I wrapped my hand around the back of my neck.

"You do understand," he explained, "that a warrant could subject your vehicle to an inspection by TBI technicians here at Nashville's central lab. Tire impressions, fiber and carpet analysis, serological and DNA samples—everything put under a microscope."

"I've done nothing wrong."

"Have I implied otherwise?"

The eyes in the dining room seemed to be turning our way. Was I being watched? Did AX have an informer in here? Paranoia curled its way up my spine.

My phone vibrated. No e-mail icon. It was a call from my shop.

"Hello, Diesel? What's going on?"

"Are we still on for tonight? Studying for our final over at Sara's."

"Sara. Yeah. Sevier. Lives off Woodmont, right?"

"You sound distracted. You ever get hold of that detective I told you about?"

"I'm staring at him."

"No wonder you sound grouchy. You're not going to bail on us, are you?"

"No. It's just...I've got some stuff up in the air."

"It's a group score. We need you."

"I'll be there." For Meade's sake, I tried to keep my voice light. "So who's doing the oral presentation?"

"Sara says she's got it covered."

"That twangy voice of hers might hurt us."

"I think it's cute."

"Tell that to Professor Newmann. The man seems immune to cute."

"Behind all the makeup, she's a smart girl. Let her run it by us at least."

"If you say so."

"Don't be late."

"I'll be leaving soon. See ya." This could be my excuse to evade Meade. I closed the phone, willed an e-mail to appear—to no avail—then looked over my glass at the detective. There was one thing I needed to know from him first to put to rest my own guilt. "Can I ask you a question?"

"Go ahead."

"How did she…" I blinked. "Did Felicia bleed to death?"

"Only the coroner's report will give a definitive answer. I've viewed photos though," Meade added in an even voice, "taken by the first officer on the scene. My guess is she suffered damage to her vitals. And the aerated blood in her mouth points to a punctured or collapsed lung as well."

I sipped at my punch.

"Skin contracture around the wounds makes its difficult to determine the actual size of the knife, but even moderate pressure with a sharp blade can do extensive damage. We do know the stabs were delivered with force, since only the hilt of the weapon could produce that type of bruising at the entry points."

Blink. Sip.

"Bruises," he noted, "indicate that her death was not immediate."

I pushed back in my seat. Had he catalogued these things to watch my reaction? Did he care that I was trying to eat? Subtly he had applied pressure to extract answers—just doing his job, blah-de-blah—but maybe my decision to open up had been a mistake.

In my pocket the phone buzzed again.

An e-mail this time. Same sender as yesterday. The game was back on.

"Gotta go," I told Meade. "Business calls."

"Personal business, judging by your expression."

I swallowed. Wadded my napkin.

He said, "I asked earlier if you were still in danger. You never answered."

"Thanks for the eats." My hand dropped a ten on the table, while my eyes swept the dining room. "That should more than cover the tip."

"Aramis." A whisper, nothing more.

"What?"

"Are you being followed, blackmailed, or coerced in any way?"

My lips felt numb.

"If the answer is yes, tap your finger once on the table."

Another quick sweep. Tug of war.

"I'll do my best to protect you," he said. "Talk to me."

I shook my head. "Easy to say now that you have a corpse, huh?"

24

Meade had his murder victim, and I had my mother back from the grave. With only twenty-two minutes till the next rendezvous, there wasn't time to retrieve my gun. Tires kicked up gravel in the plantation parking area as I followed the e-mail's instructions and aimed my car downtown. My mirrors showed no signs of the detective in pursuit, but with one call he could slap a Metro tag team to my bumper.

Which should be a good thing, right? Extra firepower.

Except the police would spook my opponent, could even endanger Mom's life. Plus I didn't want them looking on when I wrapped my hands around this psycho's throat. My Desert Eagle might be under a bush, but cops or no cops, I'd use anything in my arsenal to free my mother.

In an effort to ditch potential tagalongs, I slipped into quiet lanes of swanky Tudor-style homes, French villas, and flourishing shade trees. Despite Music City's entertainment reputation, healthcare is one of the local economy's mainstays, and in this neighborhood, doctors drive Beemers, Vipers, and Hummers to reflect their different moods. Occasional landscaping trucks break the pattern, pulling flatbed trailers and playing Tejano music. My Honda Civic—built the same year Kurt Cobain first smelled teen spirit—was the glaring anomaly.

So much for blending in.

Puttering along Woodlawn Drive, I took a turn onto Natchez Trace and let it lead me back onto West End Avenue.

Carrying tens of thousands to work each day, West End is a dividing line between the medical fortresses of Centennial, Baptist, and Metro General to the north and Vanderbilt and Veterans Affairs to the south. Set one block off this main road, my espresso shop crouches near a corner.

Black's was dedicated to Mom's memory. She always loved her morning coffee...

The hope that kept me going, the one I came back to more than any other, was that of seeing my mom take that first sip from a fresh mug of my trademark Back-in-Black roast and hearing her sigh with serene satisfaction.

———〜———

Bearing one letter each, flags rippled along the museum's art-deco exterior and spelled its name in vibrant colors: FRIST. I parked in the monitored lot. Saw I had seven minutes to spare.

Once more I read the message on my phone.

Chop, chop, Aramis. "I did not come to bring peace, but a sword."
Go to the Frist Center gift shop, 12:45 p.m. Do as instructed, and
you will see your mother again. Remember that "whoever loses his
life for my sake will find it." Are you ready to find that which you've
been looking for?

How did he know what I was looking for? The presumption of this idiot!

My wristwatch became my taskmaster, urging me up broad steps, past a landscaped courtyard, into the soaring halls of the Frist Center for the Visual Arts. Every time I enter, the facility renews my love for this city. I've seen the works of Van Gogh and Monet here, Picasso, El Greco, and Titian. Pulitzer Prize–winning photos. Last year a unique exhibit highlighted the ancient Egyptian quest for immortality.

Where in this building would my foe be hiding?

Or would he send someone else in his place, as he'd done at Cheekwood? Would he snicker as I jumped through more of his hoops?

My shoes clicked on the marble floor. I ignored the uniformed guards. From a long atrium, glass panes peered into the gift shop, and I slowed for a glimpse of those inside—groups of teens, elderly ladies, and a young couple. Rows of books and art prints sat next to Egyptian jewelry and 3-D puzzles.

Two steps through the entry, I spotted a sprightly girl to my left. She looked familiar—that profile and those eyes. I didn't realize I was staring until she popped her head from behind a postcard rack and flashed a neon green grin. Literally neon. Those snazzy fashion braces.

"Aramis."

"Do I know you?"

"Not exactly. But I know you."

"How?"

"My name's Alexia."

A and X. A coincidence? A sour laugh welled in my throat. I was now sighting letters and links in the most innocuous places.

"I was there Friday night." She stepped closer, flipping her hair from eyelashes caked with mascara. "At your brother's party in the park, remember?"

"It was kinda dark out there."

"Johnny Ray Black. Omigosh, did he sound great or what?"

"He did."

"I had him sign a T-shirt and my copy of his CD. I'm keeping my fingers crossed. Could be worth something down the road, you never know."

The lime green smile. "One of the advantages of catering on Music Row is that you get to rub shoulders with all the bigwigs and up-and-comers. Pretty cool."

"So you were one of the servers? Don't you have to be twenty-one?"

"Celebrated last month."

"Oh. Congratulations."

She winked. "Shh, don't tell anyone that I got his autograph. It's against company policy. Always supposed to keep it professional, you know."

"Which caterer was it? I forget."

"Athens of the South."

"Ahh. Playing on the Greek theme. Explains those leaf-wrapped thingies."

"Spiced figs. Weren't those delicious? I even snuck a few."

"They were...different. Anyway, I doubt Johnny minded giving you his autograph."

"I doubt he remembers." Another wink. A thumb tilted to her lips.

Gossip columnists were scavengers for such morsels, and her impropriety was beginning to grate on me.

"Are you here for a reason?" I asked.

"Keeping my grandmother company." She feigned a yawn. "She's an art buff."

"So you didn't come here to..."

"What?"

"To see me?"

"If that's a pickup line, I've gotta tell you it's pretty weak."

"Yeah. Forget I asked."

"Thanks though. It's nice to be noticed."

I scanned the length of the gift shop, wondering if my contact was already present. Should I wait to be approached? What should be my strategy?

Her eyes flashed. "Now if your brother's ever free, you let him know I'm available." She pressed her catering card into my hand, then skipped away and linked arms with her grandmother.

My watch told me it was 12:51. The adrenaline that'd pooled in my stomach was making me queasy. Was I being played here? Was this AX's way to prove he had the upper hand? Fine. Point made.

Waiting, I pretended to browse through trinkets and artsy gifts. There in plain view, a locked case held replicas of the glittery objects now on exhibit at Cheekwood.

Fauxbergé again. Another coincidence?

"Would you like me to open the case for you?"

"Uh. Sure." I looked up and met the eyes of a saleslady. "Thanks."

"Oh, it's you."

"Excuse me?"

"I saw your picture. Is it Aramis? Did I pronounce that right?"

"Air-uh-mis. Close enough. Have you been waiting for me?"

"Not at all, no inconvenience. You take your time, sweetie, and look around."

"But. Well. Do you have something for me?"

"Yes, it's behind the counter. All wrapped up, ready to go."

"I'm ready now."

"I don't mean to rush you."

"I've gotta get going anyway." Following her to the register, I trolled for information. "So this…item. You think it's a good choice? Did you see it?"

"Exquisite." She set a bag on the counter. "She'll love it. She truly will."

"She…"

"A perfect gift. I'm sure she'll play along and act surprised."

"Is this my mother we're talking about? Long black hair. Wisps of gray."

"And beautiful, soulful eyes. Actually, you favor her. You share similar coloring."

My breath quickened. "Did she seem okay?"

"I suppose so. She was quiet but very polite."

"When was this?"

"Thirty minutes ago or thereabouts."

Wonderful. The e-mail had been sent to me after the fact.

"And was she alone?"

"Yes. She said her husband was waiting in the lot."

"Her husband?" That must've been part of the act. "Did you see him?"

"I didn't. I offered to have someone wheel her out, but she insisted it wasn't necessary." The clerk was looking past me. "I'll be right with you, ma'am."

My fingers brushed the gift bag. I thought of the riverbank and that first shot that had ripped into my mother's thigh. The image of a wheelchair seemed appropriate, almost inevitable. If anything, it seemed to confirm her identity.

I heard the saleswoman tell me a price, with tax, found myself pulling twenties from my wallet. She gave me change and tucked a receipt into the museum gift bag.

"Thank you, sir."

"Wait a sec." I looked up. "You said you saw a picture of me."

"A yearbook photo actually. They're not always the best, but there was no mistaking your dark skin and wavy hair."

Had Mom got ahold of one of my pictures, saving it all these years?

"Thanks for shopping with us," the saleslady said. "And don't you feel bad, sweetie. Your mother seemed very understanding about the late Mother's Day gift."

I didn't make it past the museum's rest rooms. Standing at a hand basin, I hung my head and gathered my thoughts. Mom had been here half an hour ago.

And she had my picture.

My hands trembled on the gift bag, peeling away pearl-colored paper, exposing a Fauxbergé within. Already I'd left one of these creations tucked beneath the front seat of my car. Here was a second, emerald in color, with translucent jewels.

In the Russia of a hundred years ago, before the days of Lenin and his revolution, the Romanov family commissioned these jeweled creations to be presented each Easter. I recalled that locked within the very first egg, a tiny golden hen had represented spiritual rebirth.

Rebirth.

"Mom." I looked into the mirror. "Don't die on me again."

What now? With groping fingers, I searched for the egg's unlocking mechanism. What would I find inside?

My legs found new strength and took over. I hurried through the front doors of the Frist, pounded down the steps, and curved left toward the edifice of Union Station, an old railroad depot that's been refitted into a first-class hotel. Rising into a cloudless sky and boasting a statue of Mercury, the station clock tower said it was ten past one.

This had to be the place.

Inside the Fauxbergé, I'd found a locker-style key and a slip of paper. The printed words said: "If there's to be a union between mother and son, you will need to get on track."

A doorman ushered me into a spacious lobby where gold-leaf mirrors, bas-relief statues, and a grand limestone fireplace greeted me. Built in 1900, the Romanesque structure must've once awed train passengers. Sunlight filtered through the lobby's barrel-vaulted ceiling of stained glass, enhancing the hotel's grandeur.

"May I help you, sir?"

"The tracks."

"Sir?"

"How do I get to the railroad tracks?"

"Through those doors there," he said. "But they're not—"

I careened out onto a covered platform, found a wrought-iron railing that looked down upon numerous sets of rails flanked by barbed wire. Apparently access to this area was limited to rail workers. Orphaned cargo cars sat on one set while a Louisiana-Pacific engine purred along another. Twenty feet below me an open coal car was motionless.

I could attempt a jump, but I was doubtful of this location.

"Okay," I said aloud. "Where is it? What am I looking for?"

In my hand, the key bore numbers. Were there old station lockers nearby? I wandered back inside to the polished registration desk. An outdated train schedule hung on the wall behind the clerks, a reminder of a bygone era.

"Excuse me. Do you have any lockers here?"

"No sir, we don't. But if there's something you need stored securely—"

"Never mind. Thanks though."

I turned and stared at the clock above the lobby fireplace. The huge hands pointed, giving no true direction. What was I missing?

25

After two restless circles of the lobby, I shook my head and stalked past the doorman back toward the Frist Center's parking lot. I was so close. Over twenty years had gone by, and I'd missed my mother by thirty minutes. The vibration of my phone brought me to a halt. Another e-mail.

> By meeting with your detective friend, you have violated the rules and your mother has paid a small price. "Therefore do not be foolish, but understand what the Lord's will is." Now that I know you are not being followed, proceed to the Greyhound station. The key will lead you to the locks.

A small price? What'd he done to her?

My jaunt through Union Station had been another false lead, but at least I'd come up clean. What if the cops *had* tailed me? What price would my mom have paid then? This guy was a certified nut job, spouting Scripture as though he was God's emissary to earth.

The Greyhound station.

I hopped into my car and reached my destination in less than two minutes. Located on Eighth Avenue South, the terminal maintains a steady flow of travelers and vagabonds. I edged between the listless souls at the front doors and found myself inside the main waiting hall. Odors of urine and mildew hovered among the hard seats, while crushed cans and crumpled pretzel bags camped at the base of a trash receptacle.

The lockers drew me in. The key was warm in my palm.

I crouched, looked both ways, then opened the corresponding lock. Inside, a burnished silver tube was propped at an angle. No longer than my forearm, no wider than my wrist, the thing bore red plastic caps on each end.

Couldn't open it here. Not out in public.

I tucked the object under my arm, left the key, and strode back to my car, where I slumped into the seat.

Final instructions? Or more games?

I pried a cap from the tube and felt a feathery tickle against my finger-tips. Images of hairy-legged spiders fired through my nerve endings, awakening my imagination and barking orders at my muscles to drop this menace. I locked down the illogical fears and forced myself to hold on, lifting the tube for closer examination.

And then I understood.

Your mother has paid a small price... The key will lead you to the locks.

I braced myself against my seat, reached fingers into the opening, and grasped hold of the rolled sheet of paper that peeked through long, silky locks of black hair.

"There. Explain *that,* oh wise and older brother."

Johnny was zipping up a garment bag containing a stage ensemble of tight, torn jeans, a belt with a pewter buckle, and a black and gray striped shirt. In a box on the bed, his Stetson still contained knife slices—for publicity purposes, no doubt.

He set down the bag. "What've you got now?"

"See for yourself."

He took the paper from my hand. His eyes darted over the slanted letters and slightly open loops, then widened—just as mine had—when he recognized this as the same handwriting we'd come to cherish among Mom's old letters and scrapbooks.

"Where'd you get this?"

"She wrote it herself, sometime in the last hour or so."

"And you know it was her?"

"Yes. Did you read the whole thing? We need a few minutes to talk."

"Kid, I'm packing up, hitting the road in the morning. This is it, everything I've been workin' toward. Not trying to put you off, but..." His voice faded as he set the paper on the bed, smoothed it with his fingers. "Okay, what's going on?"

"She's here in Nashville. I'm convinced of it."

"Throw me a bone here, and help me understand."

"She's being coerced. Same way Felicia was."

"Your ex." His eyes sought mine.

I nodded.

"The one who was left to bleed to death."

I closed my eyes. "They're still not sure that's how she died."

"She's dead either way, so what's it matter?"

"It matters."

"And what's any of this got to do with Mom being alive?"

I eased the tube's other contents onto the bed, beside the letter. Black strands, mixed with some gray, slithered into a pile.

Johnny cursed out loud. "What is that?"

"Proof."

"That's human hair."

"Mom's."

He cursed again. Pacing, he grabbed his own golden brown locks and pushed them back out of his eyes. "That could be anybody's. No. I…I can't accept this."

"She was at the Frist, in a wheelchair. She had one of my yearbook photos."

"You saw her?"

"No. But the clerk did."

"You're grasping at straws, little brother."

"I have a theory."

Johnny Ray crossed his arms, waiting.

"You remember last year how that rapist collected hair from his victims, right here in Music City?"

"That was some messed-up stuff."

"At least he's behind bars now."

"What're you getting at?"

"What if he had an accomplice?" I said. "I'm thinking out loud here… But maybe I've put too much trust in my friend Freddy C."

"The bum from the park? You telling me you think he's a rapist?"

"Did you know that one out of four homeless men is a convicted felon?"

"Kid, you're not making sense."

"I'm trying to piece this all together. Remember that homeless lady who was stabbed and burned? Nadine Lott. Freddy knew her. Thing is, he's faced accusations of sexual misconduct before, and then he got mixed up in our whole adventure last year. Even had his hands on that ebony box in my room, on Mom's handkerchief too. You tell me. Maybe he got fixated and tracked her down."

"What? Some bum succeeded where her own sons failed?"

"I don't wanna believe it either. But if she's alive, who cares?"

Johnny plopped onto the edge of the bed. His hand touched the severed strands, and he jumped back up.

"You know," I added, "Freddy was alone with Felicia last night. For a few minutes anyway. What if he…did something to her?"

"She was hurt before he got there—that's whatcha told me."

"What're the odds of Freddy being out on that corner when I drove by? Maybe he was told to be there. Maybe he's working with the other guy, the one with the knife." I shook my head. "Sounds crazy, doesn't it?"

"Beyond crazy. This morning you gave the same paranoid speech about my guitar player—how he's sneakin' around in his Corvette and jonesin' for Sammie Rosewood."

"Tell me this. Does Chigger have a tat on his upper arm?"

"He plays lead guitar, so whaddya expect? He's my axman."

"A tattoo of an executioner's ax. Am I right?"

"It's a pretty common design, hardly rock-solid evidence."

"AX. That's his identity. Same as those letters he cut into your shoulder." Johnny expelled one of his when-will-my-little-brother-grow-up sighs.

"Okay then." I gritted my teeth. "Explain the note. And the hair."

"You don't want me to do that, not right now."

"I do too."

"Do not." When he saw I was serious, he pressed on. "All righty then. If you're gonna hear this, you may as well hear it from me."

"I'm waiting."

"Way I see it, Aramis, you went through a genuinely traumatic experience last night, a double shot of terror. Ain't no one gonna deny that. You saw someone special to you die—viciously murdered—and you feel responsible, feel like you coulda saved her if you had a chance to do it all over."

I looked toward the ceiling. My guilt coiled around my ribs.

"So, because you're exhausted and traumatized, that's what you've done here." He hefted the garment bag over his undamaged shoulder. "You've given yourself a chance to get it right, to ease away your shame. You dreamed up this whole scenario—the license tag, this hair, everything. By resurrecting Mom in your mind, you think you can replace what you lost and somehow make it all better."

My voice dropped. "That's insane."

"The world's a crazy place."

"No. You're implying that *I've* gone insane."

"With grief, which is a normal reaction." He picked up his Stetson, snugged it down on his head until it shaded his eyes. "Honestly, I respect your beliefs—and I've seen you turn things around like nobody's business—but you've let this Jesus talk fool you into thinking the world'll be one big, happy place. Just doesn't work that way, little brother. We gotta love people, do the best we can, and hope it all comes back to us."

"I'm not an idiot. This world's full of pain—I know that."

"Then let this go. You're just pickin' at old wounds."

"Your wounds look pretty fresh. So did Felicia's."

"Maybe we oughta just give this guy a few bars of gold to get him off our backs. I don't want to see you get hurt next. And what about our deal? To let the cops handle this?"

"The rules changed." I snatched up the note and the black tendrils of hair. "I'm going after Mom. You do whatever you want to do."

26

Written under the watchful eye of her abductor, my mother's sentences were nothing more than dictated instructions. No emotion. No personality.

Still, she had held the pen that wrote this note. Her touch, her essence...

Johnny Ray was off doing errands for his morning departure. He'd left without a word. I sat at the kitchen table, my eyes roving across the flowing pen strokes as though they held long-desired nutrients. I brushed my fingers over her cut hair.

What if I was wrong about all this? What if it was a trap?

No. Mom had survived. While I couldn't blame Johnny for his skepticism—if I were in his shoes, would I react any differently?—I refused to cave in to it.

I mulled the note's contents again. Raked through it for shreds of truth.

"It is a disgrace for a woman to have her hair cut," and you have dishonored your mother by your disobedience. To be allowed into the family, you must deliver to me the Masonic ring that was buried with your inheritance. Bicentennial Mall Park, 5:45 a.m. this Thursday—a fitting day for victory over my enemies.

He knew about the treasure. Had he wrung the info from Mom?

Two hundred years ago Meriwether Lewis had concealed the gold before his untimely death and had left clues for his descendants. But a natural dis-aster shifted the exact location. Although I'd hinted at the existence of the cache during the airing of *The Best of Evil*, only my brother and I knew the location of the family inheritance.

Could there be a Masonic ring in that cave along the Wolf River?

I thought back to yesterday's e-mail: "Perhaps you should give me a ring."

I stood and grabbed a Dr Pepper from the fridge. At the window over the sink, I guzzled while trying to put it all together.

What made a centuries-old Masonic heirloom worth killing for? And who would have something to gain from it? Yes, Lewis was a Freemason, like many of our nation's Founding Fathers. He even served as master at Lodge 111 in St. Louis. Was he linked to the Scots though? The Royal Stuarts?

Virescit Vulnere Virtus…

Who had called and threatened my brother? Possibilities stirred in my head, bolstered by recent events.

Chigger's animosity and racist leanings.

Freddy's mysterious appearance near Oak Street.

Mr. Hillcrest's self-righteous threats not only against his son's professor but against Johnny Ray and me. He'd even thrown in that bit from Proverbs, about my brother being like a dog.

I bolted up. Thought of the scriptures sprinkled throughout the e-mails.

The stove clock told me it was time for the study session at Sara Sevier's trendy Green Hills apartment. With Mom's life in the hands of a madman, I would've felt no qualms in missing it. So what if I flunked our final exam? I'd taken social psych for no other reason than to clear the muddied waters of my own thought processes. What drove people toward—and away from—doing good? What was truth?

With only one day of class left, I was more confused than ever.

Diesel, though, might be able to clarify a few things about Mr. Hillcrest.

My study partners acted surprised to see me.

"Who are you again?" Diesel gibed. "Didn't think you'd show."

"He's *alive!*" Sara called out, playing the part of Dr. Frankenstein. In her Dolly Parton twang, it sounded more goofy than anything.

"You make me sound like a monster."

"If the shoe fits," Diesel quipped.

Sara slapped at his knee. "Y'all better be civil."

"He looks even worse than when I saw him this morning," he tossed in. "Though he'd probably look worse if he'd been stranded at the airport all day, like my parents."

"Your dad's still in Nashville?"

"If you can believe that. Southwest Airlines has canceled all flights to Ohio due to the storm warnings. And he must be livid by now, demanding answers from the ticket-counter staff."

"Your poor mom," Sara said.

"She's learned to live with it."

"Diesel. You been out partying with my brother recently?"

"He invited me out to Chigger's place a couple times. Is that a bad thing?" The strands of this web kept getting more complex.

I said, "Your parents seem to think so. Your father even threatened me."

"He's just a control freak." Diesel shifted in his seat. "Here's a pop quiz for you. True or false: John Denver, that folk-singer guy, served in Vietnam as a trained army sniper?"

"Think that one's true," I played along. Best to keep the conversation casual. "Over seventy kills, from what I heard."

"You heard? There's your first clue. Denver was never even in 'Nam."

"Silly me. Denver's in Colorado."

Sara groaned, then gestured at a beanbag chair. "You gonna join us or not?"

"Sure."

Course syllabi, research journals, and varied refreshments covered the wicker-and-glass coffee table. Diesel was stretched out on the carpet with a rolled issue of *Psychology Today*, while Sara's ample frame filled the cushions of another wicker contraption. She cradled an iMac on her lap, probably surfing the Net.

"How're things looking? Is our urban legend spreading?"

"I just Googled the keywords and came up with some fresh links."

"Show him that one you showed me." From the floor, Diesel arched a piece of popcorn toward a soda can, watched it miss the opening and land on the carpet.

"I *know* you're not leaving that there," Sara whined.

I picked it up.

"Thank you, Aramis."

I tossed it in my mouth. "Five-second rule."

"Ugggh. You know, studies show that bacteria transfers as quickly in two seconds as it does in five."

I spit the popcorn into my hand and shook it back onto the carpet.

Before she could protest, Diesel swiped it up into his own mouth.

"Oh no you *didn't*. Y'all are disgusting. Go. Shoo."

Diesel was enjoying her discomfort. In class I'd wondered about his feelings for her, and now I was convinced. Typical playground antics. All very amusing, but deeper concerns were stirring in my skull.

"Boys, how can I concentrate?" Her glossed fingernails tapped the keys of her computer. "Am I the only one who wants to ace this final?"

"I know Diesel does."

"Then why is he so…distracting?"

"I'm a man," he spoke up. "We can be pretty immature."

"At least you admit it."

"Makes me sound more intelligent, doesn't it?" Diesel crossed his legs on the floor and pulled a syllabus onto his lap. There was something boyish and vulnerable in his icy eyes, something "distracting" that Sara seemed to recognize.

"Ladies and gentlemen."

No response.

"Hey," I said louder. "Let's get cracking here."

Diesel broke away from her gaze. "Sure thing, boss. Time to focus."

"And," Sara said with a grin, "it's time to take a vote. I move that Aramis do the oral presentation."

"No. C'mon."

Diesel seconded the motion. "You're the best speaker in our group."

"Every time I get up there, Newmann tears into me."

"Professor Bones? He does that to everyone."

"He's tough," Sara agreed. "But he gives mercy where mercy's due."

"You make him sound like a saint."

"Maybe that's who he was named after, Saint Boniface."

"Yep." Sitting ramrod straight, Diesel hitched up imaginary jacket lapels and spectacles. "Patron saint of turtles and tweed."

"You two. Tell him to stop, Aramis. Don't they teach y'all *manners* up north?"

Diesel's eyes narrowed. "Shoot, people around here are so polite they can't figure out who should go first at a four-way stop or how to merge onto the freeway."

"The interstate," Sara and I said in unison.

"Don't they ever teach you to form your own opinion, *down south*?"

"Ohhh! When it comes to you, mister, I *have* formed my opinion."

"Time." I made a T with my hands. "Time out."

"No," said Diesel. "Let's hear it. What's this opinion of yours, Sara?"

"You...you're rude, self-centered, and...and you're an uncultured carpet-bagger. Why I ever wanted to be your study partner is beyond me. Now, if you'll excuse me..." She lifted her chin and marched off to her bedroom.

"Smooth," I said.

"Why'd I open my big mouth?"

"Least we know one thing."

"What's that?"

"Dude. She likes you."

Diesel seemed surprised. "Then why'd she just run from the room?"

Love really *is* blind.

"I'll tell you," I offered. "But first you need to answer a few questions for me."

"Pop quiz. I'm ready."

"This has nothing to do with social psych. It's about your father."

"What about him?"

"It's nothing really. He made some comments this morning at Black's. I just wanna be sure I wasn't reading too much into them."

After rehearsing my presentation, with Sara and Diesel acting as hecklers, I swung by Centennial Park. I had the dirt on Mr. Hillcrest—including his involvement at his local lodge—and now I needed answers from Freddy C.

But he was nowhere.

The streets funneled me from Broadway to Eighth Avenue to Lafayette. I was headed toward the hotel on Murfreesboro Road. Along the way, I dialed the number for my father, Kenneth Black.

His low drawl greeted me through my cell. "Kenny here."

Though this man had raised me in the years after Mom's disappearance, his own moods often had turned hostile, and he had used me as a whipping post. He faded from the picture as I got older, and eventually he settled in Bowling Green, Kentucky, around the time my brother started playing smoke-filled Nashville honky-tonks.

Now that I'm here, there's no excuse for any of us to stay apart. On occasion Kenny does visit, and he calls when he feels like it—which isn't often apparently. In the last few months, however, we'd talked more than ever, building a new foundation where old walls had rotted and crumbled. Working on it, at least.

"Dad." I call him that, despite everything. "How's it going?"

"Just fine. Had a rash of storms this weekend."

"Went around us here, I guess. It's been warm and humid."

"Count yourselves lucky. Got me a shed roof that's all kindsa tore up."

"You need help?"

"With what?"

"The roof, Dad. I could drive up and help pound nails."

"No reason to go outta your way, boy. But I appreciate that, I do." His voice changed. "Get down offa that sofa! You don't belong up there."

I tried to sound cheery. "Is that Bruiser?"

"Stupidest dog I ever did see." Another shout: "Now look whatchu done, knockin' over my beer. Out! Out ya go."

"I'll just call back later."

"No need for that. What was it you wanted?"

"It's about Mom."

"Dianne." He made a smacking noise with his mouth. "Dianne *Lewis* Black."

"I know you've had to sort through a lot, with last year's revelations and all, but I need to know something. Did she really die that day? Did they ever find her? I mean, could she have ended up in a hospital with amnesia or something?" When he remained silent, I pressed on. "Or maybe those guys who were after the treasure found her and, I don't know, held her captive. Tried to get more information."

Dad cleared his throat. "Now you listen here. We've already had this family's laundry aired for all the world to see on that TV show. I'm not blamin' you or your brother, even your uncle, but it's gotta end. Is that clear? I done you wrong as a child. I know that, and there ain't no excuse. But you gotta let it go."

"Just like that, huh?"

"Your mother. Me. All of it."

"You sound bitter." Where had I heard those words before?

"She was unfaithful," he snapped. "You don't know what that does to a man."

"I've got some idea."

"What she did—that tore me up. No use wallowin' in it, though, is there?"

"You... Do you know if she really died?"

"Aramis." He sighed. "There's some things just don't gotta be talked out."

"Did they ever find her? Tell me that much at least... Hello?"

"These storms are somethin' fierce," he said at last. "We're losin' the connection."

Just like that, the phone went dead.

27

stared up at room 212 from the hotel lot. Less than twenty-four hours ago, I'd been parked here in the dark. Seen Felicia arrive. And then the Hillcrests. In Felicia's room, I'd found a red wig and taken matters into my own hands, dragging her down those metal stairs to this very car, playing right into my enemy's hands.

What had I been thinking?

The crisscrossed wound on my cheek throbbed. Gripping the steering wheel, I studied my blue and green tattoos. Twin swords. One on each arm. My credo.

And now it was my fault.

By choosing to live by the sword, I'd led Felicia to die by the sword.

Where was God in the midst of all this? Couldn't he have intervened somehow, sent a cop along Oak Street at that moment? Where was any sense of purpose or a master plan? Sure, I'd exercised my free will—which God gives each of us, right?—and walked into the trap. But didn't the New Testament talk about how "God causes everything to work together for the good of those who love God"?

Three words materialized through my cloudy thoughts.

I nodded. Jammed my palms against my eye sockets. Threw my head back and exhaled into the warm cockpit of my old Honda.

"Mom is alive."

Kenny and Johnny Ray could avoid the notion all they wanted, but for me there was no going back. Everything had changed last night with the locking of our eyes and the spark of recognition. Time to stop feeling sorry for myself. If I went stumbling through this gauntlet, it might provoke another killing.

Thursday. At Bicentennial Mall Park.

I had to operate under the belief that Mom's abductor would safeguard her until she could be traded for the alleged Masonic ring.

Four days and counting. In Nashville's cool, dew-drenched dawn, we would have a resolution.

If not sooner.

I climbed from the car and faced the rusty stairway, hoping to coax a few answers from the New Orleans woman in the corner unit. She'd seen me tow Felicia down the steps, and she might've spotted the person who sneaked into my car.

"Sorry, she's checked out. Her and that little boy, the poor thing."

"There must be a reason."

"A reason?" The hotel desk clerk gave me an incredulous look, then spoke with sensual lips that stood out against otherwise homely features. "Have you ever stayed in one of our units? Not that I should be talking this way, but the place has seen better days. We're lucky to get the extermination people out here once a year."

"Bugs, huh?"

"Roaches, Japanese beetles. But you didn't hear it from me."

"Any idea where she went, Miss—"

"Leake, with an E. But you can call me Geraldine."

"Okay. Do you know where she went?"

"I know the police were here, snooping around, asking questions, and they must've hooked her up with… Sorry. Wrong word."

"She was working outta that room, wasn't she?"

"You didn't hear it from me."

"So the cops relocated her?"

"That's what I was told. They hooked, I mean, set her up with one of those charity organizations, found her a place with a real sink and stove."

"Glad to hear it. Especially for the kid's sake."

"Little cutie pie, isn't he?"

"Did the cops ever tell you what they were looking for?"

"Not straight out, no. Are you with Metro?"

"I had lunch with a plain-clothes detective today." I tugged at my black T-shirt and toggled my eyebrows. "And he was picking my brain for clues. But if they've already been here, I guess I'm wasting your time."

I started to turn. The clerk seemed to be enjoying the excitement this day had brought her way—anything to break the tedium—and I was counting on her desire for a larger role in the drama.

"Sir," said Geraldine, "they didn't get to hear much of what I had to say."

"Really? Seems negligent on their part."

"They were mostly interested in the owners' thoughts. And they brought in a warrant to search one of the units."

"Number 212."

Her eyes widened. "Didn't need to tell you, did I?"

"Never hurts."

"Well, I put it all together this afternoon. Saw a news update about that woman they found dead downtown"—the clerk pointed at a small-screen TV mounted on the wall—"and her name rang a bell."

"Felicia Daly."

"Sad thing too. Just horrible. She seemed so nice when she checked in."

"She checked in alone?"

The clerk nodded.

"Tell me this. Are there security cameras on the premises or in the parking lot?"

"Not that work. Your buddies asked the same thing."

"So Miss Daly never checked out. Did she leave payment information?"

"A credit-card number, I think. But it's a family-owned hotel, sir. They won't worry about collecting a one-night fee—after a tragedy like this."

"You do see, though, how that info could be key, Geraldine."

The clerk's eyes brightened, and she began rummaging through an index-card file. "Ahh, I'm with you now. You could trace her using the number, maybe even link her activities to the person who killed her."

"Very good. Lemme guess. A fan of *CSI*?"

"No, *24*. Got the entire DVD set." She pulled out a registration card. "Here it is. That's her writing."

"I'm surprised the cops didn't take this."

"They pulled information off the owners' database. We use these cards to get the guests checked in without fuss. Later we back up the info on the office computer."

"I'd like to take this."

She shrugged. "We toss them anyway after the payment's been processed."

"Do you have the card for Mr. and Mrs. Drexel Hillcrest?"

"Middle-aged couple? They checked out today."

"That's correct."

"Hallaway, Hicks…" Her fingers came to a stop. "Hillcrest."

"What was your impression of Mr. Hillcrest?"

She paused. "You think he had something to do with this?"

"Just covering all the bases."

"Now that you mention it…" She leaned forward. "He did come in here late last night. I'd noticed his roving eyes earlier when they checked in. Made me uncomfortable, a married man looking at me like that. He had champagne in an ice bucket."

"Brought it in here? Why?"

"Said the missus had taken some meds, fallen dead asleep."

"Meds, huh? Did he say what kind?"

"He rattled off some name, but I wasn't listening."

"How'd he explain the champagne? Seems a little obvious."

"Exactly. He waited. Didn't say anything. Dangling the bait, I suppose. I didn't want to think anything about it, so I told him it was late and I needed to lock the lobby door. He apologized, said he was just looking to dump the ice somewhere. Didn't want to wake up his wife."

"Interesting excuse."

"Yeah. I suppose it was a little odd."

"And that's his registration card?"

"Here." She shoved it across the desk. "It's all yours, sir."

"Thanks for your help, Geraldine. I won't take any more of your time."

"Just catch the person who's responsible, to put our minds at ease."

"Believe me, that's the plan."

———

My appetite is a fickle beast. More than once I've worked a fourteen-hour shift at the espresso shop, pouring nothing but triple lattes down the hatch. Other times I've missed breakfast and felt like smashing things by ten o'clock.

Right now I had an appetite for something more stable.

An evening with Sammie Rosewood.

I had just under two hours before our meeting at J. Alexander's in West End, no more than twenty minutes from here. So far my "escapades" hadn't derailed our supper plans.

Sitting in the hotel parking lot, I pulled out my cell. Tapped in a message using the alphanumeric mode. Hit Send. I was hoping to goad my foe. Any reply might bear a clue and, more important, maintain the tenuous link to my mom. If AX was there, I could cling to the belief that she was too.

Instead, a prompt response said that address was no longer valid. I double-checked it, tried again. Same error message.

Like a drunkard at the bar of hope, I'd been cut off.

I departed the hotel feeling desperate. What had happened? Was AX simply covering his tracks, or was there something more sinister to it?

A crazy notion caused me to turn the wheel to the left, making a detour to the airport. Mr. Hillcrest had exhibited some strange behavior. If he was still fuming at the departure gate, a passenger page might draw him out to talk to me.

I needed ten minutes—that was all.

t Nashville International, I jogged up the escalator from short-term parking and headed through automatic doors. I mumbled an apology after bumping into a guitar-toting man in Wranglers and boots. A seasoned musician? Jilted newbie? The oversize cowboy hat suggested the latter, since most locals avoid such obvious clichés.

I followed the lines of ticket counters, where suspended banners juxtapose Tennessean images against international ones—catfish and sushi, irises and tulips, country music and classical.

Once I'd located Southwest Airlines, I requested a page for passengers Mr. and Mrs. Drexel Hillcrest.

Quick and painless. Just a few questions before supper.

Mr. Hillcrest appeared after the third page. Heavy jowls swayed with his steps, while droopy eyes stared straight ahead. He gave no acknowledgment to a woman who swerved her luggage cart out of his way.

"Mr. Black."

"You're not surprised to see me."

"I certainly didn't expect to see you again so soon, but with the mounting annoyances of this day, I would say very little qualifies as a surprise. That in no way negates my impatience with said annoyances—you being first and foremost at this particular moment."

"You're a straight shooter, aren't you, Hillcrest?"

"Pardon me?"

"You say it like it is."

"See no reason to do otherwise. At my age, I—"

"Your wife? Where is she?"

He stepped back as though physically struck by my interruption. Judging by his size, his bulldog demeanor, his behavior toward his son, I was certain he was unaccustomed to losing the advantage in a conversation. Cowards—that's what these types are. Bullying their way through life, afraid of anything that cannot be controlled.

Which meant he better fear me.

"Mrs. Hillcrest," he replied, "is waiting at the gate."

"But I paged her also."

"I instructed her to stay with our carry-on luggage. Desmond told you we were here, did he?"

"He's been worried about you guys. Diesel's a good man."

"He has no right inviting others into our family's affairs."

"Interesting word, *affairs*. Does your wife know about last night?"

"Your tone disturbs me. To what, exactly, are you referring?"

"Your visit to the hotel lobby. Champagne on ice."

"That was you who nearly bumped into me on the stairs."

"That was me."

"Would you like to explain why you were spying on me?"

"Would you like to explain why you make passes at women half your age? Was the hotel clerk the only one? Or did you start off with Felicia?"

His eyes were stone chips. His thin smile was a putty knife sliced into his fleshy cheeks. "Have you come to insult me, Mr. Black? Most of my day has been spent in this airport, and I've little desire to put up with infantile accusations."

"*Most* of your day, huh? Did you leave the airport at any point?"

"I've been waiting for my flight, young man."

"One that's been delayed. You've had time to do some sightseeing, haven't you?" I was reaching here, but I wanted to gauge his reaction. "A quick taxi ride downtown. A visit to the Frist Center."

"I haven't the foggiest idea what you are insinuating."

"Or maybe you just used the rental car. The green Hyundai."

"Your insolence is disturbing in the extreme. With your and your brother's influence, it's no wonder Desmond has slid into debauchery of late. Do you realize that 'every tree which bringeth not forth good fruit is hewn down, and cast into the fire'?"

I straightened, the nerves in my fingers prickling. "Where'd you hear that?"

"The King James Bible, son. You'd do well to familiarize yourself with it."

What were the chances he'd spout off that verse? Was he playing me? He'd made his feelings about my brother loud and clear, but how did that carry over to my mother? And what did a Masonic ring have to do with any of this?

What disturbed me most deeply was the fact that he'd been seeking guidance from the same Scriptures I was learning to read. The Bible is often called a sword of truth. But my foe had been using it as a weapon of manipulation and fear.

"You're quite the sightseer," I pressed on. "The Frist today, Cheekwood yesterday, and the *Musica* roundabout on Friday night. Guess it's fitting you'd tie my drunken brother to a statue of naked people. A bit of ironic justice?"

Mr. Hillcrest sneered. "Tied to a statue?"

"That was you circling in the Hyundai, wasn't it? No. You would've been too worried about being seen. Bet you had Mrs. Hillcrest do that bit for you."

He stepped toward me. "You are despicable."

"Dude. You still haven't answered my questions."

"I won't dignify such falsehoods with a response. I've served as a deacon at my church for years. I've been married to the same woman for nearly twenty-five. I've attained degrees from multiple universities and been accepted as a member of the esteemed Alpha Chi honor society. My only desire is to see my son excel in his studies so that he can undo the damage of the free-love, drugged-up flower children. It was my misguided peers who led this great country down the primrose path of degradation."

"And now you're fighting back."

"I hope to regain ground, absolutely."

"Using guilt and fear."

" 'Fear of the Lord is the beginning of wisdom.' Look around you, Mr. Black. How long can we call ourselves 'One nation under God' while bearing no fruit of godliness? Pandering to the whims of immoral politicians has gotten us nowhere."

"And this justifies the way you berate your own son."

"My family is *my* concern, and I'll thank you to—"

"Diesel's my employee and classmate."

"Then you should've warned him away from your brother."

"If Johnny's been a bad influence, I apologize."

"We've reached an impasse, Mr. Black. You haven't heard a thing I've said, and it's time for me to put the ax to the barren trees. I'm done here."

He turned to go, and I could barely blink.

Put the ax to the barren trees?

"Why did you kill her?" I hissed.

"Pardon me?"

"And where's my mother?"

Hillcrest cast a pitying look over his shoulder. "You're a strange one, Mr. Black. You start with accusations and end with calling out for mommy?"

A matchstick of fury scraped through my skull and sent flames charging through my limbs.

His pomposity. His mockery. The mistreatment of his own son.

I leaped, catapulted forward by emotion, and smashed my forearm into the base of his neck, driving his corpulent body onto the airport carpet. I grabbed hold of his thinning hair and lifted to slam his face down. He pushed back against my attack. He tried to roll and throw me off, but I braced my right leg on the floor and dug my left knee into his lower back.

Lift. Slam.

Aside from thin rings of pulsating red, my vision remained clear. In the past, I'd learned to focus and slow things down, and it happened again now as I anchored the man's neck to the ground.

Voices were crying out around us. Running feet were drawing near.

"Where have you hidden my mother?"

He only grunted.

This was pointless. I was attracting unwanted attention. I decided against a final thrust and let him go.

As soon as I stood, rough arms encircled me and yanked me away. I was being handcuffed. Mr. Hillcrest was stumbling to his feet, touching his nose, and shaking his head. A sheen of blood gave his teeth a vampirelike appearance, as though he'd managed to suck the honor from my veins.

"Tell me where she is!" I demanded.

"I have no idea what you're talking about."

"My mother! Where have you taken her?"

Hillcrest flashed a condescending smile and patted at his nostrils with a handkerchief. "I'm sorry, but you've obviously mistaken me for someone else." He turned his words to the police officer at my back. "There's no reason to detain this young man. In retrospect, I see how he may've misconstrued one of my comments as an offense against his mother."

"He attacked you without physical provocation."

"A simple misunderstanding."

"Would you like to press charges, sir?"

"That won't be necessary. In fact"—he still wore a smile, but his flint eyes drilled into me—"if my own family were so maligned, I might have done much the same."

The officer allowed him to go, then turned the inquiries my way.

I was concentrated on one thing only: Mr. Hillcrest's deliberate stroll through the security area. He turned his head and lifted an eyebrow, as if to remind me that cops were against the rules, as if to say he could control me better than I thought. For now, he was beyond my reach, but he'd be back by Thursday.

Five forty-five a.m. Bicentennial Mall Park. In the shadow of the state capitol.

I'd be there.

And whatever it took, I would be ready.

29

Interstate 40 took me back into the heart of Nashville. The Broadway exit fed me into the westbound lanes of West End Avenue, familiar territory and only minutes from my business supper. With time to spare, I considered stopping for gas.

No. Better wait till Monday, when prices dropped back down.

Or was that an urban legend? So many things I took for granted, so many "truths" I'd never verified for myself. Even now, my long-held family history was being called into question. Did Dad know something he wasn't telling me? Or was he simply unprepared to deal with a new reality?

I hit another red light. Was that four in a row?

I pressed my head back against the seat and told myself to stay cool.

Everywhere I turned, life was going on as though no one knew—or cared—that my ex-girlfriend had been murdered and my mother had been abducted.

Just ahead, people streamed in and out of a Blockbuster store. I wanted to roll down my window and yell, "Don't any of you read the newspaper? Don't you know how short life is? Where's your respect for a young woman whose body will be flown home to heartbroken parents? She never got to go horseback riding on the beach. And while you're at it, people, forget your stinkin' movies and help me look for my mom!"

The streets were crowded for a Sunday evening. Based on the vehicles' sticker prices, I realized they represented an influx of parents coming to sweep away their precious Vandy students for summer relief in the Florida Keys or the Bahamas or a Destin beach house facing the Gulf of Mexico's warm surf.

Ah. Poor pampered babies.

Sammie Rosewood knows that world much better than I, never wanting for material things. The family home on Tyne Boulevard was owned long before her parents' passing. The Rosewood estate includes a chalet nestled in Gatlinburg at the foot of the Smokies, and it more than pays for itself with year-round rentals. She plays tennis on the court behind her house, dines out without a second thought, and shops at the Mall at Green Hills.

If I didn't know better, I'd envy her.

But I can't.

There's something behind her eyes, a melancholy spot that cannot be consoled by monetary things. And in two years of knowing Sammie, I've seen a generous side that goes beyond the cash. She truly cares about people and invests in them. Exhibit A: Black's espresso shop. Exhibit B: Desperado Artist Development and the career of one Johnny Ray Black.

Enough said.

We're different people from different worlds. Which may be why every time our lives brush against each other is a moment I tuck away.

———

By the time I dropped in at home, changed clothes, and ran back out, I was three minutes late arriving at J. Alexander's. Passing on the golf-cart shuttle, I walked the long lot. As I entered through heavy doors, I let my eyes adjust to candle-punctuated darkness. Tall ceilings and partitioned seating areas muted the clinking of cutlery and conversation. From a side lounge, laughter trickled out.

A corner booth. That had been Sammie's request.

"You made it," she greeted me. Candlelight splashed across her eyes as she looked up. Honey accents glowed in her dark auburn hair.

"Fashionably late. Did I make you wait long?"

"Not at all."

"You'd say that even if I had."

"The evening's specials are posted up-front. Did you happen to see them?"

She was doing more than avoiding my statement. She was allowing me to take charge, to be the gentleman and order for us. Call me old-fashioned, but it made me want to step it up and become a better person.

"I did," I said.

"Enlighten me."

"It's right up your alley. Grilled swordfish served with orzo and wild rice."

"Sounds delicious."

Our waitress arrived moments later, and I ordered two specials. "Except," I said, "I'd like to exchange smashed potatoes for the orzo."

"Sure. What can I get you to drink while you're waiting?"

I glanced at Sammie. "A bottle of Pinot Grigio?"

Her lips parted, but she closed them again. She was letting me make the call. In light of my previous idiocies with her, this was a test I had to pass.

"Um, on second thought, let's go with two iced teas, one sweet and one unsweet."

As the waitress departed, Sammie said, "The wine did sound good."

"I can call her back."

"No, you made the right call."

"You know how I can get."

She tilted her head, traced a finger over her spoon. "I've had a long weekend."

"Miss Eloise."

She nodded.

"Wine might help take the edge off. Is that what you're thinking?"

"I don't know. Yes, perhaps."

Our waitress slipped cold drinks onto the table. I looked at Sammie, but she gave a slight shake of her head. I nodded at the waitress, and we were left to ourselves again.

"You," I said, "are probably the most selfless person I know."

She coiled a strand of hair around her finger. "Your point is well taken."

"My point?"

"I shouldn't let self-pity take over. I'd be thinking only of myself."

"That's not what I was saying."

"Of course it was. Shame on me for not even asking how your day's been."

"It's been…fine."

"Last night at the studio you seemed upset."

"It's all good."

"You're hiding something, aren't you?"

"No. Listen, Sammie, I was trying to give you a compliment."

"Thank you."

"You're always thinking of others, of what they'll think of you. Sometimes you're allowed to have a little fun—that's all I meant."

"You don't think of me as a fun person?"

"Now you're putting words in my mouth."

"Aramis."

I kept my lips shut and wondered if she could see my fears, my secrets.

"I have never…" She looked away, looked back.

We locked eyes, and the attraction seemed palpable. Sammie's always been the calm counterpoint to my internal wrestlings, and I've been drawn to her since that first day in the bookstore. Of course she's out of my league, and for the sake of our business, I've maintained an appropriate distance.

"I've never felt this alone," she mused.

Her eyes swam with that loneliness, stirred by the loss of her grandmother. Was there something more there? Did she feel it too?

"The memorial service will be on Tuesday," she said.

There was my answer. I was fooling myself to think anything more.

"I'll be there, Sammie. I mean, if you want me to be."

"Would you be one of the pallbearers?"

"Me? Of course."

"You could do that?"

"It'd be an honor and a privilege."

"Johnny Ray will be out of town."

"On tour, yeah."

"I couldn't take him from that, couldn't even ask."

"He'd stay though. I know he would."

"No." Her hand brushed at the tablecloth. "We've worked the past eight months to get his career to this point. I won't stand in his way now that the doors are opening. Music Row, country radio—these large venues are not sympathetic when it comes to sudden cancellations. It's an unforgiving business."

"Whatever you need me to do."

"I appreciate that."

Our dinner plates arrived, steaming with mouth-watering aromas. After sampling the swordfish—which was cooked to perfection and rivaled the seafood I grew up eating in Oregon—I leaned back and soaked in the atmosphere of rich shadows and soft lighting. Sammie and I, for separate reasons, needed this. We made an unspoken pact to skip discussions of sales figures and profit ratios.

Finishing up, I asked if she was ready for dessert.

"What I'd really enjoy is a Southern pecan latte."

"Hmm." I put a finger to my chin. "Now where could we find you one of those?"

"There's this wonderful place down on Elliston, though I believe it closes at five on Sundays."

"Too bad."

"Never fear." Sammie's eyes twinkled. "I know someone with a key."

⁓

When we first found her, I thought she was dying.

Seconds after Sammie and I had unlocked the door and pushed into Black's, I noted the glow of the kitchen light. That was unusual. Normally, only the track lighting over the espresso machine stays on overnight. As I moved around the bar, I saw that Anna Knight had polished the floors and counters to a radiant gleam. Her cleaning routine had been completed, yet lights were still shining at seven thirty.

"Hello?" I stepped past the upright freezer. "Anna?"

The sound of crying.

"Are you okay?" I pushed aside my own recent horrors and poked my head into the kitchen. "It's me. Aramis."

30

Anna Knight was seated against the tiled wall, one arm resting on the yellow mop bucket. When she lifted her chin, strands of hair slid along her cheeks and clung to her mouth. She looked shaken, but okay. No blood. No stab wounds.

"What happened?" I said. "What're you still doing here?"

Sammie flashed me a quizzical look and knelt beside her. "Anna." Her voice was low and soothing. "You're safe, honey. Aramis is going to check the rest of the property while we get you cleaned up. Does that sound okay?"

She nodded. "I was so afraid of what he might do. I feel so…silly."

"What in the world happened?" I said again.

Another look—more withering this time—from Sammie.

"What? We need to know what we're dealing with."

She circled her finger in the air, giving me the signal to move out.

I armed myself with a crescent wrench from beneath the triple sink. Since it was Sammie's investment that got this place off the ground and since she signs the paychecks, I've formed this little habit of following her orders. She rarely pushes it—not her style—but if she told me to paint the walls hot pink, I'd do it.

With some game resistance, of course.

Flipping on lights as I went, I cleared the dining room and musicians' stage in the corner, the drink prep area, storage room, hallway, bathrooms, and back office. I checked and locked front and back doors. Doused the main lights again.

"One Southern pecan latte," I whispered, "coming right up."

I turned on the grinder—nothing but the freshest for Miss Rosewood— then steamed milk as the machine extracted crema-heavy espresso into shot glasses. I measured flavoring into a black mug, added the shots, topped it with frothy milk.

She met me as I was wiping things down. I handed her the mug.

"For me?"

"For you."

She took a cautious sip. "Mmm. You're the best."

"Why, thank you, milady."

"Anna's freshening up in the bathroom. She's a bit addled."

"Did she say what happened?"

"She did. When we first came in, though, she needed assurance she was safe, not badgering for explanations."

"I didn't badger."

"You blundered blindly."

"Ouch. Okay, I should've been more sensitive." I began dispensing espresso for my own drink, though my attention was diverted by Sammie's posture with hands on hips. "What'd I do now?"

"Aren't you even going to ask what happened to her?"

I exhaled in exasperation. "First I'm in trouble for asking. Then I'm in trouble for *not* asking?"

She smiled. "All a matter of timing."

"So what happened?"

"Anna's ex is in town. Apparently he tracked her here from Orlando and came in demanding that she take him back. When she told him that was out of the question, he started yelling, cursing, making threats. She was afraid to step out of the store."

"Did she call Metro?"

"By the time they arrived, he was gone. He could be anywhere out there, and basically the authorities have their hands tied. He didn't actually commit a crime."

"Seems wrong."

"I agree." Sammie sipped again at her latte. "I'm going to take her to my place tonight in case he knows where she lives. I have good security—Miss Eloise's choice—and Digger always helps."

"The Golden Retriever Canine Alarm."

"But only you and I know he's all bark."

"I'll follow you. Make sure you get there safely."

"Thank you. In the morning I'll call the temp agency to help cover the second shift. You're opening, right? And Diesel comes in early. If I'm not mistaken, you both have classes on Monday nights."

"Our final is tomorrow."

"I'll make sure the store's covered. I'll close, if need be."

"You're the best," I echoed.

Standing in the passageway, Anna cleared her throat and gave a weak smile. She looked embarrassed. How long had she been standing there?

"Sorry to interrupt."

"Not at all," Sammie said, turning. "I'm just glad you're safe and sound."

"I feel so foolish. I didn't mean to worry anyone. Was it wrong of me to stay in the store?"

I went to her and put a reassuring hand on her shoulder. "Your safety is most important, Anna. You hear me? Your ex didn't touch you at all, did he? Anyway, I'm the one who should be saying I'm sorry." In my peripheral vision, Sammie was nodding. "I was worried about you when I came in. Just didn't know how to express it."

"I know you care, Aramis."

"I'm clumsy showing it sometimes."

"Oh, you're a doll." Anna looked to Sammie for affirmation. "Don't you think he's a doll?"

Sammie was still nodding, and I felt my heart skip a beat. But was she responding to Anna's question or still approving my apology?

Not that it mattered. That's what I told myself.

———

Atop brick-and-mortar pillars, the flicker of lead-paned lanterns illuminated the driveway's entrance. A mailbox set into the stonework bore simple black letters reading Rosewood. My headlights cut swaths between the elm and poplar trees lining the route to the two-story plantation-style home with its vast wraparound porch. As we crested the drive's gentle curve, starlight played over the fenced tennis court and a long, low building of stables. The old smokehouse, whitewashed and cut into the hill, conjured images of the ante-bellum life on this edge of modern Nashville.

Digger growled from the porch as I parked behind Sammie's Mustang. He's big and imposing, a stellar judge of character—which explains his affection for me—and protective of Sammie, who chose him from a neighbor's purebred litter. As Anna and Sammie climbed the steps, I kept close behind.

"Attaboy, Digger." I ruffled his ears. "As you can see, Anna, he's a real terror."

"He's beautiful."

Digger's ears perked up, and he trotted to her side. From the stables a horse whinnied, while crickets serenaded us with the strident sounds of old violin strings.

"Thanks for the escort," Sammie said.

"Nobody followed us. That's a good thing."

She unlocked the front door with its oval, beveled glass, then stepped inside and disarmed the alarm. "It's getting late. You're welcome to take the sofa, if you'd like."

"Appreciate it. Johnny's leaving early, though, and I wanna send him off."

"I'll be there too. Five a.m. sharp."

"Think the band's gonna be up and ready to go?"

"If not, they'll be hitching a ride to Atlanta."

"Sammie, you're such a hard-nose."

"All an act, of course. I learned it from you."

My mind flashed to the airport, to my scuffle with Mr. Hillcrest. I took one step down and turned. "For me," I said, "it's no act."

"That may be. But your rougher side's only a remnant of the old you."

"Remnants. Sometimes I wonder if they're all I have to work with."

"Aramis, honestly. Stop your navel gazing and go get some rest."

———

In the brownstone's shadows, Freddy C was waiting to talk to me. Bearded, layered in heavy clothes, he was a formidable sight.

"Hey," I said. "You shouldn't be lurking around late at night."

"That's my secret. That's how I do it."

"Do what?"

He cupped his hand into a C. "Fight crime."

"Okay. Listen, Freddy. I don't know what your deal is, but I need to know the truth. Last night did you hurt Felicia in any way?"

"If only I'd got there sooner."

"Yes or no. Did you do anything to her?"

He clenched his jaw. "No. You must believe me."

"You don't know anything about that old van or the lady who was inside? You didn't happen to go scissors-crazy today and cut someone's hair?"

He took a step back, then glanced away. "Nobody believes. No believers."

"I wanna believe you. But what were you doing out there, huh?"

"The envelope. Did you get it?"

"I got it. Tell me about that tattoo of the ax. I need tangibles."

"Too dangerous. Not till tomorrow." He rocked back and forth on his heels, stirring a stale odor. "Then he'll be gone."

"Who? The leader of the Kraftsmen?"

"I know where he lives. Might know a way inside."

"What's his name? Tell me that much."

"Tomorrow. I'll meet you at Black's."

"I open the store and don't get off till two."

"Two it is. Two o'clock."

"His name," I insisted. "Gimme something to know you're sincere."

"Just a nickname—that's all I know."

"Cough it up."

"Chigger." Freddy's eyes darted along the sidewalk. "I gotta go, gotta keep moving. Good-bye."

I slipped inside. A note from Johnny lay on the entryway bookcase, letting me know he'd turned in early and planned to see me at his morning departure. Did he believe me about Mom? Could I fault him for taking charge of his dream?

No. It wouldn't be right to keep him here, not now.

I felt alone, empathizing with the words Sammie had spoken over dinner.

As I moved toward my bedroom, the wood planking carried the sound of my footsteps in front of me so that I felt I was chasing a figment of myself down the hall. I set the two Fauxbergé eggs on my windowsill, beside the empty bullet casing, the bloody razor blade, and the ebony memento from my mom.

I tucked strands of her hair into the box, clinging to my belief.

At my bedroom computer, I decided to investigate amnesia. If Mom's mind had short-circuited during the attack at the riverbank, she may have been pulled from the water without any knowledge of what had happened, possibly even without her own identity. It was possible presumptions about her death had curtailed the authorities' search.

In the mideighties, identification techniques were less sophisticated and, by comparison, poorly organized. Maybe Mom had been stretched out in a hospital room and plugged into a machine—a Jane Doe.

I printed out some selected pages and plopped onto my bed.

I read how under normal circumstances the temporal lobe's hippocampi use a process of consolidation to move short-term memory into long-term. Chemical changes then embed each memory for future access. But in an amnesiac, physical or psychological factors interrupt that consolidation. A head injury during a car accident could terminate the embedding process so that any recollection of those moments before the crash would be erased.

In the case of dissociative amnesia, defense mechanisms and incidents of high stress can cut off the brain's storage feed. While new memories might be stored in the retrograde state, prior events are compromised.

Physical trauma. Psychological. In Mom's case, they were both present.

Despite family tensions, long-held secrets, and a bullet in her leg, she had fought to survive, throwing herself over the edge into the cold, churning river. Evidently she had avoided the second bullet. But she could've hit a rock beneath the surface, jarring her memory.

I closed my eyes and imagined her washing downriver, being discovered by some well-meaning rancher's wife. Wouldn't such a person report it to the police or local medical officials? Yet what if Mom had been found by one of her attacker's accomplices? Where would she have been hidden?

At the Frist, she had referred to her abductor as her husband.

Could that be?

I didn't want to think of the abuses she might have suffered. After all these years, was my mom still the same person? Had they stripped away everything that had made her Dianne Lewis Black?

On Oak Street, through the windshield of a Dodge van, we had locked eyes. I held on to that. Played it over and over. No matter what else had happened, I was still her son. Her blood.

Soon, at Bicentennial Mall Park, we would have a second shot at this reunion.

Please, God. Are you listening? Wherever she is, protect her for me.

If I lost her again, I hated to think what I might do.

PART THREE

OVER ICE

You are about to…witness
…one of those scenes…which
the foul fiend alone can conceive.

—Alexandre Dumas, *The Man in the Iron Mask*

nough already," I grumbled.

A slap of my arm sent my jangling alarm clock onto the rug, where it seemed to sound off in even louder protest. When a pillow pulled over my head failed to muffle the noise, I snapped upright and marched across the floor. Removed the battery. Climbed back into bed.

I was still clutching the Energizer AA when my brother shook me awake.

"Aramis, it's four twenty-nine."

"Leave me alone."

"Aren't you coming to send us off?"

"The tour…"

"On our own Prevost bus, if you can believe that."

"Okay. Gimme a couple minutes."

"Sure you're awake, kid?"

I rubbed my eyes, saw his face swim into focus. "Think so."

"Stay put, if you want. We're swingin' back through town Thursday, and you can send me off then."

"This Thursday?"

"On our way back for a show in Little Rock."

"No, I'm up." I swung my feet to the floor. "I'm your biggest fan."

"Not my prettiest."

"Wait till I put on my makeup."

"See ya there." He waved from my doorway.

"Hold on." I pulled on shorts and flip-flops. "Need to ask you something."

"Gotta go."

"It's about Mom."

He stiffened. "The band's gonna be waitin' for me."

"They're musicians. They'll be late."

"Here. Yak at me while we load up the truck."

We shouldered loads from the living room to his Ford Ranger. Lemon and violet streaked the predawn sky while birds chirped in anticipation of a balmy Monday.

"That note." I tossed a gym bag into the pickup. "Remember, the one with Mom's handwriting?"

"What about it?"

"Did you read it all the way through? It talked about a Masonic ring, something that might've been hidden with my inheritance."

"Which you won't touch."

"Just trying to make an honest buck these days."

"And I'm not knockin' that." A street lamp winked off as Johnny closed the tailgate. "Tell me this though. How'd you know about the ring?"

"You still think I made up that note?"

"Don't know what to think."

"There is a ring then?"

"Was."

"Past tense?"

"Had some Latin writing on it, dated 1644."

"You're kidding."

"Would I make that up? And, yeah, there were some old Masonic symbols. I'm into that stuff. The term *Freemason* was used as far back as the

1300s. Some people think they were tied to the Knights Templar." He climbed into the truck, rolled down the window. "Well, I noticed something on the ring's band, a family name. Fair's fair, so I did some searchin', tracked down and contacted the owner's descendants. I mailed the ring to a woman in Silverton, Oregon."

"You did what?"

"She was the youngest and most direct descendant."

"I need that ring!"

"Sorry, man. It's hers now. She sent a thank-you letter, seemed real appreciative."

"What's her name?"

He fired up the engine, combed hair out of his eyes. "Here's my advice. Drop it. Let it go. Whatever foolishness you're mixed up in, don't let it drag you down again. You nearly got yourself killed last year, and this time around you've lost an ex-girlfriend. Just leave it be."

"But Mom's alive!"

"You think I don't wanna believe that? 'Course I do."

"It's the truth."

"You're stirrin' up old ghosts, kid. I'm outta here."

I ran back inside, pulled on jeans and the special T-shirt I had printed up. Stamped in gray over a black Stetson, the name Johnny Ray Black dangles silver spurs from the tails of both Ys.

Eight minutes later I was at Desperado Artist Development, parked behind a maroon and black tour bus that dominated the curb along Sixteenth. The bustle of band members, belongings, and schedules kept me from cornering my brother again. Sammie had shown too, tired but obviously excited. She gave a little wave.

Chigger lumbered by with his guitar case slung across his back. He wore a Lynyrd Skynyrd tank top. On his thick right arm, an executioner's ax gleamed in the breaking dawn. Avoiding my eyes, he kept his head down and bumped into me as he climbed on the bus.

Through Black's panoramic windows, the Italianate Kirkland Hall bell tower on Vanderbilt's campus told me I had twenty minutes until opening. Time for the local homeless to grab a cup of joe.

"Come in, come in," I urged the raggedy line on the Elliston sidewalk.

Insulated coffeepots faced out along the mahogany counter so that each person could choose his or her own poison. Sweeteners and half-and-half stood at the end. A few slipped back to the rest rooms to freshen up after a long night on hard surfaces. A few others—the ones I really worried about—seemed beyond caring.

"Artemis."

"Hey." I turned at the tap on my back. "S'up, Freddy?"

In my experience, those who live on the streets are wary of human touch and rarely initiate it. My friend's gesture was one of trust.

"He's gone. I watched him go."

"Chigger?"

"Shh," Freddy said. "Not so loud."

"Yeah, the band just headed out for their tour."

"But his people, they're still around."

"The Kraftsmen." Resting on my metal desk, the pamphlet he'd given me was full of vitriol and hate, assuring me I shouldn't blow off his paranoia. "Go on. Grab your drink."

He poured himself a cup of Costa Rican and dropped a Sacajawea dollar in the tip mug. Seen from behind, with his brushed-back hair, oversize wool coat, and scuffed walking boots, he could've been a fireside companion of Tennessee's Davy Crockett or a trail guide for a weather-beaten explorer. An explorer like Meriwether Lewis.

My mind was still scrambling for clues, turning over stones. Who could I trust? Yesterday, despite our growing bond, I'd even suspected my well-meaning friend.

If Freddy were involved, would he be standing in my shop? He could've simply disappeared if he wanted. Yes, he was homeless. Eccentric. So one out of four such men are felons.

This was Freddy C—C for Circumstantial evidence.

"We're still on for this afternoon?" I asked. "Two o'clock?"

"You drive, and I'll tell you where to turn."

I'd done that routine before. Still had an X on my cheek as proof.

"My car's in the back alley," I said. "Just meet me out there later."

Freddy held up two fingers—the peace sign or the time?—then wandered away.

Customers kept me occupied through the morning. Diesel clocked in and helped alleviate the load. Between drink orders, he tested me on his notes from social psych and tossed in pop quizzes. I mustered some workplace enthusiasm and tried to play along, but he wasn't fooled.

"You look kind of dour today, Aramis."

"*Dour?* This is my cheery face."

"Just don't wear it around the kiddies, or you'll make them cry."

"Thanks."

"Sure thing, boss."

"How'd it go last night? At Sara's place?"

He grinned. "You were right. She likes me."

"Ahh. You owe me one, dude."

"We'll see."

"Listen, I need to ask you something." The chime of the front door cut me off. "After this," I said, and we went about handling the customers like a well-oiled machine. Business as usual.

Afterward, while wiping down tables in the dining area, I returned to my interrogation.

"You're in an honor society, right?"

"Psi Chi."

"What about your dad? Wasn't he in one of those?"

"Why all this interest in my father? Honest, my parents are boring people."

I stopped wiping. I wanted to tell him that Mr. Hillcrest was at the top of my suspects list. There was the Hyundai, his presence at the hotel, his anger toward my family, and his self-righteous attitude.

"He just seems to have a thing against my brother and me," I replied.

"He uses his intellect and moral standards to intimidate people. A control thing—that's all it is. It's part of his parenting philosophy too, but I think he probably had the same type of upbringing."

"Ultrareligious parents?"

"His mother, she was a real Bible thumper. All hellfire and brimstone."

"That explains it."

"What?"

"He threw scriptures at me like they were knives."

"There you go. That's Drexel Hillcrest in a nutshell."

I straightened a display of Back-in-Black coffee bags. Due to recent events, I'd skipped my weekly coffee roasting, and retail supplies were running low. Life slowed down for nobody. I made a note to come in Tuesday night to replenish my stock.

"In part, it's my own fault," Diesel confided.

"What?"

"The past week or two I've been hanging with Johnny Ray. He's such a regular guy, you know, when he comes in the shop. And the parties are mostly innocuous. Good luck convincing my father of that though. The first time Johnny invited me out to Chigger's, we had a few drinks, sat around listening to the guys jam."

"I've never been to Chigger's."

"Sweet place. Lots of land and one of those big, modern log cabins. He's got two dogs the size of racehorses. Bull mastiffs, I think."

"Mastiffs, huh?"

"And there's this triple-car garage. I'm told he has some amazing wheels parked in there, but I haven't been inside."

"Guess he's earned some perks, being a Music Row hotshot."

"Nah, I doubt he's earned it all himself. He has tons of pictures on his walls, relatives dating back to before the Civil War. He's into that stuff. I bet that land's belonged to his family for generations."

"Did he tell you about the Kraftsmen?"

"The who?"

"No. They were one of those sixties bands."

Diesel's expression went blank.

"Never mind. Hey, is your dad coming back to Nashville anytime soon?"

"Not that he's told me."

"No plans to be here on Thursday?"

"I hope not. That's just what I need with school finally out, him breathing down my neck."

In the early afternoon, Sammie called and told me she'd found a temp to cover Anna's shift. Anna was hidden away, comfy on Tyne Boulevard, while the cops—with gentle but unyielding pressure from Miss Rosewood—were checking into Mr. Knight's record for any history of violence or domestic altercations.

"And I'll be in to close the store," Sammie ended.

"That'd be great. You remember the alarm code?"

"The date you moved to Nashville, if I'm not mistaken."

"And the day we first met."

"That's right." She gave a warm sigh. "We were in Davis-Kidd, and you were looking for books on small-business loans."

"That's how it all started."

"A wonderful partnership. Thank you, by the way, for escorting us home last night. A very nice gesture."

"I'm learning."

"Yes, I know." She paused. "I don't want you to be worried about the shop this evening. You go to Lipscomb and pass that class with flying colors."

"Thanks, Sammie." I thought of my plans to visit Chigger's place at two this afternoon. "One other thing. You know where I could get any horse tranquilizers?"

"That's an odd question for a man without a horse."

"More like some nasty big dogs."

"Acepromazine would do the trick. ACP. My vet keeps it on hand."

"If you called in an order, do you think he'd let me pick it up?"

"She," Sammie corrected. "You taking up animal rescue now?"

"Got a couple of dogs who just need a long, lazy nap, that's all."

"I wonder about you, Aramis. Sometimes I really wonder."

32

The vet's office shrank into the distance as I passed the long perimeter of Percy Warner Park, funneling my Honda onto westbound Highway 100. In the glove box, Ziploc bags held my solution to all things furry and fanged.

I passed a sign for Cheekwood Botanical Gardens and thought about making a detour to repossess my firearm—something about that reassuring weight tucked into my belt—but the place was closed on Mondays, and a rescue mission in broad daylight would be a bit obvious. Sure to get the neighbors talking.

Hopefully later tonight.

Beside me, Freddy C had the passenger window down and remained quiet as the breeze blew his hair back like a patch of thick dune grass. The farther we drove from the city, the more contagious his increased fidgeting became.

Three days till the exchange with AX. Where was Mom right now?

I still believed Mr. Hillcrest was the culprit, but certain inconsistencies squirmed in my head. Where had he hidden my mother? for example. Had he spirited her away to Ohio somehow, driving all through the night to get back in time for his flight? That seemed ludicrous. There were also a number of reasons to suspect Chigger. His jealousy. His tattoo. His attendance at Friday night's party in Owen Bradley Park.

Was he my mother's abductor? Was she out here on his property?

Enough. Relax.

I pointed out the window. "Freddy, you ever seen so many shades of green?"

He shook his head.

Coming from Oregon, I'd seen the Cascades' sparkling snowcaps and endless evergreens, yet there's something to be said for the meandering beauty that spills down from the limestone ramparts of the Cumberland Plateau. Sycamores and red oaks mingle with box elders. Lush hillsides curl against scalloped clouds and radiant blue sky. Streams bubble beneath arches of sun-dappled branches.

It's a seductive mystery. Pulls you in unaware.

Sammie Rosewood had grown up here in Tennessee. She shared this land's qualities as if they'd been genetically passed through her.

"Tell me when we're getting close," I reminded Freddy.

"Not too far," he said.

A sign for the Loveless Café caught my eye. My brother and I had dropped by here last year for a delicious, down-home meal.

I pointed. "This is the Natchez Trace Parkway up here. Is it beyond that?"

"Little ways. Keep going."

Whole portions of my time in Tennessee have revolved around mysteries of the Trace. South of here, Meriwether Lewis died under strange circumstances in 1809.

"Slow down, my man. This gate."

I started to turn.

"Not yet. That next mailbox. There."

With its post wrapped in white chain links, the box bore the Southern Cross of the Rebel flag. Stereotyping, schmereotyping—I would've bet money that gun catalogs and truck-accessory magazines were regular deliveries at this address.

"Just as I pictured it," I said.

Freddy sat upright as we dipped down the drive. The seduction was over. We were trapped now, captured by low stone fences and vine-draped trees that seemed to hover in on both sides. My attempts at distracting myself evaporated, and my vision narrowed to this thin gravel road that cut through the foliage.

"Chigger's gone, you're sure?" I asked. "What about his buddies?"

"Meet nights mostly."

"How do you know all this?"

"I know." Freddy wore a haggard look. "I went. One time only."

Gravel crunched beneath the tires, signaling our approach. "Sure we're not heading into an ambush?"

"Should be all clear."

"Except for the dogs." I eased up to the house. "But we've come prepared."

Eyes brewing with consternation, Freddy stared at the monstrous log cabin that rose between peeling crape myrtles and hickory trees. Something about the place—the darkness behind the windows, the rack of antlers over the massive front door, the feeling of remoteness—kicked my heartbeat into an arrhythmic mode.

To the left, a cedar-planked triple garage stood just up the hill.

No sign of Thing One or Thing Two.

"You think the dogs are inside? Or maybe Chigger dropped them off with one of his pals."

"They're watchdogs."

"Meaning, they're here somewhere."

Without a word, Freddy opened the glove box and removed the ACP.

"You said you might know a way to get in. What'd you have in mind?"

He gestured toward the garage. "Need to show you. Chigger was there."

"Where?"

"By City Cemetery. On Saturday."

"When we were there? How do you know?"

"Follow me."

The sounds of our car doors clicking shut and our footsteps on gravel broke open a can of curdle-your-blood snarls. I half expected to see bull mastiffs galloping into view from the dense bushes. Instead, the *craackkkk* of hard bodies against the cabin's front door assured me they were contained.

On the door's upper half, narrow panes of smoked glass had the appearance of prison bars. The dogs sounded angry enough to vault through there, but the explosion of razor-sharp shards and splintered wood would eviscerate them on the way out, leaving nothing but bone, bowels, and fur to carry out their gruesome task.

I wondered if it was enough to stop them. These were hounds of hell, aimed at tearing into our throats and devouring our souls. They sounded ready to—

Okay, Aramis. Get a grip!

The door's mail slot beckoned. It was just wide enough to insert defrosting rib-eye steaks laced with acepromazine.

"You got the stuff, Freddy?"

"You do it." His hands shook as he relinquished the bags. "It better work."

My own pulse was galloping at double speed. *Stay calm. Read instructions.*

This medication was supposed to aid in the sedation of frightened or aggressive animals. However, treated canines had been known to temporarily overcome its effects when startled. Erring on the side of caution, I estimated each dog's weight at a hundred pounds and then added a generous gram of the compound to each steak. The tranquilizer would block dopamine nerve receptors in the brain, quieting the beasts for hours.

In laymen's terms, these puppies were going to be very sleepy after a few mouthfuls from Black's traveling smorgasbord.

———

"What're we doing up here?"

"A way in," Freddy told me. "Through this vent."

We were on the backside of the garage roof. Parked below us, out of sight of any surprise visitors, my car had done its part in boosting us to our spread-eagle positions. Before moving, I'd checked through the cabin door's glass to make sure the watchdogs were immobile mounds of placid fur. I even knocked once—a little test. Nothing but heaving sighs from inside.

"Why'd we drug the animals if we're not going into the cabin?" I asked.

"We are."

"Are what?"

"There's a way through. A cave."

"Under the garage?"

"Keep following."

Freddy pried at the vent's frame with a pocketknife. When the latch snapped, he lifted and locked the humpbacked fixture on its hinged arm. He pulled himself up, squeezed his legs into the opening, then fell through and landed.

I ducked my head inside. "You okay?" The garage was in relative darkness, but he stood in a square of light on a wooden loft just below me.

"I'm fine, I'm fine. Saw this vent the one time he brought me out here."

"Chigger, you mean."

"The axman."

"Way to be observant."

I dropped beside my companion, sending a hollow thud through the garage. Together, we descended a wood ladder to the floor. With the guidance of the vent light, I scooted along the wall until my fingers reached a set of switches.

First flick: a distant electrical whir.

Second flick: nothing.

Third: fluorescent lights winked on above a trio of classic automobiles.

"Wow."

Freddy shuffled forward. "This middle one—you recognize it?"

"Pontiac GTO. A '69, I think." The car sat on fat Firestones, ready to tear up the road and shove the driver back in the seat. "It's gorgeous."

"It was there."

"Saturday night," I realized, "as we took that curve on Oak Street."

My mind scrambled for clues again.

Chigger. Out late. St. Cloud Hill, above the graves of City Cemetery. What if he had driven that old Dodge van, holding my mother hostage and circling back toward the hill's Fort Negley area where he switched vehicles? In my run-in with the GTO, had I nearly sideswiped the very car that bore my mom away?

I looked at the other two cars.

Closest to me, the whitewall tires of a '54 Chevy Bel Air poked from beneath a fitted cloth. On the far end of the garage, the red and white Corvette convertible looked familiar. Was this the one that'd sped by two days ago on Elliston Place while Detective Meade and I met over coffee?

What would Meade think if he found us tiptoeing through this garage? After yesterday's lunch at Belle Meade, had he decided to just leave me alone? Or was he more curious than ever, surreptitiously logging my activities? Could he have planted a GPS tracker under my bumper?

No way. Not his style.

But he was a cop. Keeping an eye on me was part of his job.

"Okay, Freddy. Let's not hang around here any longer than we need to." I scanned the garage. "Where's this cave you talked about?"

"Behind you."

At my back a door opened into a tool room. A table vise was anchored to a workbench, gripping a chunk of maple. Lathes, saws, axes, and chisels hung from the walls. On the workbench razor knives rested beside a box of spare blades.

Mom, please be here. And please be all right.

Beneath the workbench, apparently released by the first switch I'd thrown, a dummy panel opened into a tunnel. The pitted stone looked naturally hewn, but light bulbs extended beyond view in the direction of Chigger's mammoth cabin.

"Is that where we're going?"

Freddy nodded.

Middle Tennessee is known for its subterranean honeycombs, places where water and the elements once carved and sluiced through rock. To ward off Indian attacks in the late 1700s, one of Nashville's founders even dwelled in a cliff cave overlooking the Cumberland River. Demonbreun Street, where Johnny had been roped up to the statue, was named after the man.

"Chigger showed you this?" I looked at Freddy. "Weren't you a little freaked?"

"We all came here."

"Who's we?"

"Men off the streets." Filling his lungs, he ducked beneath the bench and edged forward until he could stand inside the tunnel. His breathing was fast and shallow.

I turned off the fluorescent lights in the triple garage, propped a hydraulic jack in the gap between the dummy panel and the wall—I didn't wanna get trapped in here, that was for sure—then followed my partner in crime into the cave's intestines.

Heading toward the cabin.

The natural chambers had been bolstered with heavy beams and wire netting. What unlawful activities had flushed through these earthen tunnels? No doubt Chigger's ancestors had utilized this space, perhaps for Prohibition bootlegging.

The limestone cave's only warmth emanated from forty-watt bulbs in ribbed metal covers. These craggy, cold innards of earth bore whiffs of rotting flesh, and my mind conjured images of ancient ravenous creatures roaming through here.

Or, more recently, those two mastiffs.

"This place is starting to mess with me, Freddy."

"Just ahead."

"We've gone too far. The house has to be back there."

My bearded guide stomped onward, the embodiment of an old-time adventurer. His shoulders were heaving with each breath. My wider frame grazed against the rough walls. We passed tunnel openings that wormed away into darkness, and I called out Mom's name. Hoping. Praying.

Nothing but echoes.

Could Chigger be behind the past few days' activities? Had he overhead Johnny talking in some alcohol-weakened moment about the discovered gold? Could the good ol' boy guitarist have a personal vendetta reaching back somehow to my mother?

I knew firsthand that the man had some strong feelings toward my brother. According to Freddy, he was also tangled up with the animosity of the Kraftsmen who molded the King James Bible to fit their views. This morning he'd flashed his ax tattoo as though flaunting his identity. As though daring me to catch him.

Left step, right step. Breathe.

I had to keep going, stay focused.

By now, Chigger was in Atlanta, on the tour bus with my brother. They wouldn't be back in town for a couple of days. Meanwhile, my mother could be here. Held captive in that cabin.

Each step I took might be bringing us closer to each other.

ere," my companion said, his chest still heaving. "This is it."

We emerged into a domed cavern large enough to accommodate fifteen to twenty people. Three bulbs protruded at shoulder height from the walls, casting shadows across the ground like crossed swords. Equidistant between the lights, manacles hung from bolted chains.

"What is this place, Freddy?"

"They brought us here. The Kraftsmen."

"The homeless guys? Why'd you follow them down here?"

He stepped back. "You must believe. They picked us up in a van."

"A Dodge? Was it old and dingy?"

"Maybe. No. A Ford, I think."

"Did it have any markings?"

He shook his head. "But they told us they were with a mission. Quoted verses about the poor."

"Weren't you suspicious?"

"We were cold and wet. They fed us."

"So they gathered you up and brought you here. Did they tell you why? Didn't you think it was a little fishy?"

His toe scuffed at the dirt. He rammed his hands into threadbare coat pockets.

"C'mon, Freddy. You talked me into coming here. Are you gonna tell me what happened, or do I have to drag it out of you?"

"I'm…I'm afraid."

Couldn't blame the guy for that. This place was spooky. Far off, the earth's bowels rumbled, while the pitted tunnels breathed in an irregular pattern that belched cold air over my skin.

"Just say it. I'm on your side, you know that."

His watery eyes wobbled. A slight nod.

"Did they hurt you?" I asked.

"Not me. No. Not the other white men."

"How many were there?"

"Five. Or six. And the Kraftsmen. But there was a black man, just one. Older, real quiet. Sorta…slow, you know."

I waited. My eyes shifted to the manacles.

"We should have jobs, the Kraftsmen told us. Should have our wives back. Our money. Houses." Freddy C was rocking on his legs, head down. "Said it was the foreign mongrels who stole from us. And these sons of Ham, the Negroids—they corrupted our schools. Their rap music. The heathen drums."

The cavern's chill seeped into my bones. Was that blood on the iron?

"What'd they do, Freddy?"

He lurched toward the wall. I waited for him to reply, but he seemed frozen, mesmerized by the light bulbs' apathetic glare. I'd seen his sense of justice in action before, and I knew how tenuous his hold on reality was. Something had shaken him. If he didn't face it, it could permanently destabilize him.

"Don't stop now," I urged. "This is why you left me the pamphlet, right? Why you brought me down into this hellhole. You said I needed to tell the police."

"I didn't mean to."

I paused. "Mean to what?"

"I didn't know." His forehead touched the stone between the bolts. "This spot. They chained him here. I didn't know."

"The black man?"

"Can't remember his name. Can't do it."

"But you seem to know most of the homeless around here."

"Just passing through. Never seen him before."

"What'd they do to him?" I coaxed.

"Nothing."

"Nothing?" A flutter of relief. "But you said—"

"*They* didn't do anything. They made *us*. Made us do it."

My body calcified with the horror of where this was leading. "Do what?"

"*He* made us."

"Chigger, you mean."

Freddy's head moved up and down, scraping against the sedimentary rock. "He gave us a whip. He... If we didn't, we would stay down here. Left to die. And nobody would know." His skull thudded into the wall. "Just like that woman. She drowned, but no one did a thing."

A homeless lady. I knew the story. Young punks shoved her into the Cumberland at the downtown river front, and her body caught beneath a moored barge only yards from the spot of the attack. She'd been left there for days.

"Listen," I told him. "I would've come looking for you."

My friend nodded, but his finger was poking at the cavern wall. "He had a gun." Jab, jab. "Put it to the man's head. Said he'd kill him if we didn't...if we didn't..."

"Use the whip?"

His finger kept jabbing. He needed to put his shame into words before it burrowed down.

"Did you do it?"

He froze.

"Freddy. Did you whip him?"

Jab, jab, *jab.*

I waited, watched his chest swell.

In a sob, the answer erupted from his throat and reverberated against the walls. "Only once. I...did it only once." He pushed his palms against his eyes, but tears squeezed down his dusty cheeks. "Only once."

I set my hand on his shoulder, felt my own ribs tighten. Felicia's life spilling onto the sidewalk. Her lips, frothy in death. Was there anything I could've done?

Freddy shook himself. Pushed away from the wall.

"Let's get outta here," I said.

In the pale light, determination filled his eyes. "They let him go," he said.

"Was he badly hurt?"

"Dropped him at the train tracks. At the Gulch."

"What about you and the others?"

"Took us to Fort Negley, past the stone arches. That's where the Kraftsmen meet. We could be part of their plan, they said. Heroes."

"What plan?"

"The South will rise again."

"Okay. So you went last night."

"But I left." His sandy eyebrows furrowed. "And then you saw me, out on the street. I hid that pamphlet. Gave it to you. You can tell the police."

"Tell them what? They need something to go on."

"Won't believe me. Nobody believes."

"Chigger's a terrorist. He used fear to manipulate you. We need some evidence. We could go to the Gulch, try to find this guy to be a witness. Show his wounds."

Freddy flinched.

"What?"

His gaze flickered between me and the wall bolts. "He's dead."

"But you told me that—"

"Saw him. This morning."

"Where?"

"Near the Marathon Building. He was hunched over on the tracks. A train was coming, and he just looked at me. Afraid. He remembered. The train blew its horn, and he never moved. Never even made a sound."

———

On some level I guess we all want to pay for our sins. While most cultures embrace the concept of a sacrifice for wrongdoing, most of us don't want the sacrifice of another in our place. Seems unfair. Who would do such a thing anyway?

"Freddy." I tried to comfort him. "You know, Jesus was whipped too."

"Because of people like me."

"And me." I felt my throat tighten. "But he still forgave."

Whether Freddy C defied the idea or found strength in it, I'm not sure. He ran his hands over his face, through his hair, poked at the inside of his cheek with his tongue. He then pivoted on one foot and faced the black maw of the cave system.

"On through there," he said. "The cabin."

"No. Let's go back. We don't need any more of this."

"Said we need evidence."

"First, we need to get some fresh air. Clear our heads. You can just tell me what to look for, and I'll come back on my own."

"You need help. The dogs."

I hesitated. "They're sedated."

"They wake up, they'll kill you. I'll be a lookout."

"I can't let you do that."

"Friends, Artemis." He turned. "They work together. Let's go."

34

The tunnel's uneven stone walls curled to the right and came to an abrupt stop. Between two beams, the door to a small service elevator faced us. Not your usual residential appliance.

I hit the button, and we waited like new check-ins at a hotel. The whir of motors told us it was descending. The door slid open. We stepped in. There was a panel with a keyhole and three buttons. The lowest was illuminated, and I assumed the other two represented the levels of the log cabin.

"Where to, Freddy?"

"Never been in the house."

"How do you know we'll find any evidence?"

"Upstairs."

"What's up there?"

"Chigger. He said we'd understand if we saw upstairs. Said it would explain."

"Explain what?"

"Why he has hate."

"The second floor then."

The elevator rose with creaks and complaints. My heart accelerated with each ascending foot. What would we find up there? Were the dogs still in la-la land, or would they pound up the stairs and tear into us upon arrival?

No doubt Chigger had built this spacious dwelling over the ruins of his predecessors. He probably felt a physical connection, a sense of honor, living off the same land that had swallowed and crushed into dust the bones of his people. Meanwhile, racism in the name of religion continued to rise through the family tree and discolor the newest offshoots.

To rid oneself of this blight? To reprogram one's way of thinking? I couldn't pretend to understand what that would entail.

Or maybe I could.

For two years I'd been tearing free from the clutches of my own past.

The elevator slowed, bounced once, stopped. In the small space, there was no way to press back out of sight. Head-on—that's how we'd have to do this.

The door opened into a bedroom darkened by heavy drapes. At the edges, sunlight sliced through and revealed wall decorations in a country-western motif—hats and spurs and chaps. No sign of the dogs, thank goodness.

We stepped over the threshold. Floorboards cringed beneath our feet.

Still no movement.

I reached for a lamp by the window, my hand finding the switch even as it brushed the crystals that dangled from the rose-colored cloth shade.

"Hello?" A drowsy female voice startled me. "Who's there?"

The lamplight cast warm hues onto a fourposter bed. A young woman pulled herself up against the headboard, questions on her lips and fear ballooning in her eyes. A tray of food rested on the nightstand next to a pile of James Lee Burke novels.

"Hi," I said. Great start. "Who are you?"

"Who are *you*?" She lifted a baton attached to a cord. "This feeds straight to the alarm company. I push this button, and the cops'll be here in minutes."

"Hold on. Lemme explain."

"Does my brother know you're here?"

"Chigger. Uh, he's on the road, but he—"

"I know my family's whereabouts. I want to know why *you're* here."

"I'm Johnny Ray's brother. Johnny Ray Black."

"Never met you before." The baton hand motioned. "And who's he?"

"My friend, Freddy C. He's harmless."

"Afternoon, ma'am," he mumbled from just outside the lamp's pool of light. In his bulky layers of coats, he cut an imposing figure.

Trying to divert her attention, I pointed at the books on the nightstand. "You a Burke fan?"

She set her hand on the stack. "I'm a big reader. He's in my top five."

"The Dave Robicheaux books—"

"Are the *best*. His word pictures, the atmosphere... He's like a poet."

"That's what got me hooked too."

This literary connection seemed to win her over, and she lowered the baton onto the bedspread. Fellow readers share a camaraderie that goes beyond class or sex or skin color. I felt almost guilty for taking advantage of that.

Almost.

"Chigger told you to come, didn't he?" she surmised. "That hardheaded fool. He said he'd send one of his buddies to keep an eye out for me, as if I can't take care of myself. I'm nineteen years old, you know. Not a baby."

"Gotta humor the guy. So everything's okay?"

"The dogs were going wild earlier, but they quieted down." She pulled her ponytail around so that it draped down the front of her sweatshirt. "Next time you should call first. Didn't your mama teach you any manners?"

"Sorry."

"A girl needs a chance to look proper. Speaking of, where are *my* manners? My name's Trish." She extended her arm. "Not Tricia, not Patricia. Just Trish."

I shook her hand. It was cold. "Good to meet you, Just Trish."

"Funny man. And what's your name?"

"Aramis." No use hiding it now that I'd revealed my brother's identity.

"Like in *The Three Musketeers*."

"Exactly. That's where my mom got it."

"A woman with good taste in names *and* books. Ooh, I like her already."

Casual, keep it casual. "You sound like you might know her."

"Should I?"

"I don't know. I just—"

"It's not like my brother lets me out much. He's afraid something else might happen. Since the accident, I get these blackouts. That's why he installed the elevator—so I wouldn't fall down the stairs during a seizure."

Did Chigger keep her locked up to protect her? Was she the motivation for his prejudice? I'd never even heard about his having a sister. On the far nightstand, plastic prescription bottles stood in a row. Did he keep her sedated? Or maybe there was even more to this, something darker.

Trish seemed spunky enough though. Not exactly the abused stereotype.

I decided to push a little. "You ever been to the bottom level of the elevator?"

"No, and that's a perfect example of Chigger being a worrywart. He's afraid I'll go wandering around down there and get lost. Without his key, the car won't even go all the way down."

"Hmm."

"You know, Aramis, my great-granddaddy ran moonshine out of those caves. Least that's what he told us. He used to exaggerate things, but he was quite a storyteller. Maybe that's where I got my love of books."

"Well." I looked at Freddy, then back at the fourposter. "Guess we should get going now that we've done our good deed and checked on you. Anything you need before we head out?"

"I can make my way around, thanks."

"Just offering."

"I'll show you to the door." As if to prove she was capable, Trish flipped back the bedspread and hitched her legs over the mattress. The sweatshirt caught and exposed soft, youthful thighs. She shifted the shirt back down over her knees.

I found something else on the far wall to look at. "You need a hand?"

"What'd I tell you? I'm fine."

"What happened? If you don't mind. In the accident."

"My brother's never told you? I'm not surprised." She stood, slipped into a long housecoat, then braced a hand against the bedpost. "We were in New York. He'd always dreamed of going to see Radio City Music Hall and those places. When he finally signed on here with one of the big labels, he said we were going to celebrate. Of course, I had no idea that's where he was taking me."

"Pretty cool."

"I was thirteen." She took a breath. Her cheeks looked rosy in the lamplight. "It was exciting stuff—the Statue of Liberty, the Stock Exchange, Times Square, all the touristy places. The morning we were supposed to fly home, Chigger insisted on taking a cab to the Twin Towers. Didn't even care about going inside. He just wanted to look up at them. We'd never seen anything that tall. I mean, the BellSouth Tower's nothing in comparison."

"You know that Signature Tower's gonna be a thousand feet tall."

"In Nashville? Ooh, I'd love to go to the top of that."

"I interrupted you."

She stood taller, tightening her grip on the post. "He still has nightmares of that day—September eleventh. When the first plane hit, we were only two blocks away. People were in shock. Our cab stopped, and my side got speared by another taxi driver, an African American man. He was rubbernecking—not like I can blame him—but Chigger won't let it go. He thinks America's problems all stem from the 'Negroids' and 'ragheads,' as he calls them. Funny how I'm the one who suffered the traumatic brain injury, but he's the one who's still angry."

I cupped my hand around the back of my neck. "I never knew."

In the shadows, Freddy remained silent.

"Johnny Ray could've told you," said Trish. "I met him once, and he signed his CD for me. Seems like a nice guy."

"He is."

"Chigger tries, he really does. He's played nurse and cook for me through a lot of the past six years. But I worry about him. It's as if those al-Qaida guys were filled with some sort of poison that spilled down and infected him too."

Trish stepped into the elevator. "Hop in, gentlemen. And no funny business, or I'll sic my dogs on you."

"We'll be good," I promised.

The doors were closing when she turned and stared at us. "Speaking of which, how'd the two of you get past them in the first place?"

"This elevator."

"From the lowest level? From the caves?" When Freddy and I nodded in unison, she said, "Tell me again, what were you doing down there? Even better, take me down and let me look around a little."

"We can't."

"I won't tell. Chigger will never know."

"Actually"—I showed her bare palms—"we don't have the key."

"Then you're trapped." She pressed the first-floor button. "If you want to get out of this place alive, I suggest you come with me now."

35

The dogs were unresponsive to Trish's calls. "That's strange."

Praying the acepromazine was still working its magic, I followed her from the elevator into the country-style kitchen. An island stood tall beneath a brass rack of pots and pans. A built-in knife set bristled on one end of the fixture, while a dense, reddish wood served as a cutting board on the other.

"Smells good," I whispered. My nose was picking up the lingering aromas of beef and onions and herbs.

"Supper's in the Crock-Pot. You two can join me if you'd like."

Freddy's eyes snapped up.

"No," I said. "We should go."

"Where are those silly dogs?"

A huge living room opened before us, with windows stretching from floor to vaulted ceiling. Notched into the front end, the entryway was the size of a small bedroom and included wide stairs that spiraled upward. The slumbering bull mastiffs covered the floorboards at the foot of the staircase, eyes half open, jaws slack.

Trish said, "That sunshine must've zapped them good."

"Don't disturb your babies," I told Trish. "We'll just go out the back."

"Good plan. That'll get the neighbors gossiping."

"No lives of their own, I take it."

"Actually, they can't see our place through the woods, but if there's any chance of stirring their nest, I'll take it. What else do I have for excitement?"

I thought I saw one of the dogs raise an eyelid.

Trish turned and pointed down a long corridor. "The study back there has a door onto a small deck. That might be your safest alternative."

"We'll get outta your hair then. Glad to know you're okay."

"I'll tell Chigger you did your duty."

"No need for that." I winked. "Let him worry."

"Aramis, you are a troublemaker."

"So I've been told."

Freddy and I started down the corridor, nearly home free.

Of course, it couldn't be that easy. Our escape was curtailed by the clump of footsteps on the front porch. The doorbell chimed, and I was reminded that abrupt noises or movement could disrupt the sedative's effects. Snorfles and grunts came from the dogs. What were the chances they'd both wake up simultaneously?

Then: claws scrambling on waxed hardwood and low growls like machinery in need of oil.

Another ring.

The canine machines roared to life. Pistons started firing. Growls turned to deep-throated snarls.

I threw backward glances as Freddy as I hurried along, hoping to be out of here before the mastiffs realized we were in their territory. The dogs were throwing themselves against the front door with mighty thumps.

A few more steps to the study.

Circling once in frustration, one of the mastiffs moved beyond the entry-way's perimeter and spotted me. He stopped on stiff front legs, his ears upright. He bared his teeth.

And charged.

"Go!" I pushed Freddy through the doorway.

The dog was already halfway to us, powered by muscle-corded legs and back. Ropes of saliva waved from his short, square muzzle, while dark hazel eyes burned with hatred for the intruders who threatened his domain.

I stumbled into the study, tried to slam the door, but an old-style iron sat on the floor, holding it against the wall. I gritted my teeth, yanked on the knob until the impediment was moved aside by the arc of the door. Before the latch could snap into place, the mastiff careened into the wood. It buckled. I planted my foot against the base of the door, using leverage to keep things in place as the beast threw himself forward again. And again.

"Come away from there! Stop it this instant!"

Trish's calls registered somewhere in my head, but my first concern was that Freddy find an exit and leave me an easy trail to follow. My shoulder bounced against the door with the dog's continued attacks.

This battering ram was coming through. In a matter of seconds.

"Are you out?" I yelled. "Freddy?"

No answer. Turning, I saw that he was indeed out—out cold. The poor man had panicked—understandably so—and run headlong into a sliding-glass door.

I reached behind me, grasped for a low bookcase, and hooked the edge with my fingers. I pulled it toward me over the Berber carpet. Marble bookends hit the floor and shattered, but the case continued to slide, and I hefted it against the door in place of my shifting body. A temporary solution.

Ker-accck!

I dashed to the glass door, flicked the lock, and slid it open.

"Freddy?"

He groaned as I hooked his arms, swiveled, then hauled him halfway onto the deck. His coat snagged in the door's track, and I heard myself curse.

My peripheral vision registered the bookcase toppling and dusty volumes fanning over the study floor.

The dog hurdled the barrier. Veered our way.

Ripppp!

I tore the coat free.

With both hands on Freddy's wide leather belt, I yanked him through the doorway. Before I could bar the beast's path, he drove his powerful jaws and teeth down into my companion's calf muscle, pinning him to the deck. A natural behavior: subdue and restrain.

My most handy weapon now was the sliding door. It swished through its track and bit into the dog's ribs. He bellowed, caught in the vise between door and jamb, but he stayed trained on his prey—head down and fangs bared.

Through the glass, I saw Trish peering over the fallen case. She was calling to her dog but without results.

I looked away. Slammed the door one more time, with all my force.

The mastiff yelped and hopped back.

The split second allowed me to pull at Freddy and get the door closed. On the other side of the glass, the beast roared again, his black nose shoved forward, spittle flecking the pane. Behind me, I heard movement through the bushes. Reinforcements.

"Aramis! Let me give you a hand with your friend."

Detective Meade? And who was that beside him? Another cop?

Despite my reservations about their presence here—and our own breaking and entering—Meade's voice was a welcome one.

"Let's get him over the railing," I shouted. "He got tagged by that dog."

Uninsured and dressed in bum de la crème, Freddy would've been nudged to the end of the ER line at Metro General had it not been for a detective at our side. A brief exam. Sterilization of the wound. A few stitches and a tetanus shot. In no time, he'd be back out hobbling on the streets.

I stood next to Meade in the waiting room. "Thanks."

"Just doing my job."

"Interesting timing, though, showing up when you did."

"We were well within our bounds, within Metro Nashville limits. I was meaning to ask the lady of the house a few questions about her brother's relationship with Johnny Ray."

"So you weren't following me?"

Meade fixed me with his gaze.

"Dude, I should go."

"It was for your well-being, Aramis."

"You still think I'm a suspect? You know I didn't hurt Felicia."

"I've been lied to before."

"Join the club. Listen, I have to get over to Lipscomb."

"You seem nervous."

"Got a final to take. Plus, I shouldn't even be here."

"With me, you mean?"

"No offense, Detective."

Yesterday AX had chopped off my mother's hair in retaliation for my lunch meeting with Meade. I hated to guess what he'd cut next time. Of course, my prime suspects were out of town—Mr. Hillcrest in Columbus, Ohio, and Chigger in Georgia. But AX might have an accomplice. Members of the Kraftsmen perhaps. Or Anna Knight's ex-husband. He could've used bluster and threats in my shop to cover a deeper purpose.

I turned toward the door.

Meade said, "Is there anything you'd like to—"

"No. Trust me on this. In a few days I'll be able to explain."

"'Trust me,' he says." Meade filled his next sentence with a sting of accusation. "This from the same individual who skirted the truth yesterday during lunch. A lunch, I might add, that a certain detective paid for."

"Hey, you offered. That's not fair."

"Just servin' up some of my mama's deep-fried guilt," he fired back.

Though born and raised in Music City, the detective had never allowed me to hear his local accent. Cool and professional—that was his way. A man of education. Urbane. More than anything else, this change frightened me.

"What's wrong? What'd I do?"

"Essentially, you lied." The accent had vanished but left me wary. "You told me you went home after dropping off Miss Daly on Oak Street, yet we retrieved a security tape from a camera at FedEx Kinko's on Third and Broad. It's marked with Saturday's date, 10:32 p.m. You are seen clearly at the exterior phone booth placing a call to 911." He set his hands on his hips. "You tell me, Mr. Black. What exactly am I to make of that?"

36

Oblivious to the ER's activity, Detective Meade's eyes bored into me. A response—that's all he wanted. What, if anything, should I tell him?

Voice one: *If you talk, your mother will suffer.*

Voice two: *But she'll die if you try to deal with this on your own.*

"Have you gone mute?" Meade goaded.

For nearly three days I'd carried the burden of knife attacks, e-mail threats, murder, and renewed-but-fragile hope. Sammie had her own bereavement to bear at the moment, while Johnny Ray was off in pursuit of his dreams. Dad was his usual prickly self. Freddy was a victim in this game, to the extent that I'd even—briefly—considered him a villain.

I was tired.

Voice one: *Think of your mom's safety.*

Voice two: *You're running on empty, which will do her no good.*

"Okay." I stepped away from the windows, glanced around the waiting room. "You want the truth?"

"I expect nothing less."

I lowered my voice. "Yes, I lied. But only because I was afraid."

"Guilty parties usually are."

"Not for myself. For my mom."

"Your mom?" Meade leaned back. "I thought you told me… Isn't she gone now?"

"That's what I grew up believing, but now I'm not so sure."

"Wait. Are you suggesting she's alive?"

"Maybe."

He gave a caustic laugh. "Oh really. And I was born yesterday."

"This isn't funny."

"Believe me, Mr. Black, I am not amused. You"—he leveled a finger at my face—"told all of America on that TV show that you watched her die."

"Lemme explain." I gestured him into the hall, away from the waiting room's occupants. "First, you have to promise you'll answer some of my own questions."

"To the best of my ability, within the constraints of the law."

Good enough.

There's some truth in the adage that men like to communicate shoulder to shoulder, while women prefer face to face. We leaned against the wall, watching medical personnel, wheelchairs, and gurneys pass by. Meade remained stoic as I gushed forth an abridged version of my weekend. No mention of my Desert Eagle. Or of our B and E into Chigger's place.

When I was done, Meade asked if my brother believed Mom was alive.

I shook my head. "Not yet."

"You said you had some questions for me?"

"Okay. I know I'm poking my nose in here, but that witness at the hotel—was she a big black woman? From New Orleans?"

"At this point, I'm not free to divulge the identity of our witness."

"Did this witness see a third person get into my car?"

"The person you claim was wearing a black ski mask?"

"Yes."

"No."

"You're positive?"

"The witness only saw you dragging Miss Daly down the stairs to the Honda."

"What about Felicia's payment info at the hotel? Did you run it? She told me this guy had paid for her trip, so maybe it was his credit card."

"Already checked. The card was in her name, and her flight was paid for in cash two weeks ago at a PDX ticket counter."

PDX: Portland International.

"There's gotta be something though. Some clue."

"The human psyche is a delicate thing," he commented.

"You don't believe me?"

"I believe you've told your experiences the way you perceived them."

"You think I'm full of it."

"Actually, you've presented some credible details. Based on prelims from TBI's Microanalysis Unit, there were tire impressions on Oak Street indicative of a heavier vehicle, such as a van. There were also fragments on the pavement consistent with older automobile glass and flecks of gray paint on the recovered tricycle."

"There you go. I couldn't have made that stuff up."

"Please understand, Aramis. I want to get to the bottom of this too. My instincts have served me well over the years, and, no, I'm not convinced that you committed a homicide. I was upset, though, by your omissions during our lunch at the plantation."

"But you understand why. Right?"

"I'm certainly trying."

"I can't lose my mom. Not again."

He tilted his head and ran a hand over his mouth.

"Maybe," I said, "you could check with police records in Oregon and find out all you can about her disappearance. I'm telling you, they never found her body. You think the amnesia angle's a possibility? It'd be a crazy twist. Especially since her first husband—my biological father—did time in the state pen for her death."

"I remember that from your TV segment. Isn't he dead now?"

"Died of cancer. But he's the one who sent me her handkerchief. Maybe there's other stuff he held on to, more secrets. He could've passed on something to one of the guards. Or a cellmate. There's gotta be a piece of the puzzle that brings it all together."

"I'll look into it."

"Appreciate it."

Coal black irises studied me. "Don't you have a final tonight?"

"Social psychology. Ugh."

"A fascinating topic. I'm sure the curriculum's changed since my college days, but I took a similar class at Lipscomb."

"You were a Bison? Dude. You never told me."

"Did you know Pat Boone attended there?"

"Any relation to Daniel?"

"I've dated myself, I see." Meade hooked thumbs into his front pockets. "Later I completed my studies at TSU, then went through the police academy over in Hermitage. When Chief Serpas took over, Vice got rolled in with everything else, and I took the detective position at West Precinct."

"Which is how I met you."

"Next year I'm applying for North Precinct."

"Am I that much trouble?"

"Actually, it's closer to home, which would mean more time with my wife and daughter." He rested against the wall. "Family's important. I've told you that before."

"I agree."

"I'd do anything for them. How about you?"

A lump formed in my throat. "Yeah."

"And that's what concerns me. See, in your descriptions of this alleged assailant and his e-mails, you've outlined some of the classic traits of a sociopathic mind. A sense of omnipotence. Cruelty and a marked lack of empathy. Exploitative behaviors. In fact, you've even provided a modus operandi of sorts, with razor knives and these biblical references in the messages."

Where was he going with this?

"One of the first modern criminal profilers wrote a book called *Mindhunter,* in which he suggested that 'How plus Why equals Who.' It holds true, from what I've seen in law enforcement. But sometimes, Aramis, the problem is that we don't *know* the why until we know the who."

"So we need to get into the criminal's mind."

Still pressed against the wall, he turned his head toward me. "Is that what you've done?"

"What?"

"Have you immersed yourself in this situation to avoid the emotional reality? Miss Daly, a woman you once loved, is gone. It's not beyond the realm of possibility that you've created this scenario so that—"

"Felicia is dead! That's real. So is the rest of it."

"Maybe she was in the wrong place at the wrong time."

"A random victim? No way!"

"By your own admission, she was in a rough neighborhood late at night. She'd been pulled in before—"

"Pulled in? What're you getting at?"

"In Portland, her sheet contained recent prostitution charges from her involvement with a high-end escort service."

"That's ridiculous," I said.

But Felicia's breathy invitation at the hotel whispered through my head.

"With your recent studies in social psych," Meade rattled on, "is it possible you've fabricated this sociopathic character as a means of not only protecting your ex-girlfriend's honor but also protecting your heart from its very real grief by seeking a maternal replacement for her loss?"

"Meaning, my mother."

The sympathy in his voice was real. "It's been over twenty years, Aramis."

"I saw her. There's no doubt in my mind."

"I know how much you cared about her."

"You think I sent those e-mails to myself?" I hissed. "I don't even know what some of them mean. 'Thursday—a fitting day for victory over my enemies.' What the heck is that about?"

"Thursday," Meade mused. "Named after the Norse god of thunder."

"Thor's Day. Okay. But I don't know who conquered Thor."

"Your subconscious could've dredged up repressed knowledge."

"I never would've written that."

"I can't let friendship blur my objectivity."

"Explain the cuts on Felicia's back. And the matching initials on Johnny Ray's shoulder. You witnessed both of those wounds firsthand."

"That's the one thing that doesn't fit."

"Back at my place," I said. "I have a blood-stained razor this guy left for me in an envelope. Maybe it'll help. Would that make you believe what I'm saying?"

"I'd like to see it. If there are any latent prints, we can search them against the AFIS database." He clapped his hands together. "We both have a lot to think about, Aramis. I'd better let you go."

37

The pressure was on. Seventy minutes till my final. With Thursday's confrontation still three days away, I figured I might as well finish out this course and earn my credits for the semester.

Sara and Diesel, please don't hate me if I bomb this.

After Freddy C's stiff-legged exit from ER, I gave him a ride to Centennial Park en route to my brownstone. Meade was close behind, intending to collect the razor-blade evidence I had offered.

"How's the leg?"

"Not bad, not bad."

"Meade covered the cost, you know. Or talked them into comping it."

Freddy wore a look of panic. "I can't pay him back."

"Just tell him thanks. That'll make him happy."

"We in trouble? For breaking in?"

"Is that what's got you nervous?" I turned into the park, gliding toward the Parthenon. "Don't worry. Trish thought we were supposed to be there all along, and she was beside herself after her dog took a chunk out of you. Sure, it looked strange that we'd parked back behind the garage. But if there's any trouble, I'll deal with it."

Freddy was ready to disembark. "Right here."

"Take care of yourself. Come by for coffee in the morning."

"I got it," he said.

"Got what?"

"Evidence. You said we needed it."

"To build a case against the Kraftsmen, yes. What'd you get?"

"You were talking to her, keeping her busy. So I took it from the wall."

"In Trish's bedroom? I didn't even see you do it."

"C for Crime-fighter," Freddy stated.

"Let's see what you got."

From musty layers of clothing, Freddy drew out a coiled leather whip. "It's the one. From the cave."

"Are there bloodstains on it?"

"Can't tell."

"Well, I'm sure they can figure it out in a crime lab. I bet Chigger thought it was safer in plain sight than hidden away somewhere. I mean, how many people go into Trish's bedroom in the first place?"

Freddy pushed it toward me. "Give it to the detective."

"Okay."

"My payment. Tell him thanks."

"No." I nudged it back. "You should do that yourself. Tell him what you told me, how Chigger put it in your hand and forced you to use it on another human being."

In my rearview mirror, the exchange played out between the detective and my friend from the park. There was a shaking of hands, a nodding of heads. When it ended, Freddy C carried himself a bit taller as he melted away into a copse of trees.

"Legends and Lies: Cultural Susceptibility in a Secular Age."

Our project's title filled a mobile chalkboard. Against the green background, Professor Boniface Newmann cut an imperious figure as he watched students file in. He hitched his tweed lapels over a wide-ribbed turtleneck and waited for the wall clock's minute hand to point straight up.

"Yes then." He took a step forward. "If any student is late—meaning those who enter from this moment on—he or she will receive a ten-point deduction. Moreover, anyone who leaves before the last group's presentation will suffer the same penalty. Consider yourselves fortunate for having demonstrated a degree of promptness."

Roll call commenced with military precision.

"If they're late," Diesel muttered, "how will they know about the deduction?"

"Seems like a contradiction. How can you even *receive* a deduction?"

Sara Sevier shot the two of us a sideways glare.

My nerves ratcheted up a few more notches when I heard the order of presentations. We were last. Fifteen minutes per group, with eight groups of three. I had a good hour and forty-five minutes to stew in my anxiety.

Diesel slipped a drawing to me. "Professor Bones," it read, over a cartoon sketch of a human skeleton with a tortoiseshell.

"Leave me alone," I mouthed.

He let his eyelids fall, then jerked his chin as though waking up.

"To avoid difficulties, I will be the timekeeper for each group," Newmann was explaining, lifting an antique stopwatch. "As the designated speaker comes forward, he or she will submit the group's written outlines, then proceed to the podium. The clock will start at that point. The group's score will be adversely altered by any presentation lasting under fourteen minutes or over the allotted fifteen."

"And you think *I'm* a stickler," Sara Sevier whispered to Diesel.

Staring ahead, he said nothing. Crept a hand toward her stacked books. Poked at them till they were out of alignment with each other.

She fidgeted. Tried to ignore them.

From the podium, the first group's speaker was halfway through a Power-Point display when Sara caved, rolling her eyes and straightening the stack. Diesel gave a knowing nod that could've been in response to the PowerPoint but more likely to Sara's compulsive quirk.

When the next group's presentation kicked off with a skit in full costumes and regalia, my mind scrambled for ways to spice up my own fifteen-minute segment.

It kept snagging, though, on the conundrum of AX.

What was the value of a centuries-old Masonic ring? Monetary? Sentimental? How was this person connected to my mom? What was the goal of the whole charade?

The problem is that we don't know the why until we know the who...

Who then?

I played mental hopscotch, jumping from the outrageous to the plausible.

Athens of the South: a catering company with an obsessed young employee named Alexia—A and X. Beware the poisoned fig leaves? *Yeah, right.*

Reginald Meade: a straight-arrow detective. But he knew details of my long-lost inheritance. Had greed or power corrupted him? *No way. I refuse to believe it.*

Anna's Ex: AX? A messy divorce. Disgruntled husband. Domestic flare-ups. By employing Anna, had I painted a target on my chest? *Seems a bit far-fetched.*

Chigger: an ominous tattoo. A jealous guitar player. An axman with an ax to grind—and a religious grindstone for the task. *Certainly seems capable of it.*

Mr. Hillcrest: an arrogant, controlling parent. A zealot. Thumping his King James Bible, using an ax to clear away the so-called barren trees. *A very good possibility.*

None of these suspects seemed to have a solid alibi. With an accomplice, any of them could be involved. My hopes of narrowing the list were inhibited by limited resources and dwindling time. And while investigating, I might dig up more suspects.

For that matter, Sammie could be involved. Or Johnny Ray.

I couldn't trust a soul. Learned that last year, the hard way.

What about myself?

Perhaps my brother and the detective had hit upon the truth, poking beneath my layers of emotional protection. What if I was losing touch? Concocting alternate, safer realities? If, in fact, a hinge had come loose somewhere in my psyche, would I know it? Would I hear the parts rattling before they simply fell apart?

"Group eight?" our professor called from the front. "Snap to it."

"Aramis."

I blinked and found Diesel waving a hand in front of me.

"I'm fine." I gathered up my papers. "I'm here."

"We've had some creative presentations to this point," said Newmann. "A mix between mildly and wildly entertaining. Unfortunately, the success of most groups' urban legends has sputtered due to ineffective means of dissemination. Perhaps group eight will reverse the trend."

"I'm ready, sir."

Professor Newmann peered over his tortoise-shell rims as I approached and turned over our trio's project outlines. "Frankly, Mr. Black, your lethargy disappoints me."

I nodded at the podium. "If I may…"

The moment my hand touched the lectern, he clicked his stopwatch with exaggerated force.

"Legends and lies," I began. "Does our present culture promote our susceptibility to them? We've seen seven groups already. They've worked hard, I'm sure. But I suggest we've been simply entertained."

"As your instructor, it is my job—mine *alone*—to make such judgments."

"Not meaning to be rude, Professor, but"—I gathered my notes and threw them to the floor—"I've come here to learn. Not to outdo the last circus act. Not to get a good grade so that Mommy and Daddy will buy me a Lexus. If this class is really about navigating our way through society's lies, then we should be allowed to sidestep your browbeating and speak freely."

Mouths dropped and eyes widened around the lecture hall.

"Browbeating," Newmann echoed.

"I don't mean any disrespect, but this country was built on the exchange of ideas, and many of the religious denominations that came over here formed from the soil of protest. Thus the name Protestants."

Expecting a rebuke, I saw instead a bemused expression tug at the professor's lips. He repositioned his spectacles, ran two fingers over a pasty eyebrow, and said, "For the first time this evening, I believe a student has tapped my own frustration with the spineless, amoral equivocations we see daily all around."

I stood in shock.

"Proceed please, Mr. Black."

"Uh, thank you, sir."

38

Nearly nine p.m. End of semester. And I had the full attention of the class.

"Quoting a friend"—I nodded at Diesel—"here's a pop quiz. True or false: the glam rock group Kiss once published a comic book printed in their own blood?"

My peers rustled in their seats, hesitant to speak.

"C'mon," I prodded. "If this is your great show of courage in seeking out the truth, then we're in more trouble than I thought."

"Amen," agreed Professor Newmann.

"True."

"We've got our first vote," I said. "Anyone else?"

The final tally ended in favor of the comic book's authenticity.

"Yes," I said, "it's true. The band members agreed to the promotional gimmick and donated some of their own blood to be mixed with the comic's red ink. A notary public confirmed the stunt with a sworn statement. That issue, which appeared in June 1977, went on to be one of Marvel's best-selling issues of all time."

Gasps of disgust went up.

"Real blood? Oooh."

"Snap," one kid exclaimed. "Everything cool happened in the seventies."

"Yeah, you moron," said another. "Like the Vietnam War and Watergate."

I raised a hand until the room had quieted. "I bring all this up for a reason. If this really is a secular, godless age, why are we so willing to idolize almost anything? When something entertains us or gains some sort of popularity, we shower it with praise—until the next big thing comes along. We sacrifice our standards. We stop thinking for ourselves. We let the media and marketers tell us what to love and to believe."

"All noteworthy comments," Newmann interjected. "But tell us, Mr. Black, what was your group's urban legend? What was it that *you* would have us believe?"

"My study partners and I chose a local subject. After fine-tuning the idea, we went to multiple Web sites and Internet forums and proposed that General Nathan Bedford Forrest, the Confederate mastermind who later spearheaded the Ku Klux Klan, was born to a poor white woman and a slave boy from a local plantation. At delivery, his mother's parents took young Nathan and drove the slave away to cover up the, uh, forceful nature of the pregnancy. Nathan grew up believing his father had abandoned him."

A student piped up. "You tellin' me the leader of the KKK was half-black?"

"That was our urban legend."

"Dawg, that's a work of genius."

"It's not true," I emphasized. "But it started spreading."

"It is true," said another classmate. "I read about that on Wikipedia."

"Students!" the professor barked.

"Diesel gets credit for that particular entry," I noted. "We'll be editing it from the site after tonight, if they haven't flagged it already. But that's the danger, isn't it? Once the truth's been tampered with, it's hard to separate out the lies."

My own words precipitated a dizzy rush, and I lowered my head. Both hands gripped the podium as images flitted across my closed eyelids: the riverbank...the gunshot...Mom kneeling, falling...splashing beneath the surface...

Most of my life had centered round that one moment.

Was I lying to myself about her reappearance? Even our legend involved an estranged mother and son. Was it another subconscious machination of mine?

God, only you know. Help me uncover the truth.

"Truth." I lifted my head, took a breath. "It's the very foundation of friendship, marriage, government, and society. By testing it, we still have some hope of seeing through the lies. Meanwhile, my group's urban legend is floating around out there, like most of yours. Too late to call it back."

"Tha's messed up."

"And that, my dear students, is the point." Professor Newmann joined me at the podium and clicked his stopwatch with a flourish. Panning the class while avoiding my eyes, he clapped a bony hand against my back. "Well done, Mr. Black."

I thanked him. Awkwardly patted him back.

He gritted his teeth—or did I just imagine it?

"Prof—"

He shook his head.

My suspicion flared.

"Come see me afterward," he mumbled.

He squared himself. "Students, your final grades will be calculated and in your boxes by the end of the week. For those wishing to receive them via mail, please inform the office. If you prepurchased a yearbook, those will also be available."

Kids started shuffling around, scooping up books and supplies.

Newmann rapped his knuckles on the lectern. "Hello, class, you have not yet been released." He hitched his lapels and said in his reedy voice, "For years I've set out to instruct others and to show them the pitfalls of deviating from the truth. Some of you have already made corrections. Others have lessons still to be learned."

My eyes were glazing. I needed food and something to drink.

"In these last moments, I want to express my gratitude to those of you who accepted me—no matter how begrudgingly—as your substitute. For personal reasons, I will not be returning after the summer. Godspeed."

If he had hoped for sympathy, he didn't get it. A few thank-yous and good-byes, one "Peace out, Prof, " and Ward Hall 150 was empty.

Save the two of us.

———

I gathered my notes from the floor. "You're leaving us, huh?"

"For my own protection," Newmann replied. "And for the sake of my ideals."

"You lost me."

"I've been persuaded to leave by ignoble means but persuaded nonetheless. After the verbal intimidation of one particular parent, I became victim yesterday to his escalated tactics of coercion."

"Mr. Hillcrest."

Newmann nodded.

"What'd he do to you?"

"It's immaterial. The point is—"

"No no no. This is important."

The professor pursed his lips, drawing deeper hollows in his gaunt cheeks. "On more than one occasion, Hillcrest warned me that his son's scores were vital to his further education. I made it clear that my grades reflected the work of the individual students, nothing more and nothing less."

"So what happened yesterday?"

"He found me at home. Roused from an afternoon nap, I was foolhardy enough to open the door without checking who was there."

"And he forced his way in."

"He did."

"I can guarantee you that Diesel had nothing to do with it."

"I never thought so. And thanks to the strength of your group presentation, I'll be raising Desmond's scores without violating my own ideals."

"That's a good thing. So lemme guess. Did Mr. Hillcrest cut your shoulder?"

"I tried to resist, naturally. But—"

"He's a big dude. Show me the cuts."

"There's no need for that."

"I think he might've done the same thing to my brother."

He sighed. "I feared as much. It's what I warned you of on the phone, Mr. Black. Of course when I saw in the Sunday paper that Johnny Ray was leaving on tour, I had hopes he would escape this man's holy terror."

"If only it were that easy."

"There is something to be said for a person who's willing to act on his convictions."

"Oh, there's something to be said all right."

"In your offhanded manner, Mr. Black, you did address that very thing in your oral presentation—the need for personal conviction. It's disconcerting in the extreme, the way it decays further each year in our homes, churches, and schools."

"Yeah? Well." I drew in air. "It doesn't justify what he's done."

Blond hair…a slack mouth…pinkish blood…

"Show me the cuts," I demanded again. "Don't be shy."

Wearing a sheared sheep's expression, Professor Newmann slipped an arm from his jacket and tugged the turtleneck down to reveal an all-too-familiar pair of initials.

Five cuts. Thin, but deep, in his pasty skin.

"AX."

"Yes, I examined them in my mirror." He slipped back into his jacket, trying to appear unfazed. "Of course, in light of Mr. Hillcrest's collegiate accomplishments, they came as no surprise. Alpha Chi is a prestigious honor society."

"Alpha Chi."

"In Greek the initials are AX."

"What?"

"A for Alethia, meaning 'truth.' X for Xapakthyp, meaning 'character.' The society's limited to the top echelon of the nation's universities. With his boasts of being a member, is it any wonder that he derives from this such narcissistic pleasure?"

heek Road cuts south off of Harding Pike and, less than a hundred yards later, passes the old entrance to Cheekwood Gardens. No longer used by the public, the spear-tipped iron gate is rusted, chained shut, and shaded by juniper trees. Statues of American eagles perch atop tall stone pillars where moss and grime have collected over the years.

All very imposing at first glance.

But I'd taken second and third glances.

With my car parked outside an animal hospital on Harding, I walked along Cheek—a neighbor out for a late-evening stroll—then slipped to the trees left of the gate. Here, behind the greenery, a chain-link fence stood between me and the estate. Between me and my Desert Eagle.

I scaled the fence and dropped down beside a pump house. Blue plumbing fixtures curled from the soil like periscopes searching for possible invaders.

This was one invader who would go unseen.

The Cheekwood estate spans fifty-five acres, its various gardens dotted with offices, greenhouses, a learning center, a museum, and a restaurant. Security cameras eye such structures, but they have little need to probe the outer darkness for petunia-stealing grannies. Uniformed guards patrol the property—maybe even my ol' friends Taciturn Chuck and Jolly Jerry—but by hugging the vegetation and moving slowly, I was sure of recovering my pistol.

That is, if I could locate the exact shrub.

My advance from the pump house, past flowers and bushes and box-woods, over trails and a paved drive, brought me to the Perennial Garden within ten minutes. I spent an equal amount of time creeping along hedges, trying to recognize terrain that had seemed so distinctive in daylight.

Where was the stinkin' thing?

The fountain, the feel of the spray... If I just followed the sound of water.

When at last my fingers stretched beneath the correct shrub and snagged my treasure, I was dirty and sweaty. I brushed it off and reassembled the pieces.

Recovering my .40 caliber would've brought a smile to my face under normal circumstances, but I could think of nothing other than Thursday morning and my confrontation with Mr. Hillcrest. He had my mother.

The way he'd looked at that hotel clerk while toting his ice bucket...

The way he'd carved into my ex-girlfriend and left her to die...

What had Diesel told me about his father a few days back? *He's got it bad for women, young or old. Maybe it's wrong to say, but that's a fact.*

Lost in these thoughts, I almost exposed my position to a passing guard. I reared back against a tree bole, took measured breaths.

Did he know I was here?

When he lifted a leg to pass gas, I was pretty sure I had my answer.

Fifteen minutes later I was back over the chain-link fence and headed toward Harding Pike. My skin crawled in the humidity of this Monday night. I slipped into the driver's seat. Sat silently.

With the safety on, I wrapped my right hand around the Desert Eagle's black plastic grip and its imprinted sword insignia. I let my finger rest on the trigger, while my other hand came up to brace the gun's weight. Extended over the dash, the fixed dot sights guided my eyes to an inanimate target, and

I imagined drilling round after round through the abdomen of Mr. Drexel Hillcrest—one to match each location of Felicia's stab wounds.

Live by the Sword...Die by the Sword.

As he would soon discover, that was a credo that cut both ways.

I turned the engine over and headed home for a meal, shower, and sleep—if sleep was even possible.

———

"Hey, Johnny." I was towel-drying my hair. "This is Aramis."

"Can't go one night without calling your big brother, can you?"

"It's late there, isn't it?"

"An hour ahead, but the party's just gettin' started."

Part of me resented that. By willful denial, he was free from the concerns that had sucker-punched me the past few days. Another part of me worried about him, knowing the amount of alcohol that boy could throw down the hatch.

"Just take it easy on the drinking, would you? For my sake."

"Got it under control."

"If you get roped up to any more statues, don't come crying to me." I switched gears. "So how'd it go?"

"The show?"

"No. The trip to the Hardee's drive-through."

"Whoa now, you're the junk-food connoisseur."

"You have a good turnout?"

"Get this. We had over three thousand payin', singin', boot-scootin' fans."

"That's incredible!"

"You're tellin' me, kid. Had a few equipment problems, being the first show and all, but the band was on fire. Chigger had 'em rockin' from the get-go."

"Chigger, huh? You never told me he had a sister."

"You met her? Heckuva nice girl."

"You ever heard him talk about the Kraftsmen?"

"Nope. What sorta craftsmen?"

"Never mind. Have you been into those caves beneath his cabin?"

"Caves? Can't hear you too well." Female giggles bubbled up through war whoops and sounds of clinking bottles. "Things're fixin' to get rowdy around here."

"Who've you got with you?" I inquired.

"Wouldn't you like to know. You shoulda come with us."

"You know me, Johnny. Trying to keep clean. Turning a new page."

"I'm just sayin', is all."

"Actually, it's nice having the house to myself."

"You're jealous."

"No, I'm not."

"Yes, you are."

I said, "Okay, wise guy, guess what I'm doing right now. Eating Twinkies by the boxful and slamming six-packs of yummy, sugary Dr Pepper."

He turned serious. "One day you're gonna wish you'd heeded your older brother. You'll wake up with your hair fallin' out and your belly saggin' like a triple stack of flapjacks. Gotta take care of yourself, kid. Your health's one of the few things you got some say over."

"Considering the brain-numbing activities you're about to dive into, the concern is touching. And look who's talking—Tanning Booth Man."

"Count your blessings. What you got naturally, I have to pay for." The noise was growing in the background. "I gotta go."

"Don't hang up. Please."

"What is it?"

"That woman's name in Oregon. You have to help me, Johnny. I know you think I've gone loopy in the head or something, but this is Mom I'm talking about. I need that ring. For one day, that's all."

"Too late for that now, isn't it?"

"No. She could FedEx it to me tomorrow. I'd have it by Wednesday."

"Can't we talk about this when I swing back through town? I'll be at the studio real early, stocking up before we head toward Little Rock."

"I can't wait that long."

"What? You gotta speak up."

"Please, just give me her name!"

"And watch you throw yourself into trouble? Not this time, Aramis."

"Hold on. You're not even—"

"See ya Thursday."

The phone went dead in my hand, and I threw it against the cushions. On the coffee table, the box of Twinkies remained unopened beside a single soda can.

***

After a fitful sleep, I bolted up from the sofa with anxious energy.

Two days to go. Less than forty-eight hours.

With Johnny's departure early yesterday, I'd missed my walk through Centennial Park. But I made up for it by pausing a few extra minutes on my way to work.

A warm breeze stirred over the lake, ruffling the feathers of waddling ducks. Huge blankets of grass bristled in the first rays of sun, as though the earth were coming awake underneath. In a Christian sense, there's nothing spiritual about the Parthenon—in fact, the building houses a huge statue of the Greek goddess Athena. But I usually find peace in the stillness there. Jesus was all about ushering love and forgiveness into the most pagan of places.

Still is. That's what won me to his side.

This morning, though, I wasn't sensing that peace. Revenge was on my mind.

Between the killer's e-mails and the text of the Kraftsmen's pamphlet, I'd read a number of scriptures these past few days. It was disturbing to think that words of truth and life could become weapons for evil in the wrong hands.

Of course, the same tug of war was raging inside me.

Love for my mom. Hatred for her abductor.

I walked toward Black's, more prepared than ever to kill my enemy. With my gun. My bare hands. With a stinkin' thumbtack, if that's what was given to me.

Diesel helped me through the morning rush, his voice cheery, his eyes dancing. It was good to see him like this, free of the pressures—for a short time anyway. But how would he handle the revelation of his father's depravity?

"What's got into you?" I said. "You're like a new person today."

He grinned, kept working on a mocha order.

"Nice to have finals outta the way, huh?"

"Got that right, boss."

"Bet your dad's gonna be proud of you," I said.

"If he is, he won't show it."

"You don't think so? Even if you snag an A?"

"Nah. Always another hurdle for his favorite little racehorse."

He turned to hand over the mocha and to help the next customer. We worked our way through a stream of harried professionals and sleepy-eyed coeds—deadlines and hangovers colliding in our line.

"Pop quiz," Diesel said as the crowd subsided.

"No. We're done with that."

"True or false," he went on undaunted, "after class last night, Miss Sara Sevier and I grabbed some ice cream at Cold Stone Creamery?"

"Sweetness."

Diesel's eyebrow lifted with rakish flair. "That's what I've been learning, I guess. No matter what issues my father grew up with and how much he wants to shove those things onto me, he can't live out his expectations through me. I have my own life."

"Dude. Definitely."

"Of course, my grade would've been sunk without your presentation."

"Don't sell yourself short. You and Sara aced those written assignments and outlines. Way I see it, we all played a part."

"When you threw down your notes, I thought you'd killed us for sure."

"Me too."

"Then what made you do it?"

"I was just tired of it all. It was like our class itself had become this big urban legend, and we had to discern what was real and what wasn't."

"And therein lies the genius of Professor Bones."

I put a lid on a to-go cup and handed it to a customer. "Got a question for you, Diesel. You remember when you called me on Sunday, during my lunch with the detective? Did you tell your dad about that?"

"Why would I?"

"You called your parents at the airport. Maybe you mentioned it in passing."

"I could've. I don't remember. But get a load of this. You know how you asked if my father was coming back to town anytime soon? Well, he called this morning. Say's he's driving down later this week."

A vein throbbed in my neck. "Did he tell you why?"

"Says he has a gift for me. Shoot, I think it's his excuse to be here when my grades get posted. If they don't meet his standards, he's threatened to pack up my dorm stuff and send me to his alma mater."

"Call him," I ordered.

"Right now?"

"Use the work phone. I don't care. I have a message for him."

Diesel eyed me, then picked up the cordless and punched in the numbers. "It's ringing. What am I supposed to say?"

"Tell him that—"

"Hello, Dad. Yes, I'm calling from the shop. I think my boss has a message for you." Diesel covered the receiver and said to me, "He doesn't want to talk right now."

"Big shocker." I snatched the phone away. "Mr. Hillcrest."

"Mr. Black, I presume. Until you've issued an apology for your outburst at the airport, I have no wish to—"

"Here's the deal." There was no use kissing up to this guy. To give in to fear was to give him the edge. "Are you listening? When you come into town in a couple of days, stop by and I'll give you a free drink. I'll put as many *shots* in it as you need."

He scoffed. "To do so would only *cut* into your revenue." And he hung up.

40

The casket was heavy. From the memorial service to the cemetery, the hearse bore along Miss Eloise Rosewood in confines of burnished metal and red maple veneer. The pallbearers and I reconvened at the back doors of the parked vehicle.

I looked up and found Sammie's eyes. She tilted her head, gracing me with a thin smile.

"Okay, gentlemen," said the minister. "Nice and easy."

We found our places, shouldering the weight as the casket slid out. Our dress shoes stepped in unison on dew-soaked grass. Insects hummed all around—in the leafy chestnuts, along age-blackened tombstones, around our heads.

The casket was heavy. Would we drop her? What if one of us lost his footing?

I found my focus narrowing to the strain on my arm tendons and the lint clinging to the suit of the man in front of me. The thoughts seemed so wrong, so irreverently ordinary.

Anything to forget.

Here. City Cemetery. Three nights ago.

On our way through the corner gate, I'd spotted nothing on Oak Street to indicate the loss of a young woman's life. Detectives, coroners, and crime-scene specialists had come and gone already, picking the pavement clean. The question remained: if I had stanched the bleeding, would it have saved her?

Focus, Aramis. A few more steps.

After words from the minister, the casket was lowered amid stifled sobs. This graveyard has been closed for a hundred years, and only longstanding agreements allow for any more burials here. Miss Eloise would be one of the last laid to rest on this hill. She marked the end of a generation, of a way of life.

"It's up to me to carry on," Sammie had told me.

A ceremonial handful of dirt broke the glint of sun on the casket. I glanced at Sammie again, but she was turning to shake the minister's hand. Her chin was set, her eyes moist with tears. Who was I to share in her grief?

I aimed across the lawn toward my car.

"Aramis." Her footsteps came up behind me. "Thank you."

I turned. "You're welcome."

"You men were all so gallant." Sammie's gaze lifted beneath her auburn highlights. "It meant a lot to have you here, and you were particularly presentable in your suit and tie."

"This old thing?"

"I hope you didn't go to any great expense."

"Found it in my closet."

Which was true. I'd found it there after renting it for one hundred fifty dollars from a place in West End. The entire ensemble was due back tomorrow.

"Is there anything I can do, Sammie? You need help out at your place? Someone to pack things up or whatever?"

"Let's not think about that right now."

"Bad timing, huh? But if you ever need me…"

"I'll let you know."

"You're a rock. You have been since I met you." I rubbed my neck. "It just doesn't seem right."

"What?"

"That you've been left alone."

"I'm not alone."

"You know what I mean." I took a step away, my head swimming. "Forget it. I'm sorry. You've got your own things to deal with, without my moaning."

She rested her hand on my arm. "I don't pretend to understand it either. I'm not sure God intends us to."

"Seems pretty convenient since he makes the rules."

"Miss Eloise led a long, pleasant life."

"But not everyone gets that option, do they? It's like he's swinging this sword around, and you'd better duck or suffer his wrath."

"You think he strikes people down in anger?"

I kept silent.

"The Bible shows God's judgment—that's without question—but it also shows large amounts of grace." Her hand slid into mine. "Over and over he reached out in love to people. If we stop recognizing that, we'll lose all hope."

"In here"—I pulled our joined hands to my chest—"I believe that. I do."

"But you're a thinker, Aramis. That'll always be a struggle."

The words cut to my core. She'd pinpointed that which defined my past couple of years. The past couple of days.

"Are you hearing me?"

I squeezed her hand and let go. Why was I the one falling apart here?

"It's the two sides of your sword," she explained. "The Bible says God's Word is 'sharper than any twoedged sword...a discerner of the thoughts and intents of the heart.' Only he knows how to strike to the truth of a situation.

As fallible humans, we usually slip too far over one edge or the other—all wrath and judgment or all grace and love."

"Hellfire or the holy hugs," I joked.

She gave a short laugh. "If you say so."

"Forgive me, Sammie. I shouldn't have gone off like that, especially today."

"I understand. In fact, last night Anna and I discussed the same things at length. She's a blessing. She may even stay with me while she gets back on her feet. Her divorce has devastated her."

"Any word on her husband?"

"The police found him at a local motel, and he was strongly encouraged to return to Florida and let bygones be bygones."

"That's right. He better not come back into my shop."

"Our shop."

We locked eyes. My heart was racing again.

"My bad," I said. "*Our* shop—that's what I meant."

In the back office at Black's, I went over inventory sheets and yesterday's sales receipts. I was reminded of Sammie's decision to come in last night to close the store while Diesel and I took our social psych final. She was a bulwark.

So why had I vented out there on the City Cemetery lawn? What kind of idiot was I, airing my doubts when she needed my strength?

I logged on to my computer. Checked my e-mail. Nothing from AX.

While placing my weekly online order—cups, hot sleeves, sweeteners, etc.—I received an invitation to accept a new friend on my instant messenger.

Reginald Meade, that wily detective.

We went back and forth for the next few minutes. As far as I knew, this

communication couldn't be tracked by Mr. Hillcrest. When Meade asked for
the story behind the coiled whip that Freddy C had handed over, I typed a
reply.

> A: "Check for bloodstains. Could match homeless black man killed
>   by train."
> M: "Where?"
> A: "By the Marathon Building. Racial violence involved."
> M: "Were you a witness?"
> A: "No. Freddy was."
> M: "The whip came from the house on Highway 100?"

This question was troublesome. An affirmative could lead to further
probes into our methods of obtaining the item. I decided to skip forward.

> A: "Chigger is possible ringleader. White supremacist group called the
>   Kraftsmen. Meets Saturday nights, Fort Negley. Please investigate."
> M: "Already some suspicions. Will follow up."

Switching the topic to Mr. Hillcrest, I cited my knowledge of the man
and his menacing behavior. Meade wanted to know why Hillcrest would
attack Felicia. I noted his apparent weakness for the opposite sex and—going
against my desire to believe otherwise—conceded there may have been a
physical relationship between the two of them. My mom's safety took prece-
dence now.

> A: "Can you put surveillance on him?"
> M: "Possibly. I'll talk to Columbus police to see if he has any priors."
> A: "Check in Oregon too. Felicia said he found her there."

M: "Which city?"

A: "Don't know. Remember ticket paid for at PDX."

M: "Will investigate. Thursday deadline?"

A: "5:45 a.m. Be careful. He can't know he's being watched, for Mom's safety. If he drives here, I think he will bring her too."

Seconds rolled into a full minute.

A: "Still there?"

M: "A hard sell with my commander. Limited resources. I'll try to link razor blade with Oak Street homicide. Info on latents coming soon."

A: "He's smart. Maybe under the radar all these years."

M: "What connection Nadine Lott?"

A: "Same. Sexual contact and repressed guilt. Violent rage to cover his sins."

M: "Was he here last year, at time of Lott's death?"

A: "Maybe visiting Diesel at school."

M: "Checked. Desmond transferred in this year."

A: "Business trip? Don't know."

M: "Will check flight records."

A: "One more question."

My fingers hesitated over the keyboard, frozen by the potentially condemning nature of his answer. Did I really want to know? Could I live with myself?

A: "Coroner's report? Cause of Felicia's death?"

M: "Brought on by pneumothorax."

A: "She bled to death?"

M: "No. Collapsed lung. Bloodstream unable to absorb oxygen, no supply to vital organs. Death within minutes of lung-tissue damage."

Tingles spread through my jaws as my throat clamped shut. Sorrow and relief brewed together in my thoughts. Out on that sidewalk on Saturday night, those few minutes I had left her made no difference. There was nothing I could've done to keep her from sliding away.

I tilted my head back and drew in some air before continuing.

A: "Thank you, Detective."

M: "Anything else?"

A: "Please check Hillcrest. Very careful please."

M: "Do my best. Stay in touch."

A: "Will do. TTYL."

M: "What?"

I grinned. Obviously I'd been weeding out IM hieroglyphics for good reason.

A: "Talk to you later."

M: "Right. CYA."

A: "See ya?"

M: "Cover your ax."

That wily Detective Meade.

41

Anna, it's good to have you back."

"Thanks."

Anna Knight had come in for her closing shift with no sign of the cowering fear from Sunday night. That was encouraging. She's a good woman who can do without some creep diminishing her. She even went so far as to ruffle my hair as I passed by the espresso machine.

"Would you like a nightcap, hon?" she asked.

"Sounds vaguely naughty."

"You"—she pointed and winked—"are the naughty one."

"If you're making me something, I'd love a good double latte."

"At your service."

"I'll be roasting in the back. We're running short on retail inventory."

"The Back-in-Black blend? It's popular with the college kids."

I looked toward the ceiling, cracked my neck. "Not sure. Maybe a new blend, in honor of a special lady." I was thinking of my mother.

"Not too fast, Aramis. Don't get me wrong, Sammie's a wonderful person, but she's at a vulnerable point."

"Of course. I know that."

"Maybe in a few months—a friendly date, a night on the town."

"Don't worry. No sudden moves on my part."

"And you'll remember to treat her like a lady."

"Haven't you seen how far I can shove my foot into my mouth?"

"I've heard."

I let that comment pass. "But, yes," I said. "I'll do my best."

"So there's a future for you two?"

"You are a little troublemaker."

She topped off my drink with a dollop of foam, handed it over. "Sometimes it's just a way of taking my mind off my own problems."

I hefted the cup. "Thanks a latte."

"You mocha me laugh," she answered back.

In the roasting area, I found comfort in the routine. I scooped raw coffee beans—Venezuelan, Brazilian, and Ethiopian—into the rotating drum, then reset the time and temperature for something a little milder, but with good complexity.

I'd name this blend after my mom.

With the aroma seeping into the room, I printed new labels for the shiny black retail bags and affixed the first label. An act of faith.

I still had no ring. I'd failed to sway my brother. How would AX react, less than thirty-six hours from now, when I showed up empty-handed?

Please, Lord. Just bring Mom through this alive.

In the room's stillness, through my six-year-old eyes, I saw the smile she used to give me as she sat with her morning coffee and took that first sip.

Time for some late-night research.

The store was closed, Anna had gone home, and I'd double-checked the timer on the roaster. From my office computer, I ran some Internet searches.

"Knights Templar"…led to Rosslyn Chapel, the Crusades, and so on.

My brother was correct that the Knights Templar, self-proclaimed protectors of the church and her relics, had been associated with the Masons.

After years of secrecy, the knights faced growing persecution in Europe, where they were viewed by many as a cult. They survived, in part, by fleeing to Scotland during the fourteenth century. They imported great wealth and secrets, which they used to form alliances with the Royal Stuarts and the Sinclairs, cupbearers to the Scottish throne.

"Freemasons"…led to Scottish Rite and secret societies.

Their modern permutation was traced to 1717, when the first Grand Lodge in London brought together other smaller lodges. Before that, the trail is less clear. It's a matter of record, however, that as far back as 1425 England's King Henry VI issued a decree banning their annual gathering.

Our own nation's foundations were built by numerous Masons, from the presidency on down. Even the Lewis and Clark expedition, which expanded American territory from the Mississippi River to the Pacific Ocean, was touched by the Masonic influence of Meriwether Lewis.

Lewis was an explorer, a governor, and Master of a St. Louis lodge. A museum in Missouri alleged to hold "the Masonic apron that belonged to Brother and Captain Meriwether Lewis and was in his possession at the time of his death on the Natchez Trace."

Last year I discovered my own blood ties to Lewis, which led to the cache of gold, trinkets, and documents he concealed before his demise.

By my way of thinking, acts of treason and murder had desecrated the find.

My brother took a different view. With a few hints, he'd tracked down the treasure near Memphis and found this centuries-old ring among the loot—a Masonic heirloom, dated 1644.

How had anyone else found out about it?

A mythic voice sounded in my head: *the ring is a dangerous thing, Frodo.*

Not funny.

With only a day till the exchange for my mom, I was starting to feel panic. I clicked on link after link, cross-referencing my information. Although I came across numerous legends and conspiracy theories woven through the history of the Masons and Knights Templar, I found no specifics about this ring.

I rubbed my eyes and headed home. Still empty-handed.

———

My chest is wet, sticky—that's what first catches my attention. I'm standing on a battlefield, the clash of swords and shields ringing in my ears. At my feet, a dead woman's eyes stare upward. She's attractive, not much more than sixteen, and my heart bemoans a world that preys on its young.

Labored breaths grow louder behind me.

I turn to see a warrior stumbling forward. Friend or foe? I'm not sure.

He's in chain mail. His helmet is crushed down over his skull, indented from the blow of a heavy object—a mace, perhaps—and he is mortally wounded. That much is clear by the copious blood dripping along the raw wound of his right cheek.

He says something to me in French.

"I don't understand," I tell him.

Adorning his white tunic, a splayed red cross indicates he is one of the Knights Templar. My own tunic displays the same shape. We are brothers in arms, I realize, joined by a history of protecting the church's treasures while warding off the heathen horde. We ourselves will plunder and kill—if that's what is required—all in the name of the one true God. Amen!

"I don't know French," I tell my comrade. "Do you speak English?"

We resort to primitive hand gestures.

What?

There, you fool! Take it.

I follow his pointing finger to the dead girl's clenched fist. I kneel to pry it open and take hold of a ring, one marked with dates and inscriptions. Behind me, the warrior drops to his knees and plunges facedown into a pile of dry horse dung.

He is dead, I realize.

And so am I.

The charging steed is upon me before I can react. I'm already wounded in the chest, but my mounted foe's sword catches up under my chain-mail skirt and nearly slices me in two. I rise through the air and come down hard, already leaving the world behind.

As I've heard in stories, I feel my spirit rise. Spiraling, like the flight of a bird.

A curious sensation. Then…

Coming back down, falling, spinning against the grain.

My body quickens, with fluttering eyes. The ring remains in my grip, warmed from the heat of battle. With halting movements, my corpse rises to its feet. Steps over the dead and dying. Reaches the bank of a crimson-tinged river.

I am driven by a need. A desire to be renewed, made clean.

Legs march at my command, taking me down into the water, out into the rinsing torrent. I go all the way under. Open my eyes. I see swords and a crucifix wedged between stones along the river bottom.

Then the current tears at me, ripping the tunic and armor from my body. I watch my stains wash away. My wounds pucker and begin to draw closed.

I come up to the shore again, naked and new.

In my hand, the ring sparkles.

"You're not listening to me, Johnny Ray."

"What time is it?"

"Five fifteen," I replied.

"In the morning?"

"I had this crazy dream. We need to talk."

"Can we do this later, kid? Had a show last night in Tallahassee, and now we're on the road to Birmingham."

I switched tactics. "How'd that go? You pack the place again?"

"To the gills."

"You get to try out that new song?"

" 'Livin' with Your Ghost'? Crowd loved it, even had 'em singing along."

"And then you stayed up late and partied. I know the scoop." I paced the bedroom, my eyes playing over the items on my windowsill. I knew that a tired and hung-over Johnny would be easier to press for information. "Listen. Can you just tell me where that ring is? I'm begging you."

"Done told you already. It's in Oregon."

"The lady's name—that's all I'm asking. Then you can go back to sleep."

"Aramis—"

"And don't give me that line about stirring up trouble. I'm a big boy. I can handle it. There'll be a lot more trouble if you don't cough up an answer."

He yawned, long and unrestrained. "Don't mean to sound like one of them prima donnas, but this tourin' stuff'll wear serious holes in your hide."

"Give. Me. The. Name."

He sighed and surrendered.

"Thank you, Johnny. Thank you. That wasn't so hard now, was it?"

Jillanne Brewster...

One call to Oregon's directory assistance, and I had her phone number.

With less than twenty-four hours till my meeting at Bicentennial Mall Park, I knew of no delivery service that could get Ms. Brewster's ring to me in time, assuming I could talk her out of it in the first place. And considering the gap between Central and Pacific Time, I knew I'd have to wait before dialing her number.

Six thirty a.m. here. Four thirty there.

Catching my brother half-asleep was one thing, but waking a complete stranger was a different matter. I'd take no chances. I might have only one shot at coaxing information from her.

"Diesel, am I ever glad to see you."

He clocked in and stepped behind the counter. "Are you leaving me?"

"I'll try not to be too long." I grabbed a cheese Danish from the bakery display. "Just something I have to do."

To his credit, he faced the line of customers without complaint.

I hurried to my computer, intent on fitting together the final pieces of research. I took one big bite, then started tapping at the keys.

"Virescit Vulnere Virtus… Courage grows strong at a wound."

Mary, Queen of Scots had used this phrase in the 1500s, and as I panned through her history, I realized she was my link between the Freemasons, the Knights Templar, and the present Brewster family.

I fixed my eyes on the screen.

"Mary, Queen of Scots… Royal heir to Templar secrets."

Born in 1542 to Mary of Guise and King James V of Scotland, she became queen six days later upon her father's death. With bloodlines linked to French, Scottish, and English thrones, she was a threat to many. A triple queen.

After years of turmoil, she became a long-term prisoner to her relative, Queen Elizabeth. Many of her jewels and royal baubles disappeared. Eventually, she was put on trial at Fotheringhay Castle and beheaded.

With many Scots claiming—even into the present day—that England's throne had been built on this brutal injustice, Queen Elizabeth realized she needed a scapegoat. She threw forward her secretary of state, a Mr. William Davidson.

By doing so, she cut short the diplomatic career of his assistant.

William Brewster...assistant to Secretary Davidson.

This was same Brewster who once served as a local English postmaster, faced harassment for involvement with religious radicals, and later joined the *Mayflower* expedition to the New World in 1620.

He became Elder William Brewster, spiritual leader to the Pilgrims.

Thoughts swirling, I gobbled down the last of the Danish.

Had Mary, Queen of Scots tried to bargain for her life with the ring? Had an illicit romance caused her to lower her guard, as she'd been prone to do in the past? What secrets had been handed down, stolen, or coerced from the ill-fated queen?

At nine a.m., I called Jillann Brewster in hopes of answering that question.

42

The fourth ring, the fifth. Maybe caution had gotten the best of me. It was seven a.m. on her end, and she might've left for work already.

Sixth ring.

C'mon, answer. Someone, anyone.

On the seventh ring, a breathless voice came on the line. "Good...ahh... morning...Jillanne speaking."

"Jillanne. Sounds just the way it looks."

"Yes...ahh... Do you mind telling me who's calling?"

"Sorry if I caught you at a bad time."

"Out for...ahhhh...jog."

"A fitness buff, huh? I used to live in Oregon. There's a lot of that."

A long pause. Jillanne said, "Yes, I'm trying. Who did...you say is calling? Or did you tell me that already?"

"Name's Aramis Black. I'm calling from Nashville, Tennessee."

"Oh, really? I'm a big country-music fan."

"Not my thing," I admitted. "With one exception."

"Don't tell me," she said in a resigned tone. "Shania Twain."

"Sorry. Couldn't tell you the name of one of her songs."

"Oh? I'm liking you more by the minute. Why'd you say you were calling?"

"You know the name Johnny Ray Black?"

"Isn't he that new guy, the one who sings 'Tryin' to Do Things Right'? That man's got prettier hair than I do."

"Yeah. Lotsa shampoo and conditioner."

"Hold on there. You're a Black, you say? From Nashville?"

"Yeah, Johnny's my brother. He called you a few months back."

"If he did, I never got the message." She sounded flustered, disappointed. "You sure it was me he was after?"

"He says he sent you a ring that belonged to your family."

"A ring." She breathed into the phone. "Yes, I did get that. But he never told me his name. If I'd known, I would've at least asked for an autograph."

"I can arrange that."

"Really? I don't mean to be a burden."

"Not at all. He…I mean, we just need one thing. It's about the ring."

"Please tell me he's not asking for it back. It's a family heirloom, Mr. Black."

"No no no. Nothing like that."

"It's very precious to me."

"Yes, I'm sure. All I need are some details. The symbols, the Latin inscription—that sorta thing. After that, I'll leave you alone."

"And you'll send an autograph, you say?"

"Even one better. How about a signed T-shirt?"

Jillanne started to talk, stopped, then blurted, "Can you make it an extra, extra large?"

"No problem."

"You need a place to send it, but I don't feel right giving out my street address. Nothing personal, of course. Here's a PO box instead."

"Good to be careful." I jotted down the info. "One T-shirt on its way."

"Oh, I can't wait. Now if you'll hold on, I'll go get the ring and tell you anything you'd like to know. Even better, I can e-mail a picture of it."

―――――

On my monitor, the photograph was clean and simple.

Brewster and *1644* were stamped into the heavy gold band. Intricate patterns were carved into the signet circle, wrapping around a *B* monogram. Inscribed along the inner circumference was the favored Latin phrase of Mary, Queen of Scots.

Did those patterns form a map or something? Was there some priceless bounty to be uncovered? Maybe a relic with miraculous powers.

Based on my research, the ring seemed to have passed from the Pilgrims to Founding Fathers with Masonic ties. From generation to generation, it had worked its way down into the hands of Master Meriwether Lewis of St. Louis Lodge no. 111.

Before his doomed final journey, he hid the signet ring with the rest of his cache. I was sure he meant to come back for it, to continue guarding its mysteries.

But fate had another plan.

―――――

My workday dragged along in inverse proportion to the speed of my thoughts. Minutes ticked by, monstrous thunks of a clock hand, mocking my anxiety.

I dropped off my rental suit and reflected on yesterday's dialogue with Sammie. Something had changed between us.

Or was I just hoping it had?

Cloistered back in my cramped office, I went online in hopes of IMing Detective Meade again. I was still hesitant to contact him in person. Somehow

AX had known of our lunch at Belle Meade plantation, which resulted in my mom's hair getting chopped.

Meade wasn't logged in. But he had sent a detailed e-mail.

Mr. Black,

Bear with us. Investigations involve a lot of time and paperwork, not nearly as exciting as on TV.

We've found no criminal record on Mr. Hillcrest, no fingerprints on file. During his childhood, his father faced domestic-violence charges more than once, but on paper Drexel himself is clean as they come. He makes occasional business trips, including to Oregon and Washington, but I find no indication he was in Nashville around the time of Miss Lott's homicide.

Our witness at the hotel has identified his photo and remembers see-ing him the same night you were present. She cannot confirm that he tampered with or broke into your vehicle.

I've convinced my commander to aid your cause. The Columbus police are also tentatively on board, posting surveillance on Mr. Hillcrest. He does have a single-car garage and a small utility shed. So far, though, they've seen nothing of a suspicious nature, no sign of an abducted woman.

A judge has agreed to the undisclosed placement of a GPS tracking device on Hillcrest's primary vehicle but was very concerned about the violation of personal rights and has limited its use till 5 p.m. on Thursday. If indeed Mr. Hillcrest appears headed for the rendezvous point, we'll have officers and a sharpshooter in place. Make no attempt to engage him on your own.

I've also initiated contact with Oregon law enforcement regarding your mother's death and any potentially related incidents with Mr. Richard Lewis, the man once incarcerated for his part in her disappearance. Records show that Mr. Lewis spoke very little to cellmates, but he did allow occasional visits from a chaplain.

As for the original investigation of Dianne Lewis Black's disappearance, it was concluded that she suffered fatal wounds on the riverbank— based on blood spatters and witnesses to the shooting—despite the failure of diving teams to recover a body. There was no evidence of cerebral matter or cranial splinters, casting some doubt on the actual entry of a second round. Bullet casings were cataloged on the evidence sheet, but they are now missing, "probably thrown out long ago with similar junk," I was told.

I hope this helps. You have my cell number if you need it. I've called in all my favors on this, so please don't take this lightly.

Detective Meade
West Precinct, Metro Nashville Police Dept.

I fired back a note of appreciation.

The sly dog was going beyond the call of duty. A few years back my anarchist buddies and I saw the cops as the enemy—and now look at me. If Meade had been in the room, I'd have hugged him.

The Brewster ring was still in Oregon, and I needed a substitute to wave at Hillcrest during our confrontation. Something to buy me time.

So I went ring shopping.

Branching from West End Avenue, Murphy Road crosses I-440 and boasts a number of unique storefront businesses. The Ooh La La Boutique caught my eye and greeted me with a whiff of perfume as I entered. Purses hung on the wall. Custom clothing ranged from feminine and exotic to stylishly casual—like something Sammie might wear for an evening at the Schermerhorn Symphony Hall.

"Hi. How are you doing today?"

"Good." No use dragging others into my troubles.

"My name's Liorah. If there's anything I can help you find, let me know."

She had a friendly face and eyes that seemed to dance with ideas. On a normal day, I might've asked about her handcrafted wares. Right now, however, I had one specific need to fill. I moved to the jewelry case, leaning down for a look at necklaces and bracelets beside sets of colorful earrings and rings.

"There. Can I see that one?"

"Sure." She set my selection on the counter. "Is it a gift?"

"Something like that. It's for a man."

The ring was solid and simple, fashioned from gold, with twining patterns along the band. A few modifications, and it might pass a cursory glance.

"Do you have anyone who does engraving? I need it by tonight."

"I'll call a friend of mine," she offered. "I'm sure we can arrange it."

When I returned, the ring had been transformed. It bore the Brewster name and monogram, Masonic symbols, and the 1644 date. From a few feet away, it could pass as the real thing.

"Looks good," said Liorah, scanning my debit card. "I'm sure he'll like it."

"He'd better."

———————

Four fifteen a.m. Only ninety minutes till the confrontation. In this predawn hour, the trees and cars were drained of color. The world slept in dreary monochrome. As for me, I couldn't sleep for fear of missing the rendezvous. I stood at my windowsill, cradling one of the Fauxbergés. It was so delicate, this symbol of new life. So fragile.

In my other hand, the empty bullet casing represented deadly force.

Where was Mom now? Lying in the trunk of Hillcrest's car? Was he cruising down the interstate from Ohio, watching his speedometer to avoid attracting any police? What would he do if he suspected that he was under surveillance?

Already Hillcrest had shown that he operated on his own sense of superiority. It's no urban legend that most psychopaths endure a childhood of detachment. They lose connection. Become self-absorbed. For some, low birthweight results in a lack of bonding to parents. For others, that bond is severed by degradation and abuse.

I had to believe I could rescue her. Somewhere south, my brother's bus was also headed this way. I could just imagine his shock if I greeted him with Mom.

She was alive. For now.

As long as I produced the Masonic ring, AX would allow us to reunite. What did he want from the ring? Scholarly prestige? Riches? A map that would lead him on some religious pilgrimage?

Whatever.

Once I knew Mom was safe and alive, all I would need was one good look at Alpha Chi member Mr. Drexel Hillcrest.

A .40-caliber round, and this sicko was going down.

I flashed back to the gospel account of Jesus's arrest in the Garden of Gethsemane. I thought of the apostle Peter dropping his sword after a rebuke from his master.

But that was different, I told myself. Jesus knew that he was headed for the cross. When it came to my family, I had an obligation to protect them, didn't I?

You better believe it.

43

ar off between the trees, the first shades of pink and light gray stippled the horizon. Time to do this. I shoved back from the window, pulled on a knitted cap and a black, hooded sweatshirt. I dropped the boutique ring into a Fauxbergé felt pouch, then tied the strap to a belt loop and tucked the bag into my pants.

Armed with my cell, my loaded handgun, and a multifunctional pocket tool, I stepped out into the fading night. The rendezvous point was only five minutes away, and I planned to arrive early so I could reconnoiter the park.

How would this play out?

In last night's dream, I'd died on the battlefield but risen back to my feet. I'd gone under the water. Been baptized and cleansed.

My intentions in this moment felt much grittier.

I was marching down the walkway to my Honda Civic when a husky shape materialized from the shrubbery alongside our brownstone. He came at me in a bullheaded charge. He was a blur. Before I could identify him beneath his ball cap, he drove into my side, catching me midturn and driving me off balance.

Mr. Hillcrest?

Not so fast, old man.

I planted my front foot. Swiveling, I brought my left arm around and deflected the attacker's weight. As he stumbled past, my right fist pistoned into his thick belly, and air exploded from his lips. He started to go down. I slipped. Together, we landed in a sprawl of limbs on the dewy lawn between my building and the next.

Did he think he'd just slice me early and swipe the ring from my corpse?

Not gonna happen! This was a violation of our agreement.

With one arm propping him up, he scrambled for a foothold. From a pivot point on the ground beside him, I swung my leg and took out his lone pillar of support. As I brought the leg back, I hooked his neck, flipped him hard onto his back. I sprang up. Lifted a knee. Stabbed it down into his ribs, pinning him to the turf.

His eyes bulged, and we stared at one another.

On the grass, dislodged during the scuffle, his cap showed three letters: C.S.A.

"Chigger?"

"Hand it over!" he seethed.

Hold on. Had I been looking at this all wrong? I ran back through the clues: the e-mails and religious quotes, his presence at Owen Bradley Park, not to mention his voiced envy of my brother and his violence in the caves beneath his cabin.

Other things didn't sit right though. Such as his lazy English.

"What're you doing here?"

The tour bus must've arrived back in Music City a short time ago. With DAD's studio only a few miles away, Chigger could've slipped away in the sleepy-eyed activity. Had he orchestrated the Thursday confrontation with me, working it around the tour schedule? Was it his way of throwing me off his scent?

"Just give it to me!"

"What? Are you after the ring?"

"Don't you play dumb with me."

He ran a stream of curses at my face and tried to break loose. I leaned the knee into him, held his arms down with my own. His gaze burned with fury in the dim glow of the walkway's lanterns.

"What're you talking about?"

"Hand over whatcha stole from me. I'm outta town, playin' shows with your brother of all people—and that gives you the *right* to break into my cabin?"

Is that what this was about? Had Trish told him of our visit?

"I was checking on your sister."

"Don't you lie, you scum sack! She tells me that she never let ya in, that you came up in the elevator."

"I didn't do anything wrong. We just talked."

"Well look at you, all smug and innocent." He squirmed against my grip. "You just gimme that horsewhip, you hear? It ain't yours."

The coiled whip. The evidence smuggled under Freddy's clothes.

No wonder Chigger was concerned.

"What? You're gonna threaten me?" I stood back and released him, reaching into my belt for my pistol. I kept the safety on as I brought it into view. The barrel pointed up at clouds the color of fresh bruises. "Not a good idea."

"Whoa there." He scrambled to his feet.

"That's right, Chigger. Back off."

"You trespassed on my land." Keeping his eyes on me, he scooped up his hat. "What were you doin' down in them caves?"

"That's what I was going to ask you."

"None of your cotton-pickin' business."

"How do you justify hating other people in God's name?"

"You're as blind as the rest of 'em." He slapped his cap against his thigh, punched his fist into it before returning it to his head. "Y'all think you're some kind of saints, comin' down here to clean up the good-fer-nothin'

rednecks. Look at you, waving your gun. You're no better than the next guy.
'Thou shalt not steal,' that's what the Holy Bible says."

"What about 'Do not judge others, and you will not be judged'?"

"My Bible's the King James authorized."

"Popular version," I noted.

He brushed dirt from his knee, started to turn. He looked over his shoulder at me. "You stay away from my land and my people, you hear? Your
brother, he's one thing. But you're not welcome."

"Better keep your nose clean," I said. "That whip's already in Metro's
hands."

History is full of lessons to be learned, and I'm a tree drawing nutrients from
those who have gone before.

Nashville's past is riddled with such lessons. Some rich. Some foul.

Over a century ago, Hell's Half Acre was a blight on this city's landscape.
Ramshackle huts and shanties spilled over with loose women, smudge-faced
orphans, whiskey runners, and malcontents. This blister swelled at the foot of
the state capitol, burst with a short period of criminal activity, then subsided.

Today park lawns and gardens stretch like bandages over the old blem-
ish. Completed in 1997 in honor of Tennessee's two hundredth year of state-
hood, Bicentennial Mall Park runs northward from Capitol Hill toward a
group of Grecian pillars. In the hot summer months, Johnny Ray and I have
played Frisbee on the lawns near the amphitheater and bought fresh produce
from nearby Farmers Market.

My favorite part of Bicentennial Mall is its long granite wall, engraved
with details of the area's past and quotes from notable figures.

This is where I parked.

Five twenty-seven a.m. Eighteen minutes to go.

I'd already circled the terrain twice, searching for signs of Hillcrest, my mom, or the cops. At this hour, the place was empty except for two men sleeping off bouts with booze near a clump of bushes. They could've been undercover officers, but I doubted it. The dirt rolls in the creases of their necks went beyond the imagination of most police makeup artists.

My cell quivered against my thigh. Detective Meade's number.

"Morning," I said.

"Get any sleep last night?"

"Tried. Didn't work."

"I'm headed over to Bicentennial," he told me. "Should be there in ten."

"What's going on? Is Hillcrest coming this way?"

"Yes, he's been on the road since very early."

"Any idea if my mom's in the car?"

"That has not been confirmed."

"She could've been in his garage or basement. Out of sight."

A cautious tone. "That's possible."

"Where is he now?"

"State troopers took over surveillance about an hour ago as he crossed in from Kentucky. They're in unmarked vehicles, well back—a safeguard really, in case he pulls off and tries to switch cars or anything."

My eyes were surveying my environs. "Don't spook him. Please."

"They know the situation, I assure you. Either way, I'm carrying a GPS unit that's got Mr. Hillcrest's number pegged. Can't hide from the satellites, and I see that he's coming down I-65 as we speak. Won't be long before his arrival."

"I'll be waiting."

"You stay put while we get into position. And do nothing—I repeat, nothing—that will endanger yourself. I'd rather not wipe up your blood for breakfast."

"It's the other guy you better worry about."

"I don't like the tone in your voice, Mr. Black."

"He's got my mother."

"We don't know that, not yet."

"I know it."

In the spreading dawn, something caught my eye.

"I've acted on that belief," Meade was saying, "but don't think I've been fully convinced. This is a long limb I've gone out on."

"And I appreciate that. Really. Bye for now."

"See you shortly."

I flipped the phone shut. Swallowed hard. I leaned forward to reposition my weapon in my belt under the sweatshirt, then climbed from the car and forged over grass and concrete toward the gray black wall. A specific section of the words carved into granite jumped out at me. They spoke of Lewis and his death in 1809.

Below, attached with packing tape, a sheet of paper gave me my orders.

I tore it free.

AX was still playing games, toying with me. Obviously, he'd put this here much earlier. He got off on this manipulation, pretending to be God. What he didn't know was that even if he changed location multiple times, it would still do him no good. Wherever Hillcrest went now, he was being tracked from the sky.

Which raised a serious question.

I shoved the note into my pocket, then speed-dialed the detective even as misgivings flooded my stomach with a sudden wave of nausea.

44

You're positive?" I asked, as I drove from the park.

"Absolutely. This is the first time he's left Ohio since flying back on Sunday."

"And you're sure it was Hillcrest who got in that car last night."

"There was visual confirmation, yes."

"Then tell me," I pleaded, "how he got a message taped to the wall here."

"I'm still a few minutes away. Don't move."

"Too late. I'm already heading to the new location."

"Where?" Meade wanted to know. "What's the note say?"

"Says to be at Fort Nashborough at 5:50 a.m."

"Down at the river front, less than two miles from your position."

"I have two minutes to get there."

"Won't matter if you're late, Aramis. Hillcrest is on I-65, already beyond the I-24 turnoff. He doesn't appear to be headed there, and if he is, he's delayed on his timing. Either way, we've got our eyes on wherever he goes. Hold up, if you would, and I'll catch up to you at the park."

"Can't wait. Sorry." I followed James Robertson Parkway, veered right onto Third Avenue. "Plus, you still haven't answered my question."

"About how the note got there? I have no solid answer."

"I do."

"Are you planning to divulge this information?"

"Diesel," I said.

"Desmond Hillcrest, you mean. Drexel's son."

"Meade, I've been blind. Just didn't wanna believe it. Diesel's the only one who knew I was having lunch with you on Sunday. He also knew you'd come into the store to talk about the e-mails I sent you." Church Street carried me over cobblestones and right onto First Avenue. "He's lived his whole life under his father's thumb, trying to make that man happy. Probably just acting as an errand boy."

"I'd be cautious about that assumption. Children have been known to do unspeakable things for the sake of a parent."

"Got that right." I swerved into a parking spot. "I'm signing off."

"Wait."

"I'm at the fort. Made it just in time."

"Keep talking to me, Aramis. Don't disconnect or do anything rash."

"But if Mr. Hillcrest's still on the road, there's nothing to worry about, right? I'll just check this out." I dropped the phone into my pocket.

For some reason, I was dead set on facing this alone. Was I doubting my own convictions about Mom's survival? Preferring to face my self-deception in private?

Or maybe I believed I'd find Diesel here. He'd been through a lot with his control-freak father, and my empathy with his mistreatment made me hope that if he was involved in this, there might be a chance of winning him over, of building on the friendship we'd started.

A nice idea, sure. But I was in for a surprise.

———

I stood at my car, peering up and down First Avenue. My Desert Eagle pressed against my spine, and I adjusted it beneath my sweatshirt. My pockets still held my cell and the multitool. The ring dangled in the felt bag between my jeans and thigh.

What now? Was anyone here?

Thursday. Five fifty a.m. The streets were mostly vacant.

On First, downtown buildings face the Cumberland River in an unbroken line, their historic facades brightened by the neon of the Wildhorse Saloon and Graham Central Station. Grass terraces descend to a vast concrete pier on the river front. Supply vessels used to dock at these banks, with porters walking up and down wooden planks, laden with burlap sacks and crates.

I crossed to the gated entrance of Fort Nashborough.

The stockade is a replica of the original fort that stood on this bluff above the river. Plaques tell the story of Colonels James Robertson and John Donelson who led a party of settlers here in 1780, then fought off Indian attacks and inclement weather so this seedling community could grow into present-day Nashville.

Through metal bars, I looked in at the stockade's courtyards and dwellings.

Not one human in sight.

On three corners of the fort, blockhouses rose from the spiked walls. I wondered if my mother could be in one of these defensive battlements, held hostage by Diesel. When Mr. Hillcrest arrived, he would ask for the ring and then release her.

"Diesel!" I strode around the log structure. "Diesel, are you here?"

No answer.

"Mr. Hillcrest?"

Of course there was no response to that. He was still out on the road.

Another phone call to Detective Meade. "No sign of anyone here," I said. "Where's Hillcrest now?"

"Are you certain you have your facts straight, Aramis? Times, dates."

"Positive."

"Then I'm not sure what to think. He's still on 65, proceeding south, and he's bypassed all the downtown exits."

"Maybe he's kept my mother locked up locally. Could be going to get her."

"Back to the theory of his son's involvement?"

"I hate to even think it. But, yes."

"We're still on him. Hold tight, and I'll keep you posted."

"Thanks."

I circumnavigated the stockade once more, then took a seat on a bench beneath a group of trees. Clouds were moving northeast. Across the Cumberland River, the sun was cresting over LP Field, home to the Titans football team.

I pulled the crumpled note from my pocket and read it again, wondering if I'd missed something in my rush.

Chop, chop, Aramis. Prepare "to put off your old self, which is being corrupted by its deceitful desires...and to put on the new self." You desire to see your mother, and indeed you shall. Take the ring to Fort Nashborough, 5:50 a.m.

The old self. And the new. A continued tug of war.

The scripture's phrasing seemed to be from a more modern translation, going against both Chigger's and Hillcrest's stated preferences. Hillcrest had compared my brother's drinking to a dog that "returneth to his vomit."

Maybe I'd been mistaken about this.

From behind, in the deceptive stillness of the dawn, approaching footsteps caused my pulse to jackhammer. I spun on the bench and saw a gaunt figure less than ten feet away. Even in the shadows beneath these branches, I recognized the tweed jacket and tortoise-shell glasses.

I jumped up. "Professor Newmann?"

He seemed more relaxed than in class, his look less pinched, his walk easy.

"Did I startle you?"

"I… Well, I thought you might be Diesel."

"Desmond," he said in his thin voice. "Is there a reason you'd fear him?"

"Never mind. What're you doing here?"

"Morning strolls can be quite invigorating." He came alongside me. "Why don't you join me, Mr. Black?"

"Got something else going at the moment."

"I'd enjoy the repartee."

I stepped back and looked around. "You live down here?"

"Honestly, I have a certain fondness for this time of day." He waved an arm toward the swirling hues of the sunrise. "It's that moment when night fades and the new day dawns. It's a true privilege to witness this transformation, the putting off of the old for the new."

Heat rushed up my neck. "What'd you just say?"

"Time to become a new man."

Professor Boniface Newmann removed the spectacles, dropped them to the cobblestone path, and crushed them deliberately beneath his heel. Thin fingers reached through his plastered hair and shook it until it hung into his eyes.

"Professor Newmann?" I said.

"If you prefer the alter ego." His voice had turned deeper, devoid of the characteristic reediness.

"That's not your real name?"

"In a sense. I've been renewed—a new man—so I'm no longer bound by such facades."

I glanced at the trees and the stockade's perimeter, where sunlight poked at the foliage. If he wanted surprise on my part or an angry denial, I could not—would not—give him that satisfaction.

I'd been so blind. My overactive mind had misled me.

Soon Diesel would be showing up for work at Black's espresso shop. Mr. Hillcrest, at this very moment, was probably pulling into the student housing area at Lipscomb, hoping for the first glimpse at his son's grades. Chigger was simply guilty of hating those whose skin didn't match his. In his shoes, if someone had broken into my place with my sister alone in her room, I'd have been irate too.

"Where is my mom?"

"Nearby." Newmann avoided my eyes.

"Is she alive? Tell me that much."

"Life, as a concept, is greatly misunderstood."

"Is she *alive*?" I repeated through clenched teeth.

"She is, Mr. Black. To come alive, though, one must be broken."

"Take me to her!"

"The Romanovs, tsars of Russia, valued their heralded Fabergé eggs as symbols of new birth, and yet an egg must be broken to provide sustenance. The shell must be destroyed to accomplish its purpose. Am I wrong?"

"Your brain's been scrambled. That's what I think."

This all had a strange sense of inevitability. His manipulative demeanor. The shifts in mood. His grandiose pontificating. Even his gaunt features suggested the low birthweight that could lead to a newborn's detachment.

The detachment nurtured by psychopaths.

"Our culture has succumbed to lies," he said, "trading the straight and narrow road for one of carnality. I'm disappointed actually. Your oral presentation on Monday indicated you were latching on to this insight."

"You! I can't believe you stood up there so self-righteous."

"Most students are simply interested in scraping by—"

"Like you had any place to be talking to us about deception."

"Yet Desmond was different."

"Did you arrange for our instructor to get nailed in that hit and run?" My eyes narrowed. "Or did you do it yourself?"

"For his father's sake, Desmond was desperate to succeed," he pressed on, undaunted. "I gave him a role in my social experiment, with extra points available toward his final grade if he would monitor you for me."

"He told you about my lunch with Detective Meade."

"A flagrant violation of the rules you and I established."

My hands were begging to act, to lash out, but I forced myself to remain rational. Listening to this was the only way to get to the truth. And I might discover a chink in this man's defenses. Or provoke him into a careless mistake.

"So, Professor, tell me. How does someone get like you? So seriously sick in the head?"

"I'm no one special. Like anyone, I've felt the burn of ungodliness."

"Did you feel it with that homeless lady?"

He tilted his head, rubbing at his eyebrow.

"The one you set on fire," I hissed. "Nadine Lott. Did you even know her name, you pathetic *runt*? Just couldn't resist her, huh?"

"Yes. Very good. Which is why I, too, had to suffer at the edge of the blade."

"Cutting yourself to fool me? That doesn't count."

My cell phone vibrated in my pocket. Detective Meade, no doubt. I hoped ignoring it would serve as a distress signal.

"What about Felicia?" I said. "How'd she get dragged into your schemes?"

"It was your lack of attention, Mr. Black, that drove her into my office."

"What?"

"In Portland I had a small ministry. She was quite vulnerable at the time."

"You? *You're* the one she dumped me for?"

"It was short-lived. When she saw you on that television segment, she became obsessed with seeing you again, absolutely refusing to let go of the notion. And so I granted her that opportunity."

"And then killed her for it."

"She was alive when I left. If I recall, you were the last one with her."

"There was nothing I could do."

"Succinctly stated. The human condition in a nutshell."

Only three cars had passed along First Avenue as I stood here beneath the trees. I was trapped here with a madman, hostage to his knowledge of my mother's whereabouts. I could feel the gun tucked into my jeans, but I told myself to stay calm, wait.

"Felicia did not deserve to die like that," I said. "No one does."

"That's where you're mistaken. We all deserve that. There are no saints in this life."

"Oh really? *Saint* Boniface."

"Granted. But are you aware that he, too, received theological training?"

"What?" I scoffed. "You really think you're some kind of priest?"

"He was an apostle to eighth-century Germanic tribes, distinctly aware that conversion required unorthodox, even drastic measures. One day he took an ax to a huge oak tree, their tribute to Thor. When the tree fell and split apart, he taunted the Saxons: 'How stands your mighty god? My God is stronger than he.'"

"A fitting day to face your enemies," I mouthed.

He grinned at me.

"And that's why you get to chop into people?"

"The ax is a tool of salvation, as shown by Saint Boniface himself. We must all die to the old self."

"It's a *metaphor,* Newmann. You die figuratively, not physically."

"Is that what you think?"

I watched him pace from the bench to the low fence overlooking the Cumberland, then back toward me with rage painted into every pore, every crevice of his face. Despite his thin frame, he carried himself with an imposing air. Gone was the weak demeanor that had served his disguise.

"You have *no idea,* Mr. Black. None whatsoever! I lost my first wife long ago. She was nineteen, I was twenty, and she was struck *down,* instantly dead. Taken from me by the sword of judgment."

"And you think she deserved it?"

"Nooo!" He shoved a bony finger into my chest, staring at it as he pushed.

I swiped his arm away.

"Don't you see?" he went on. "*I'm* the one. *I* deserved it."

"That much I believe."

"We were newlyweds. She was out for the afternoon, on the golf course. While I was fornicating with her best friend beneath our own bedsheets, my wife was struck by lightning. Only *nineteen.* Dead. Blown *right out of her shoes.*"

I considered his words, the agony behind them. "So now the rest of the world has to pay."

He filled his lungs and brought his voice down to a level pitch. "God took her from me—a severe lesson. Woe is me if I fail to show others the true wages of their sin. It's much more than a metaphor, Mr. Black. Much more."

"And that's what gives you the right to kill people? That's crazy."

"The shell of the old self must be destroyed. Few ever comprehend that."

"Okay. Stop. Take me to my mom."

"Earlier I invited you for a stroll. Have you changed your mind?"

I ground my teeth. "I'm dying for a stroll."

"The Masonic ring. May I see it?"

"I have it. But what's so important about an old heirloom?"

"You have your family secrets. I have mine."

"In your e-mail you said I could join the family circle."

"The ring, please. Assure me that you've followed through on your end."

"Not till I see her."

"I can live without the ring. Can you say the same about your mom?"

I shrugged. "It's been over twenty years now. She's a stranger to me."

The words were sour in my mouth, biting in my throat, but I ignored the taste of them. I would eat my words—eat the bile of my own past sins—if it would give me back the one woman I'd ever loved without reserve.

"She's no stranger to *me*," he taunted. "She's my wife."

My hand slid around my back, trembling. In seconds, I could end this.

"The incident at the river crippled her. The first gunshot put her in a wheelchair. I cared for her, fed and bathed her, filled her prescriptions."

"I saw you punch her full in the face!"

"We all require correction at times."

I swung my Desert Eagle into view. Clicked off the safety.

"What is this, Mr. Black?"

"Oh, I'm sorry. Did you think I would come unarmed? Lay a hand on her again, and I'll blow a hole through your skull."

"The old self is still very much alive, I fear."

"It's not your place to change it."

He shook his head as though his star pupil had failed an exam.

"Which way?" I snapped. "Take me to her now, 'new man.'"

45

Daylight splashed over the pitched roofs of the stockade and dribbled across the courtyard through cracks in the log fencing. I followed my foe along the walkway, behind and to the right, just out of his reach. His arms moved with military stiffness.

Where was Mom? What had she endured?

We rounded the corner of the blockhouse. My eyes ran ahead, hoping for an indication of her whereabouts. I had to stay focused. The details of her forced captivity—if she'd been married to him, that's exactly what it had been—were more than I could handle right now.

First things first. Breathe, evaluate, act rapidly…

"Do you consider yourself a student of history?" Newmann asked, looking back at me. "Would you care for an abridged lesson on the Pilgrims?"

"Are you even a real teacher? Or was that part of the disguise?"

"Lipscomb is an accredited university. Don't be foolish."

I waved the gun. "Keep walking."

He continued straight ahead along First Avenue. "A number of the Pilgrims were imprisoned for their secret gatherings of worship. Some went into hiding for printing religious tracts critical of the king. As a group, they were looked upon with suspicion by the Church of England, and they—"

"Would you shut up?"

"You asked about the ring."

"The Stuarts. The Masons. Yeah, I know. And Brewster ended up with it."

"Elder William Brewster—that's correct. An intuitive bit of research."

"Keep moving. This better be leading to my mom."

"My wife."

"Move it!"

He turned at the end of the stockade, led me up a set of steps back toward the river. "Initially," he said, "Brewster's boss, Secretary of State Davidson, received the ring from Mary, Queen of Scots as a bribe to aid in her defense, which he failed to do. After the execution, Queen Elizabeth shifted blame to Davidson for the entire debacle."

"So why's it so valuable?"

"Brewster removed the ring from Davidson's belongings and claimed it as his own, even engraved his family name into it. He recognized its importance as a Masonic emblem and as a signpost leading back to Templar mysteries in the Holy City."

"Jerusalem?"

"There are secrets still buried there."

"On the phone you told my brother it'd been stolen from your family."

"Mr. Black, in seeking to break loose from England's restraints, many of the Pilgrims lost their lives. When Elder Brewster boarded the *Mayflower,* he understood the price they'd have to pay."

"The old for the new."

"Yes. I'm privileged to be a descendant of his wisdom."

I realized we had circled and arrived back near our starting point. Beyond the low fence, the bluff dropped off toward the river's muddied currents. "If you've hurt her"—I reached forward and pushed the .40 caliber into his back—"you'll never see your precious heirloom. Where *is she*?"

"Doing penance."

I followed his gaze over the edge just as he spun away from me with his own weapon, the tapered blade glinting in the early sunlight.

"You put her down there?"

"The ring first."

"Where is she?"

"If one only has eyes to see." Newmann moved to the fence and pointed with his knife at a rope knotted to the upper horizontal support. It disappeared into the thick foliage below. His hand snaked under the braided strands and brought the blade up underneath it, severing a few strands of the twisted fiber. "She's in the water."

"No!"

"She's been baptized before, though the last time was warmer."

I leaned out over the rail, tried to track the rope through leafy vines.

"Her mouth is taped, as are her hands," he explained. "She's almost completely submerged. If you were to pour one of your coffeehouse creations over ice, it would be no colder than she is now."

The slope plunged forty feet to the river's edge. Where did the rope end?

"The surface may look calm," he went on, "but it hides a strong current. There are rocks and submerged hazards below. I've heard that search teams often discover corpses miles downriver, though that may just be urban legend."

"I can't see her."

"If I were to cut the rope—and that would take very little, I assure you— she would plunge twenty-seven feet to the bottom. Assuming the measurements there are accurate."

I followed his nod. Where the pier jutted into the Cumberland, a corner pylon showed depth readings in feet.

My eyes ran back along the bank, still finding no sign of her. Was he lying? Had I been played again? For six days I'd clung to a hope so ridiculous it strained the limits of credibility. It could all be one horrible deception.

The time had come, at last, to winnow out the truth.

"You're full of it, Newmann." My grip tightened on the Desert Eagle. "You've lied to me from the start."

"Are you willing to take that risk?"

"She's not down there." I aimed the barrel at him. "She's dead. She's been gone for twenty-one years."

"Oh?"

"And now so are you."

My heart pounded in my throat, nerves jangling beneath my skin. My arm began to shake. The only thing keeping me from drilling a round into his smug head was my concern it would endanger my mother. If she wasn't alive, if this was my psyche coming apart at the seams, then I had nothing to lose. I'd give this man a taste of his own religious psychobabble. The shell would be destroyed.

The old self into the new…

Yes, God transforms people. I was living proof. But rebirth didn't come through my own good deeds or sacrifice. It happened through the redeeming act of God's Son on the cross.

So why did I still struggle, wallowing in the sludge of my past? In the guilt? Why did I still feel the old credos dictating my emotions?

And what was I doing with this gun in my hands?

"Okay, listen." I clicked on the safety and laid down my weapon. "I'll play this your way. Just take me to her. Please."

"She's there. Try looking from that angle." He jutted his chin.

My phone shook in my pocket. I ignored it, keeping an eye on him and craning for a view over the rail. Bushes, vines, and—

There!

Through a gap in the foliage, forty feet below, I spotted her. *Mom?*

Six years old…helpless…watching her plunge forward…

Salt-and-pepper strands obscured her face as she slowly twisted at the rope's end, struggling to keep her chin above the water. Her body turned toward me, her hair parted, and her eyes crept up the slope to mine.

"Mom!" I yelled. "It's me. Hold on!"

In that split second, she dropped, and Newmann's grunt snapped my attention back. With one upward slice, his blade had severed the taut rope.

No!

I dashed forward, my scrambling sending the Desert Eagle out beneath the fence and over the edge into the thick greenery.

Newmann lurched toward the fence, his foot braced against the creaking post. The cut rope was twined around his other arm, digging into his skin.

He chuckled, her life now in his hands. "Take it," he commanded. "I'm starting to slip."

As the cord slithered from his grip, he turned aside, yelling in pain, and I grabbed at the rope, twisting my left hand around the remaining length before it whisked away. The fibers tore into my hand and wrist, and though it couldn't have been more than 130 pounds cantilevered on the riverbank below, it was enough to demand my full attention.

My feet dug for purchase against the wood post, and I angled back, using the horizontal beam to fulcrum the tension. From this position, I could hold on forever. Till my tendons snapped. Till I sweated blood and it pooled in my shoes.

"The ring," Newmann whispered in my ear. "Where is it?"

"Search me."

"My pleasure," he said, feathering his knife along the hair at the back of my neck.

I cracked my skull into his cheek.

He stumbled backward, growled, then moved closer. "You don't realize the predicament you're in. Do you want her to drown? Believe it or not, my wife has expressed a desire to see you."

"She's not your wife."

"I assure you, she is." The blade crept along my ear. "I labored for a time at God's work in the Oregon State Penitentiary, where I met your father." A hand dug into my back pocket. "Richard Lewis was a parishioner, if you will, who confided in me as though I were his priest. He led me straight to her."

I felt the rope slacken a bit, and I wondered if Mom had found a narrow ledge beneath the water to pull herself up against. Hindered by soggy layers of tape, she wouldn't be able to hold on for long.

"Did he talk about me?" I asked. I'd never known my biological father.

"Before the cancer? I don't believe so. No."

"He died in prison, serving time for her murder."

"A pitiful irony, since she was very much alive." His search moved to my front pockets. "An accomplice of his fished her out. The town assumed she was gone—and, yes, she did suffer short-term memory loss due to acute physical and psychological trauma—but she survived. She needed someone to watch after her, in her condition. And I filled that need."

"You need serious help."

The knife scraped at my cheek. "What I *need* is your cooperation."

I wanted to turn and throw this guy off me, but I couldn't let my mother slip into the powerful current. The rope was digging into my arm through my sweatshirt, cutting off circulation, and the fingers of my other hand were growing numb. But I had to buy her time. If she went under, if I lost hold of the rope, I doubted I would have time to plunge down the slope into the water and rescue her from the murky depths.

"Gifts for me?" Newmann was removing my cell and multitool and slipping them into his pocket.

If he wanted the ring, Jillanne Brewster's number was in that phone.

"I'm moving my knife away now, but I'm sure you're smart enough to keep holding on." He knelt and patted at my legs, fishing his fingers into my shoes. "In your father's soul-searching, he told me of a family treasure that had eaten at him with greed. When I realized the historical tie-in to Master Meriwether Lewis, I knew God's hand had guided me to him."

"How appropriate."

He ran his hands across my back, staying low to search my abdomen. "The ring was guarded by the Masons and was last known to be in Master Lewis's possession. When he met his end on the Natchez Trace, it was feared the Templar secrets had died with him."

"Until you saw my story on that TV show."

He stood and pressed against me. The knife was touching my ear again.

"The ring, Mr. Black."

"I won't propose till you get tested," I gibed.

The razor edge was so thin, so sharp, I was unaware he had cut me until a hot droplet of blood splashed against my collarbone and ran down my chest.

"Last chance, Mr. Black. The next cut will dramatically compromise your ability to sustain your grip."

"A felt bag." My voice was beginning to quiver from my exertion. "Pull it up by the drawstring on my belt loop."

To his credit, he did only as told, then backed up and emptied the contents into his hand.

"Yes, this is it!" The excitement in his voice suddenly caught. "Wait."

I searched the river's edge below, hoping to catch my mother's eye again. I wanted to tell her the words I hadn't been able to say in years—*I love you!*— but something about the gesture would feel like surrender. Like saying good-bye all over again.

That was unacceptable.

"Isn't that what you wanted?" I said.

"No."

"It's gotta be. The name, the date—it's all there."

"No!" From behind me, the force of the cry shook my throbbing earlobe. "This is a counterfeit! Nothing more!"

"How was I to know?"

"There's only one way you could've crafted such a fake. You had to have seen the real ring. And I don't believe for a second you would have risked your mother's life by leaving it behind." The blade circled round my neck, shaking. "Tell me. *Where* is it?"

His voice had a dangerous edge now. His mind was set.

My eyes ran down the slope once more and locked with my mother's.

Mom.

Somehow she had pulled herself up and was clinging to the edge on her elbows. Dianne Lewis Black. Forty feet of treacherous incline separated us. We were bound together in this moment. Warmth, longing, and fear passed through our gaze.

Mom, can you hear me? Stay down!

"It's gonna be a little harder to get to," I said.

He tore at my sweatshirt, lifting it with my T-shirt in one decisive motion. I was defenseless. His other hand slid in from the right, drawing the blood-wet blade up my abdominal ridges. "Is it possible you swallowed it? Perhaps a C-section is required."

"I prefer a natural childbirth."

The razor crept higher until it jabbed at an angle against my nipple.

I peered off across the Cumberland. As a small boy, I'd given my mom heart palpitations every time I ran in with a new scrape or bruise. She didn't need to see this. Didn't need to see the pain when it flared in my eyes.

"I've played your game, followed your rules," I whispered.

"No, you haven't." The razor broke the skin, and I felt my blood trickle down. "Haven't you learned? Don't you see how Felicia had to pay for her sins? I really thought we might have something, you and I—as father and son. This is your final exam, Mr. Black. Will you do the right thing?"

The right thing.

In that last phrase, I found the shred of truth I needed.

The right thing was to protect my mother, to fight for her life. I had set down my weapon—and that, too, was the right thing—yet I could not let this madman continue unobstructed.

"You win," I said.

"I always do. You cannot stand against God's hand of judgment."

We'll see who's left standing!

I flexed one hand over the rope, twisted the other arm through the cord again, and took a short step forward as though losing my balance. The agony was intense where I'd been cut on my chest, but I'd felt pain before.

"Up here," I groaned. "Check beneath my left sleeve."

Newmann's breathing quickened in anticipation. He came around on my side and tried to free my sleeve from the coils of rope. With hands clasped around the lifeline to my mother, I heaved my arms upward and dropped them down over my enemy's shoulders in a suffocating embrace. Surging forward with my legs, I drove our joined bodies into the railing.

Fence joints popped. The wood cracked.

Together we plummeted down the incline, caught up in the flailing rope and rag-doll thrashing of arms and legs. Everything was spinning. Lush leaves and veins cushioned us near the cliff top, but protruding stones met us farther down, cracking against ribs and hips.

The rope, Aramis, Don't let go!

A blade flashed, sliced across my sleeve, then ran in a long, blood-spurting track across Newmann's chest before spiraling through sunlight toward the river.

Our awkward embrace came undone. Alternating gasps and moans punctuated the final seconds before the Cumberland roared up to slap my face.

Going under…

Nothing but bubbles exploding around my head, green-tinged darkness, and a horrible ringing through my battered body. I thought of my dream—the medieval battlefield, my corpse wandering down into the water, the stains washing away. Beside me, another body writhed in the murk and then slipped away, caught in the undertow, the way my mother's had been all those years ago.

Air!

Caught in the current myself, I thrashed toward the surface, fighting the river's desire to devour me.

Don't panic. Act rapidly.

I carved my hands through the cold depths, pulling my weight toward the dim light above. The rope slithered beside me, still entwined around my arm.

Desperate for oxygen, I sensed a ring of blackness tightening around my vision. My thigh brushed against something—an old grocery cart? a creature?—triggering another burst of adrenaline.

I broke the surface, gasping, filthy water pouring from my face. My fingers found loose stones on the steep bank. I scrambled for footing on uneven rock, then turned and started pulling on the rope. Reeling in against the pain.

Slack, slack, slack… *tension.*

How long had Mom been under? How deep had she gone? Bound as she was and with her useless legs, she could have done little to resist the current. Ignoring the burn in my palms, I waded back a few steps and cranked on the rope, willing her to surface.

"Come on!" I screamed.

Something splashed nearby. Voices called out. I was too focused to pay attention.

My bottom lip was split, bleeding.

My arms near spent.

My legs and torso aching.

Shaking, I could feel my body giving way to the pull of the hungry river at my feet.

A glimmer of color sloshed beneath the Cumberland's muddied palette.

Mom!

Feet came crashing through the shallows, and then Detective Meade was at my side, tugging with me. The snap of the rope resonated through my bones. The rope's angle grew sharper until she was there, rising from the water into the land of the living.

She came up, gasping, crying, sputtering for air—but alive.

I stumbled toward her, peeled back the soggy tape, and lifted her body into my arms. She was lighter than I'd expected, yet so tangible. So real. Tears spilled down my cheeks as she breathed my name.

There was no sweeter music.

46

*B*lack's espresso shop, 2216 Elliston. This was the place to be.

Glistening coffee bags stood in the retail rack beneath a sign introducing my newest blend. At a table beside the display, Dianne Lewis Black shook customers' hands, accepted hugs, and signed bag upon bag of Mom's Memory Blend, putting my brother's autograph lines to shame.

I crouched beside her wheelchair. "He's on his way."

"He'd better be," she said, eyes twinkling. "My wrist is cramping."

I laughed, fearing it might unleash another rush of emotion I could not control. This scene was surreal. Despite all the years, we'd been brought together again.

Mom was here. In my shop. Sipping my coffee.

"Mom,"—it felt good to say that—"you wanna take a break?"

"What? No. I'm making you money hand over fist. Which is a good thing, considering your fists are out of commission." She nodded to my bandaged hands, and I smiled. She asked, "How much longer till Johnny Ray arrives?"

"Not long now. He's canceled tonight's show to be here."

"I hope I'll get to hear him play."

I pointed to the corner stage. "You're gonna get your wish."

"He always dreamed of being a big music star, you know? Even as a little boy. I had to scold the two of you for jumping around on the bed, playing air guitars."

"Me? I don't remember that."

She touched my cheek. "There's a lot I don't remember, Aramis. A lot I don't wanna remember. But that picture's one I'll never forget."

———

Coffee beans are among the most studied natural substances in history. A number of researchers believe the aroma of brewing coffee can release mood-enhancing endorphins. Some say these chemicals can trigger the healing process. And all agree that smell is closely linked to memory.

I ground another batch of Mom's Memory Blend, breathing in the rich aroma, praying for healing of my family's memories. We had so much to look forward to. So much to be thankful for.

And a few things to be aware of.

Earlier, Detective Meade had stopped by. He hinted at a coming shake-up among the Kraftsmen. Even if not admissible as evidence, the discovery of blood on the horsewhip had stirred the suspicions of local law enforcement.

"In the weeks to come, Freddy C may be called as a witness."

"I'm sure he'd be honored," I said.

Meade also explained that Mr. Hillcrest's trip to Nashville had involved the gift of a new computer system for his son. Diesel's grades proved he was climbing the academic ladder. He and I would have a few things to discuss, but I couldn't be too hard on him. He'd never meant to cause any damage.

Most of us never do.

"Oh, and one last thing, Aramis." Meade's coal black eyes froze me in place. "We found some evidence downriver."

"Spill it."

"Fresh footprints and bloodstains along the bank a quarter mile beyond the Fort Nashborough site. We've sent alerts to medical facilities throughout Middle Tennessee. The man using the alias Boniface Newmann has been wounded, but I don't think he'll be foolish enough to stay in the area. Not with police bulletins out for his arrest."

"What about my mom? Do you think he'll come after her?"

"If he does, he'll be walking right into my handcuffs and a loaded Glock."

"Speaking of."

Meade anticipated where I was headed. "It's been recovered as evidence from the scene, a .40-caliber Desert Eagle registered in your name."

"It scared me," I said, recalling the surge of adrenaline. "I thought I was going to kill him."

"To hold the law in your own hands is a powerful thing."

"Yeah." My eyebrows furrowed. "I don't think I'm cut out for that."

Johnny's set was unannounced, but the shop started filling as word passed around West End. Fifteen minutes before he kicked things off, the place was packed with friends, regulars, and fans of his brand of modern-edged country music built around traditional mandolins, fiddles, and an upright bass. Chigger was there too, his showmanship and artistry bringing the set to life.

No denying the man had talent.

I noticed Trish working at the music-merchandise table, and I walked over. "I see your brother actually let you outta the house."

"Miracles never cease. I met your mom, by the way. I can see where you got those expressive eyes of yours."

"Uh. Thanks."

"I brought something for you."

"For me?" I accepted a small bag. "If anything, I owe you an apology."

"For sneaking onto our property and tranquilizing the dogs?"

"Yeah."

"Just another day on the farm. Besides, you got me up and moving. Chigger's other so-called friend never showed. What about Freddy's leg?"

"He was here earlier. Said the stitches come out next week."

"That's a relief." She waggled her finger. "Now open it."

"Should I guess what's inside?"

"I'll give you a hint. Can you spell the name Robicheaux?"

"Burke's new hardcover?"

She beamed as I pulled out the book and flipped through the pages.

"Thanks," I said. "Hey, before I forget. Can you put aside one of the double-X T-shirts for me? Need to send it out to a lady in Oregon."

"You bet."

I went back to check on my mom.

"I'm fine, Aramis. Go on. You have a duty to your customers. We'll talk more later."

Reluctantly I weaved back through the crowd and took my place behind the mahogany bar.

Anna pulled two shots from the espresso machine. "There's barely a seat left out there," she said.

"We're gonna be busy tonight."

"You're telling me, hon."

"If it keeps up like this, I'll have to give you that raise."

"Really?" Her eyes brightened.

"Oh no. Wait." I scanned the crowd behind me. "Hold on a sec. Sammie?"

Samantha turned from the other side of the counter, her hair sweeping the shoulder of her black satin top. "Yes?"

"Did you get that thing?"

"For that one thing?"

"Yeah, that thing."

"Signed and sealed."

"Well, Anna," I said. "Look's like your raise will be on next week's paycheck."

"You jokers." She winked. "But thank you."

I slipped around the bar and nudged next to Sammie. "Played to perfection."

She leaned into me to be heard over the rising clamor. "Your mother's a sweetheart. You think she'll be okay with the crowd?"

"She wouldn't miss it. Johnny's about to take the stage."

"You certain of that?"

I followed her eyes. A black Stetson dangled from the microphone, but my brother was at the foot of the platform, his arms wrapped around Mom, his face buried in her neck. He'd been here nearly half an hour and had barely left her side. She brushed her fingers through his long hair, patted his back, then nudged him up.

"Go," she mouthed. "Go."

He nodded. Took a deep breath. Turned and hopped up to the mike.

The shop buzzed with anticipation as he combed back his golden mane, sniffed, and pulled on his hat. The band assembled and took up their instruments behind him. With one hand covering the mike, he addressed the crowd. "Thank y'all for coming. And thanks to my little brother for pulling this together at the last minute." He nodded at me, and I nodded back. "Tonight"—he gestured with his hand—"is dedicated to my mother, who was taken from us years ago but has never left our hearts. And to my brother." He looked my direction. "Thank you for bringin' her back."

Sammie squeezed my hand, and Mom threw me a smile that was full of pain and hope and love that had never died.

On the stage, Johnny Ray grabbed the mike in a dramatic sweep and called out, "So y'all ready to make some *noise?*"

———

Our brownstone was quiet. Mom was asleep in my bed, exhausted by the events of the day. I'd poked my head through the door, watched her eyes flutter with unknown dreams before settling into a peaceful state. She was beautiful. More beautiful than I remembered.

When I moved into the kitchen, I found my brother standing at the counter in his Tabasco boxers, draining a glass of vegetable purée.

"How can you stand that stuff?" I asked.

"Don't start. When it comes to our diets, I betcha Mom's on my side."

I changed topics. "You did a great job tonight."

"Thanks. It's good to be home."

"Home."

"Got a whole different ring now, doesn't it?" He leaned back against the sink and crossed his arms. "Guess you've got another story to write."

"I don't know. It takes a lot out of me."

"You gotta do it, kid."

"Because you said?"

"Because Mom's here. This time it's not just for her memory. It's so she can read it for herself."

"Hard to argue with that." Already ideas were forming in my head.

"You gonna leave me more clues to follow?"

"That's exactly what I'll do, but it won't be so easy this time."

"That a fact?" Johnny Ray studied me.

"This time you'll have to string together the *last* letter from every chapter and see what it spells."

"Another treasure to find?"

"You'll just have to see."

ACKNOWLEDGMENTS

Carolyn Rose (wife extraordinaire)—for backrubs, for energizing laughter, and for loving me despite everything you know about me.

Cassie and Jackie (daughters)—for your joy, for your ideas, and for protecting Dad's writing time even when allowances were put on hold till the book was turned in.

Dudley Delffs (editor and friend)—for continued faith in novelists and words and for giving me that first opportunity.

Mick Silva, Shannon Hill, and Carol Bartley (editors)—for partnering to make this a better series in ways I could never conceive.

Commander Louise Kelton and Officer Bo Smith, Metro Nashville Police Department (North Precinct guardians)—for allowing a nosy novelist to ride along.

Linda Wilson (mother)—for ice-cream memories, garden tours, memorable cars, and years of encouragement to keep these fingers typing.

Mark Wilson (father)—for incredible support over the years and for recent insight into the world of law enforcement.

Sean Savacool (friend and writer)—for unconditional friendship and provocative ideas... May the Tennessee Inklings (the Tinklings) keep tinkling.

Valerie Harrell and Davin Bartosch (friends)—for insights from a Southern perspective and for putting up with this daydreaming co-worker.

Roosevelt Burrell and Hudson Alvares (management at FedEx Kinko's)—for continued flexibility and full support of my writing goals.

Randy Singer, Kathryn Mackel, River Jordan, Robert Liparulo, Gina Holmes, Jeremiah McNabb, Todd Peterson, Ted Dekker, Vennessa Ng, Rick

Moore, Chris Well, and many others (fellow novelists)—for honesty, friendship, and needed support.

Liorah and Kevin Johnson (friends and creative types)—for sharing your music and artistry for the cause of a local novelist... Ooh la la!

Ian Monaghan (brother-in-law)—for gallons of gas sacrificed on the altar of my research and for hands-on weapons knowledge.

Nashville Public Library (Edmondson, Bordeaux, and Main branches)—for places to study, daydream, and write in relative solitude.

As Cities Burn, Switchfoot, Demon Hunter, Mat Kearney, Flyleaf, Project 86, and Underoath (musical artists)—for sonic rejuvenation in the late-night hours.

I-Dragon-I (rock group)—for including my debut novel's title in the lyrics of an honest, powerful song... Sweet!

Readers everywhere (the ones holding this book)—for following me on these journeys of plots, people, and ideas... Each word is dedicated to you.

I welcome your feedback at my Web site or e-mail address:

wilsonwriter.com

wilsonwriter@hotmail.com

The first in the
ARAMIS BLACK SUSPENSE SERIES

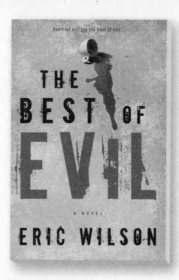

Also available from Eric Wilson

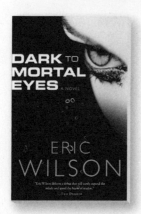

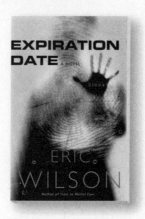

Available in bookstores and from online retailers.

WATERBROOK PRESS
www.waterbrookpress.com

To learn more about WaterBrook Press and view
our catalog of products, log on to our Web site:
www.waterbrookpress.com

WATERBROOK
PRESS